All Roads South

Roan Poulter

Other Titles by the author

The End of the Road (2012)

DEDICATION

To my great friend Kelly.
If only this were how your story ended. A thousand times I have
wished you would have called. I miss the world that had you in it.

I hope you found peace.

To my great Molly who supports me in every way a creative person
can, Thanks, you help make me a better writer.

Chapter 1

"Click"

Clark sat back in his chair with a smile spreading across his face. He pressed back hard to stretch the knots that had accumulated in his ergonomically unfriendly computer posture. Someone was always telling him that he was leaning too far forward, all hunched over like an evil minion. Then they would ask about his eyes, tell him that he sat too close to the monitor, that he needed glasses. Clark could see fine from further back, not as far back as he might have once been able to, but today he was leaned in close because he had just transferred the last remaining amount into his hidden account.

Not just months, but years of planning completed in that moment. When he pressed the left key on his mouse, all the hours of research paid off. He had been tracking costs and secretly squirreling money away for almost three years. Tonight would be the night, when all his plans would be revealed to his family for the first time. He looked around for someone to share the news with, but Marjorie was not at her desk. Tim was at his desk, but Clark knew Timothy wasn't the kind of guy you share good news like this with. He was a crab guy. Clark had been told by his father that most people were like crabs, and crabs had an interesting trait. You couldn't keep one crab in a bucket. One crab would claw its way out, yearning for the crushing depths of the ocean where it could live out its little crab life with its little crab wife. But two crabs was a whole different matter. Two crabs could be kept in a bucket. When one crab would attempt an escape, the other would pull them back down. When the other tried they would simply reverse roles, content to ruin each other's chances of escape until they could be boiled properly. Tim was that kind of a guy. He was always the first person to say why something wouldn't work. Clark had worked next to Tim for almost twenty years and in all that time Tim had only gotten worse, seemingly as he lost more and more of his hair. As the hairs fell out and the comb over got longer, so did Tim's desire to crush everyone else's dreams.

The more Clark looked around his area, he realized that same assertion applied to almost everyone there. Not hugely surprising he guessed, since they all worked as IRS auditors. Every day they worked to ensure that every American paid their fair share of the tax burden. Not exactly a pleasant workplace most the time. Clark didn't really consider himself to be at work until the second person had asked him how he could live with himself. Regardless of when that happened, he would take a break. As if the coffee just somehow wouldn't be savory without the slowly fading memory of a Mexican restaurant owner screaming that Clark's questions were unconstitutional.

Clark always thought that was unfair. Not that anyone wanted to be notified that their taxes were being audited, but he did his utmost to be fair. He was more than fair; he gave the benefit of the doubt. If someone could produce even a shred of documentation he would give it due process. Many of the other Auditors were real hard asses. Clark had regularly gotten people money back that they didn't know the government owed them, albeit a small percentage. Still, he was always courteous to people on the phone, even telemarketers, why couldn't people at least do that for him?

But never mind any of that now, he needed to find Marjorie. If someone could be happy for him, it was her. Heck, she had found over half of the places herself. She was the opposite of Tim, the kind of person who longed to be happy for someone. Her life had been hard and sad, but somehow she always came to work with a huge smile and a new piece of outrageously gaudy jewelry.

Clark locked his computer and tried to peek over the cubicle walls to see if her red hair was visible. She was shorter, but occasionally she would jump with excitement at someone's story and he could spot her.

Where the hell is she, she should have been here for this. She was just there at her desk; she knew this was the big day.

Clark walked around the campus for twenty minutes, always thinking that she would be right there. His mood was dwindling for lack of a common candle to hold the vigil. He had been more excited to tell Marjorie than his own wife.

Wait, what? That can't be right. I must have meant that she was the second most, right? How could Marjorie be better to tell than Karen? Now I'm just being silly.

Standing in the corridor lost in his thoughts he started to get the sadness, he looked around desperately, thinking that there must still be time to fend it off. He knew he couldn't go back to his desk, not like this. He needed some air, so although he was not technically on break he headed toward the courtyard. The twenty by fifteen foot section of grass and benches that constituted their outdoor exposure, conveniently positioned so they didn't leave the secure area. As he approached the glass doors he saw Marjorie there.

Why the hell didn't she tell me she was going on break? I can't even think of the last time she went without me.

But the closer he got the more he realized something must be wrong. Her head was hanging down and she was staring at the ground. She looked upset. Clark hoped it didn't have anything to do with her husband. He had been sick for as long as Clark had known her, maybe this was it. Clark opened the door slowly.

"Hey Marge, can I join you?"

"Of course you can", Marjorie immediately peaked up, pressing her hands under her eyes in a vain attempt to fix the damage the crying had done to her makeup. She really looked a fright. Marjorie had always been known to be excessive on the eye makeup, so any amount of tears left her looking like street art being washed away by the rain.

"Are you okay? Is Jim alright?"

She smiled at him as though he had tried to make a joke and not known it.

"Jim's fine, why do you ask about him?"

"Well, I saw the, well never mind. I, uhmm, transferred the final amount."

"I know you did."

"Well, I wanted to tell you, I've been looking for you forever."

Marjorie just smiled at Clark. It was the kind of smile that is meant to impart something, but is usually wasted upon men, who understand little to nothing. Like a radio that's not tuned to the right station, this message was also not received.

"We should go to lunch today, on me. After all, how many lunches have we sacrificed to make this happen?"

Again Marjorie tried to broadcast the signal, but like a broken radio, Clark just smiled and nodded like an idiot.

"Oh Clark, what am I going to do without you?" Suddenly the water works kicked on again and Marjorie's head folded down into her hands. Soft sobbing sounds and a slight shake were all that Clark needed to understand. His radio might not be tuned into the subtle frequency, but he understood that when a woman cried and his name was even remotely mentioned, it was his fault.

"Well I'm coming back; it's not like its forever."

Again Marjorie's head picked back up, now she was really a mess. Clark wished he had a handkerchief to hand her, something to help repair the damage. He would have given her his shirt if it would have stopped her from crying.

"Clark I won't be here when you get back." Suddenly Clark felt the world shift under him. As if the gravitational field on Earth wasn't totally constant in that instant. Marjorie had been there when he started so long ago. He simply could not imagine going to work and not seeing her there. She was his constant, the unflagging presence that made it all tolerable.

"You can't retire, you just can't." She smiled again, this time warmly as if she had been hoping that he would say this. He had also been her rock, her work spouse. In a place that tended to sap the life force from people, his optimism and charisma had kept her coming to work long after she would have left.

"Clark, I would have retired last year if you hadn't been here. I need to spend more time with Jim and your leaving is the perfect excuse to retire. Don't be sad on your big day, I wasn't going to tell you, but I'm a silly old woman who's always looking for a good excuse to cry. Now tell me how you're going to surprise the kids."

Clark tried to pull himself from the ashes, but it was hard. He needed time to process things like this. He couldn't just turn on and off his feelings. He would miss Marge, but what most drew upon his mind as he laid out the banal details of how he would spring the news on the family was that she had called him her work spouse. Part of him was repulsed by the idea, she was at least thirty years his senior. He had simply never thought of her in that way and to picture her in anything but a coworker role was shocking to his system. But then he supposed that she was talking about something different, that they shared things with each other, took care of one another. There was nothing sexual, just an earnest relationship that sought to protect the other from the miseries of the workplace.

"…then I'll show them the account sheet and just wait for them to go crazy." He finished, mouth dried from the monologue. Marjorie had smiled hugely through the whole thing. Her face had almost been wiped back to pre tears Marge. She patted his folded hands.

"Your kids are so lucky to have you as their dad." Marge smiled again. She loved every detail about the kids, from pictures they drew to hearing about their grades. She had never had children of her own and it seemed she lived vicariously through Clark sometimes. She had however, now mentioned the kids enjoying themselves without mentioning Karen, Clark's wife.

"Karen is just going to go crazy, I think." Marjorie's eyes flashed something different at the mention of her name. Marjorie was not the biggest fan of Karen and Clark knew it. She never came right out and said she didn't like her, but there was always an undercurrent of dislike in her responses about her.

"I'm sure it will all go just like you want it to." She smiled so hard that Clark felt she was saying the truth, although something in her tone made him think she didn't believe a word of it.

So then why would she have helped me plan this thing? She could have doubted me earlier and killed the whole thing.

But he didn't ask her about what she thought. He went back to trivial small talk, an attempt to have a retirement luncheon for Marjorie, which she strictly forbade. She also made him swear not to tell anyone. She would put in her paperwork and just walk out those security doors a few minutes early one Friday. Clark wondered how many more of these conversations they would be able to have. He wondered what would happen in the months ahead, the future becoming a darkening sky, uncertain in its nature. He felt the wind changing direction for the first time in as long as he could remember and it felt great.

Chapter 2

When Clark arrived home that night he had his briefcase nearly busting with pages of details and a rolled up parchment tucked under his arm. He was trying to play it cool, but the smile was leaking through his guise of everdayness.

Karen was on the computer when he walked through the door. Jack was at the dining room table working on his homework, Chloe was somewhere else, but at seventeen years old, that seemed appropriate.

Clark tried not to make too much noise or any scene as he put his things on the counter.

"I'll make dinner tonight", he announced to the room. Karen didn't even look up from the computer.

"Knock yourself out." From the tone Clark interpreted that she had a bad day. The list was endless as for the reasons for it, be it slow pickup line at the school, the internet was too slow to play Facebook videos, or the power bill was more than expected this month. He knew that if he asked it would just get her ramped up and further invested in her bad mood. Not tonight, he needed everyone happy and ready for an adventure.

In the kitchen he was whipping up an epic dinner. Actually he was making breakfast for dinner to be exact. Belgian waffles, French omelets, Spanish rice, English tea, he hoped that the dinner would get everyone in the house ready for the news he had.

Timing would be everything. He needed everyone no more than thirty seconds away from ready to eat when he started the waffles and omelets. He prepped everything he could before realizing it was a suicide mission to start the cooking without knowing where Chloe was.

He eyed Karen at the computer, but decided it was best to let her Facebook herself toward happiness or at least away from irritation. He approached Jack hard at work, staring furiously into his math book.

"Can I help?" Clark asked. Jack smiled as he always did. He seemed to be working on some kind of area problem, computing the square feet of an irregular shape.

"I think I got it, but could you check it when I'm done?"

"Of course I will. Math is my specialty after all." Jack smiled again and went back to his work. The boy was fiercely independent. He would learn it or die trying. Clark laughed, his daughter Chloe had been almost the opposite. She would have happily let her father do all of her homework, continually asking him to do just one more of the problems so she could finally get it.

"Have you seen Chloe?" Clark braved. Now Jack did not smile.

"Her and mom are fighting. I'd stay out of it if I were you."

"Is Chloe in her room?"

"Mom says she's grounded until she goes to college." Clark smiled, he was sure that this was the thousandth time she had been grounded until she was either married, in college or paying her own bills. The women in his life it seemed were destined to fight each other for dominance.

"Do I want to know what it's about?" Clark interrupted. Jack looked up again, with just the faintest look of annoyance.

"Some boy, or something; I tried to ignore both of them." Clark kissed him on the head as he got up from the table. A small part of his stomach clenched as he walked out of the dining room and toward his daughters room. This was dangerous ground, who knew what kind of crazy storm he might walk into. He took a couple of deep breaths and knocked softly on the door.

"GO AWAY." Somehow he never got used to that. Even as an IRS auditor, the sound of his daughter telling him to leave her alone broke his heart every single time it happened. He remembered a little girl who was always so excited to see him after work that she would dance and sing, but that time had passed. That cute little girl had been replaced by a walking hormone disaster zone. Loving one moment and homicidal the next, he had thought that the stories of hellish teenagers was overblown. Turned out that they had understated just how bad it would be.

"Honey, I'm making dinner, will you please come help me serve it?"

"I can't, I'm grounded til I die."

"I think you're exaggerating, I heard it's just til you graduate college."

"Whatever."

"Will you please come help; I can't do it without you." He had learned from years of having a high maintenance wife that flattery was the only possible remedy.

"Alright, but I'm not serving HER."

Clark set to work on the waffles and prepped the omelet pan. Chloe set the table, with only two minor shoving matches with her brother. Since Jack was only eight there was less rivalry that most siblings. He liked to tease her occasionally and the inverse on occasion, but mostly they got along.

When half the waffles were made, Clark started on the omelets. The key was to have all the ingredients minus the cheese already cooked and ready. Three lightly beaten eggs into a medium high buttered pan, swirl and peel down the edges with a silicone scraper. Once it was settled toss the ingredients in the middle, fold over the sides and slide it out onto the plate. The whole process should take less than a minute if you're doing it right. The omelets were coming out perfectly. Fluffy and still a little runny, but the cheese looked fully melted.

It's all about having a high quality pan and the right heat. Calphalon pans and a gas stove.
Finally all the items were assembled, Jack and Chloe were finishing setting the table and getting everyone a water.

"Karen dear, let's eat." Clark was doing his softest and least insistent. Karen was doing her best to ignore him.

"Honey, it's omelets, they're not good cold." Now Karen looked up from the computer.

"Omelets, are you doing breakfast for dinner, again?" She gave him a disgusted look.

Heat flushed Clark's face, but he was doing his best to keep it in check. He wouldn't let her ruin this, not after everything he had sacrificed to get them to this point. He took two long deep breaths to check his tone. She had a short fuse tonight and she would be storming into the bedroom to lock the door at the slightest note of confrontation.

"Please come eat dear." With that Clark sat down at the table with the kids. The three of them looked at each other questioningly. Unsure of how long they should wait, the omelets wouldn't wait forever. The window of time that the butter would actually melt on the waffles was also quickly diminishing. Clark looked over and Karen had still not moved.

"Go ahead and eat", he finally told Chloe and Jack. They looked at each other for a moment, shrugged and started their meals. Clark's food sat on his plate, untouched. He cleared his throat twice, tucked his chair in noisily, but to no avail. Finally Karen looked up from the computer, groaned and walked over to the table.

Clark got up and pulled her chair out. She looked at him like he had a second head growing out of his armpit. As he pushed her chair in there was just the slightest exhale groan from Karen. Again Clark was trying to deny its existence. *Keep it positive.*

Now that Karen was there at the table eating her dinner Clark felt much better. The food wasn't totally cold so at least she couldn't use that against him. Breakfast for dinner wasn't really that unusual for him to prepare, but someone would have to say something about the Spanish rice. It was just such a standout, surely someone would notice. But as everyone ate in silence it began to occur to him that they didn't seem to be taking the hint to ask about the unusual combination of food.

"So how is everything", he asked in the most leading way possible.

Karen smiled a flat lipped smile. "It's great daddy." If he had closed his eyes he almost would have believed she meant it.

"The waffles are really good dad. I can taste the vanilla in the waffles." Jack was always quick to offer a complement. Chloe didn't feel it necessary to say anything, allowing her silence to speak for her.

"I thought this would be an interesting combination of food. Belgian waffles, French omelets, Spanish rice, even English tea." *Now I'm just being blatant. I'm giving them too many clues.*

But still no one was jumping up and down, hoping what this might mean. Clark wanted to slap them, get them excited. *I wish I had some kind of music to get everybody pumped up for this. That's what they need.*

Then it was just too much. He couldn't contain himself any longer. He had wanted them to guess what was happening, but it was obvious they weren't going to.

"I'm taking us all to Europe for a month!!" He realized at that moment that he was standing and shaking with excitement. The three still seated at the table looked at him and at each other.

"That's nice honey, we all appreciate it." Karen turned her face back down toward what remained of her omelet.

"No, not just this meal. I'm taking our family on a two month vacation to Europe. Look here's all the stuff." With that he ran to the kitchen to get his map and the accompanying paperwork. He was far too excited to eat now; he shoved his plates out of the way to roll out the map. It had been traced by his fingers so many times that it looked like an antique. There were at least three separate routes with so many thumbtack holes that the whole thing looked like it might fall apart at any moment. For the first time Karen pushed her plate to the side and slid the map toward herself.

"See we're going to fly into Rome, then stay at the Eurocamp..." he started but Karen cut him off immediately.

"We can't afford this, we can barely pay the bills as things are." She sharpened her gaze at the map and then at Clark.

"Well, uhmmm, it's already paid for. I've been secretly saving money for this for the past three years." Karen's eyes widened for a second. Clark tried to continue with details of the trip.

"We're going to stay at Eurocamp, you get these great tents with.." he started.

"How much money have you saved for this?" Her question was simple, but it was barbed and her gaze had narrowed again.

"Well, I've been planning this for awhile, finding the best airfares and such. Marge and I have worked the whole thing out, buying souveneirs and all. We've got it planned down to the penny." He didn't seem to be helping his wife's gaze.

"So how much did you TWO save up?" Her voice was just slightly louder than her usual. Clark started to sense that he was in danger, better to be out with the details.

"Thirty seven thousand, four hundred and fifty dollars" as the words finished coming out of Clark's mouth, Karen's eyes widened and she laughed slightly. Clark sighed in relief, thinking he had dodged a bullet.

"Wow, that's amazing Clark." She sat back in her seat looking around the room.

"Yeah, it's gonna be great. The camp has waterslides and you can catch a bus into the city, then after five days we move onto..."

"Just how did you save forty thousand dollars? I mean, where did the money come from?" The kids looked at each other. Clark realized that he had not saved himself, this was just getting started.

"I had money held from my check and put into a secret account." Even Clark cringed to hear it stated like that. That sounded like a confession, not the surprise that he had hoped. They should all be dancing right now, but somehow he doubted that happy moments were just around the corner.

"Secret accounts daddy", Karen now spoke directly to the children, "what are you some kind of Goddamn spy now?"

"Honey, this was supposed to be a surprise, something for us as a family. A chance to spend some real time together." Clark hoped that his face was conveying what he meant, he was having a hard time not crying. He could feel the disappointment welling up in him like a huge geyser ready to blow. This was supposed to save them and now it was all going wrong.

"Quite the surprise Clark." With that Karen got up from the table and walked down the hallway to their bedroom slamming the door once she was there. Chloe got up and cleared the plates, most were still almost full of food, but Clark didn't say anything. He was done eating for the night, his appetite satiated with self-doubt and disappointment. As she cleared the last of the plates she bent over and kissed her father on the head. She quickly turned back to the kitchen, no one noticing the small tear that escaped the lid of her eye.

"I thought it looked like a lot of fun dad", Jack said.

"Me too", Clark said as he put the papers back into his briefcase. He tried to roll up the map, but it had gotten stuck to the table, probably some spilled syrup and the map tore a large hole where Austria should have been. Clark sighed hard and removed the small scrap of paper with his thumbnail.

Suddenly the bedroom door flew open and Karen came back out with vengeful steps.

"Why don't you take your girlfriend with you, since I'm sure that's what you planned all along!!" Then she was gone again, another great reason to slam the door. Clark found a spot on the couch and stared straight ahead at the empty television. He didn't need to watch anything; his mind was already racing and tormenting him. Suddenly Jack was sitting next to him, tucking his small body next to Clark.

"Wanna watch Spongebob? Nobody can be sad when they're watching that."

With a nod Clark passed Jack the remote control and did his best to forget the world in his head and journey to Bikini Bottom.

Chapter 3

"Shoot, my back is killing me", Clark wailed as he leaned back in his chair to stretch his painfully cramped muscles.

"I told you Karen doesn't like surprises," Marjorie said with more than a little of that 'I told you so' look.

"Well, like always, I should have listened. She wouldn't even look at me this morning. Just threw my clothes into the hallway and told me to use the kid's bathroom." Marjorie looked at Clark. She thought he was just a little more handsome this morning. He was always a good looking man, but a day's beard was quite becoming on him. Not that she thought about him that way, but it never hurt her feelings to look at him.

They both went back to work, it wasn't break time yet, Clark had only been told off once so far today. The stack of files on their desks was just as high as it had been the day prior, just as high as it had been for the past two decades for Marjorie. She wouldn't miss that, not a bit. But she would miss Clark, he had been a true friend to her. When her husband had gotten sick he had picked up the slack that had piled up on her desk. He had never mentioned it, working late hours and coming in early so that no one suffered because of a shoddy Audit. Marjorie was never sure if he was like the son she never had or the lover she always pined for. It would seem unnatural to say something in between, but that felt the most correct. She wanted to pick him up and rock him like a baby today. She had known him long enough to sense when he was in pain, and he was howling today. The whole room almost smelled of failure and dismay. She wanted to do something, but wasn't sure what would possibly help this mess.

Suddenly the phone rang at Clark's desk. Marjorie was trying to ignore it until the tone of the conversation made her stop typing. Clark was talking to Karen.

"Of course I can come home, but why won't you tell me why? Okay, okay, but, alright dear. I'll come right away, love you." Marjorie thought she noted he hung the phone up too soon to have been treated to a return 'Love you'. She hated Karen, although she had only met her twice at the Christmas parties, Marge had been forced to deal with that woman's fallout for far too long. She would have tried to get Clark to leave her years ago, but was one of those silly people who was head over heels in love with his wife, it was a little disgustingi6. He would have done anything for her. He let her sit home on her ass all day long, then let her complain that he didn't do his fair share of the housework. Marjorie had worked over twenty years for the IRS and now she was supporting her sick husband, no one hated a stay home wife more than one who was the sole breadwinner.

Clark was grabbing his jacket.

"Cover for me will ya?" Marjorie nodded her head, it was after all the least she could do. Somehow this whole thing was being blamed on the two conspirators. She walked Clark to the security door.

"Good luck", she said to his rapidly shrinking outline as he walked toward his car, "You're gonna need it".

Clark was trying to be hopeful. When they had first gotten married Karen had called him to come home for 'nooners' several times. True, it had been almost fifteen years since then, but it still seemed possible. He really hoped she had come around on the trip idea. Maybe she felt bad about how she reacted. That was what he was counting on. Karen was really quite a loving woman when it came down to it. She wouldn't have ever denied the children the opportunity to see Europe over a silly misunderstanding.

In the driveway there was a Silver Chevy Malibu.

That's strange, it looks just like our Pastor's car. Wait, that is the Pastor's car, in fact there he is.

Clark pulled in beside him and waved. This seemed odd timing for a visit from him. Clark walked up to him and extended his hand to shake.

"Good to see you, what are you doing here Tom?" Clark asked.

"Karen said she needed me to come over immediately, some kind of spiritual crisis."

Clark was confused, just how bad did Karen feel about her outburst. Suddenly he was very concerned for Karen. She must have been home torturing herself, thinking that he was mad at her. But Clark wasn't mad, he was just disappointed that she hadn't been more excited.

The two men walked to the front door of the small modest home Karen and Clark had lived in for almost their entire marriage.

For no good reason Clark rang the doorbell, it just didn't seem proper to walk someone in unannounced, even if it was the Pastor.

Karen answered the door, opening it fully.

"Please come in both of you and have a seat." *She is being awfully formal for someone in crisis.* Clark had expected tears, or at least for her to be red eyed and hoarse. She looked like she was ready to go out on the town. Clark and Tom sat down as they were told and looked at each other. Neither knew if they were supposed to start or what.

"I asked you both here so I wouldn't have to say this twice. I have met someone, I love him and I'm done with both of you."

Time shifted and Clark thought he might pass out. Had he heard what he thought he just heard? He thought he must be having some kind of a bad dream, that he should pinch himself and wake up. The silence lasted for an excruciating amount of time after Karen's declaration.

Then like a dam bursting everyone was talking at once, Clark begging Karen to think about what she was doing, Tom trying to make a case for counseling, but Karen's voice was louder than both of theirs combined.

"I SAID; I'M DONE WITH BOTH OF YOU".

Clark looked at Tom as if he could somehow fix all that was falling apart before his eyes. Tom's mouth was opening and closing but no words were coming out.

"I packed your clothes into some bags, take them with you. You have twenty minutes to get your stuff and get out of my house. My lawyer has an injunction ready to file if you don't." Karen's face did not belie any kind of bluff. Suddenly Clark realized that he was being kicked out of his home, he couldn't even begin to imagine where he would go.

"Where am I supposed to go?" he stammered.

"Well Clark, you have your secret money, it's yours. Buy yourself a small condo and figure it out."

"Is that what this is all about? I saved that money for us to fix our relationship."

"There's no fixing this; I'm in love Clark. I didn't know how to tell you and I didn't know how we could possibly separate when we could barely make ends meet. So when you told me about the money, I saw our way out, or my way out I guess." Her words had softened, so much that he was startled by them. It was almost sweet, much kinder than she had spoken to him in a long time. Now his tears would not be held back. Clark held his head and felt the tears running down his cheeks. He was ashamed to let Tom see him like this, but there didn't seem to be any stopping it. Tom's mouth was still working furiously on some words that just didn't seem to materialize. Suddenly Tom got up from his couch and walked to the door.

"Karen, Clark, I'm sorry. I wish I could have helped. Remember that God loves you both. Clark, my home is always open for you or the kids." With that he turned and exited the door. Now it was just the two of them.

"What about the kids?" Clark asked, now sounding resigned.

"Just pick the kids up like usual and go to a Hotel. Tell them it's a surprise test for your vacation. When you drop the kids off Sunday night I'll explain it to them."

"Will you explain it to me too", Clark now looked at her, pitifully as it might have been.

"You've been here; you know this marriage died a long time ago."
There it was. Stated so simply, Clark could not deny the truth of it. He
had been in a slump for a long time, she had been too. Maybe this was
the way. With great resolve he stood and went to the bedroom to
collect his things.

"It's all in the garage", Karen yelled after him.

"I need my papers, it's only fair." Karen nodded toward the room.

Inside Clark looked around the room. All the pictures had been taken
down. He looked at the bed and wondered how many times he had
been betrayed in his own bed. He felt nauseous and thought he might
throw up. His shock and sadness were starting to turn to anger, he was
glad. The sadness had started to weigh him down. Anger at least had
some force behind it. He walked to the safe and opened it, wondering if
Karen even knew the combination. Inside he saw his file with birth
certificate, passport etc. Next to it were the kid's stuff. For a moment
his mind raced, and in a moment of impulse he grabbed the passports
and tucked them into his jacket pocket. He closed the door and spun
the combination.

"I'm just going to get a few clothes for the kids."

No answer came from the living room, he wondered if she was
watching the same blank television that had so enthralled him the night
prior. He went to each room and threw what he assumed were clothes
they might need. Socks, underwear, jeans, t-shirts everything got packed
into the garbage sacks then thrown into the garage.

"Okay, I'm leaving." Clark's declaration sounded hollow and pitiful to
his ears. He waited for a response, but no sounds came from that
direction. Twenty years of marriage almost and he wouldn't even be
treated to a goodbye. He was angry, so completely filled with rage in
that moment that he could taste blood in his mouth. He had suffered as
the loving husband while his wife worked her way through the phone
book, fucking anyone who came calling. Well, this was to be the end of
the it; he wouldn't be anyone's victim anymore. It was time for a new
Clark.

Chapter 4

Ring, Ring.

Marjorie's phone had been ringing off the hook since Clark took off. Her hair was more frazzled than usual. It seemed like a law that when someone had you watch their area, everything went straight to shit. Without proper answers for the people being audited, her percentage of thank you to screw you was going way down.

"This is Marjorie, how may I help you."

"Marge, its Clark." Relief washed over Marjorie. He was on his way back, she would not indeed have to pull her hair out.

"Get yourself back here, things are crazy." There was an abnormally long pause on the other end of the phone. Marjorie wondered if maybe he was distracted by some bad driver.

"She left me Marge, Karen threw me out, it's over." Marjorie was sick, not so much for the news as she was for the anguish in Clark's voice.

"Come back and we'll talk it through, everything's going to be alright."

"Marge I need a favor. I need you to log into my computer and send a request for an emergency leave of absence. I need sixty days." Marjorie blinked for what seemed like a full minute, trying to comprehend what her friend was asking her to do.

"I can't log into your computer, I don't have your access card."

"Remember when I thought I lost it last month and got a new one, I found it. Open my top drawer and under the sliding drawer is the extra one, my password is on a sticky note on my monitor. Marge I gotta go, I appreciate everything. I'll be in touch." With that he was gone.

The phone line was silent. Marjorie had hours of reasons why everything would be alright to tell him, he had just to listen to all her wisdom. She thought about calling him back, but thought better of it, he had asked her for this one thing and she would not let him down. If he was found absent before his emergency request was put it, he would not have a job to come back to.

She found the card just where he said it would be. She could have guessed his password, he worshipped that boy. She wondered if he was still intending to take the kids to Europe, some crazy plan to see this last thing through.

She grabbed her phone and sent him a text, just so that she knew he had a plan that didn't involve a length of rope. Her text read, 'So still on for Europe?"

The response took longer than usual and left her no clearer than when she had no details.

'Trip on, destination changed Tierra del Fuego'

"What the hell is a Tierra del Fuego?" Marjorie opened her browser and put the words into Google. The results had varied responses, so she shifted to a map view. Suddenly she was looking at the furthest tip of South America, her eyes blinking repeatedly.

She texted her response, 'flying to Argentina?'

Now she had to wait almost ten minutes for the response to ding her phone.

'Road trip'

"Oh hell". Marjorie quickly located the extra card and sent the emergency leave request. Once she was done she looked at her own monitor blankly for a moment. Then she shook her head and walked over to Clark's desk to collect his files, if she was going to cover for him until he was back, she had best get started with it.

Chapter 5

Chloe tried her best to carefully fold the banner before she put it in her locker. It was inexplicable why she had to store the stupid thing; after all, Mrs. Fleisher had her entire classroom. She regretted joining HOSA every time she went to the meetings, but her parents had drilled into her that if she wanted a scholarship she needed something to put on the application. But why a membership drive the last week of school? To her it felt like a massive waste of time. She should have been doing something real, even an after school job would have been better than this. She could be volunteering at a hospital, but her mother had been too freaked out about Swine and Bird Flu epidemics, so here she was painting banners to encourage people to join HOSA next year. What was the point anyway, Health Occupations Students of America? It was mostly filled with girls who dreamed of emptying bed pans or holding babies. She was better than this, smarter than this. Her grades might not always reflect it, but she was smart enough to be anything she wanted to be. And more than anything she wanted to be a Psychiatrist. It was like being a brain surgeon, without all the blood and grey matter. She could figure out how just how screwed up people were, and then do her best to fix them.

It was a closely held secret that she had first become interested in Psychiatry after reading the Red Dragon by Thomas Harris, that book had totally blown her mind. She had seen the movies at a friend's house, which would have royally pissed her mother off, and thought they were alright. But the books, they had opened up the field of possibilities further than she could have ever dreamed. Of course, it was a closely held secret, like to herself. No one trying to become a psychiatrist should tell people they idolize a fictitious serial killer, no matter how brilliant a Shrink he was.

With her bag out there was just room to set the banner in and slam her locker closed. She tried to run through the to-do list in her mind, making sure that she had taken what she needed, only a few days left. She frowned just slightly, thinking that she must be forgetting something. Her mother would not be happy if she forgot some crucial piece of homework. Then she frowned even more as she thought about her lack of a car, almost preemptively arguing with herself. It was completely and totally unfair that she didn't have a car. Everyone she knew had one. If her mother had gone out and gotten a job like everybody else's mom, they would have had plenty of money to buy her a car. Chloe could have gotten a job, wanted to get a job in fact, but both her parents had forbidden it, telling her that this was her time to learn. Now instead of being happy school was over for the week, she was once again angry at her parents. Sometimes they just made her crazy.

As she made her way down the hallway the internal debate raged. She had argued those points so many times against the immovable wall of her mother that she didn't even need her to fight. Mid stride she stopped herself. She tried to will the negative energy out; no one seemed to care anyway. She knew her dad would be out front waiting for her and he had enough problems without her adding to the load.

The bright light almost blinded her as she walked outside for the first time in eight plus hours. She expected to see the familiar grey-beige insert whatever domestic car her father drove, but the drive was empty. This was highly unusual; he was not the kind of person to be late. Something must have gone horribly wrong. She pulled out her phone to text him and noticed she already had a text from him. She must have put her phone on silent for the HOSA meeting. He said he would be a few minutes late, so Chloe went over to find a spot in the shade to wait. Inside was air conditioned, but like all free spirits, she found it difficult to willingly go back in the cage once she was out. Under a large tree she found a wonderful spot that didn't have any gum or garbage. She set her bag down and lay on the grass, propping her head on the bag. Looking into the sky beyond the clouds seemed extra billowy. It made her think of how her dad used to take her to the park. They would lie on the grass and look at the clouds, trying to come up with the most unusual shape coincidences. Any fool could find a dinosaur or an elephant, they would try to find castles with buses parked in the lot, or a giant cup of coffee with a motorcycle protruding. She smiled, this was much better than thinking about the car. Damn, she was thinking about it again.

Go back to the clouds. Look that one looks like a human thighbone being eaten by a laptop computer lying on an inflatable raft. Better.

She played the game so long that she didn't notice the time passing and before she knew it she was drifting off. Whether or not she was asleep, the earth rattling sound of a horn woke her with such a start that her heart raced. She looked around for the nefarious character that had tried to be funny. In front of her, in the parking lot that had been empty sat a sad old piece of crap motor home. It was yellowed and covered in so much dust that it looked like Pig Pen from the Charlie Brown cartoon. Chloe looked around with a mischievous smile. Which of her classmates was lucky enough to be picked up by such a sweet ride? Only there wasn't anyone around. She looked hard, it seemed like everyone had gone home. Suddenly the horn blew again. She strained her eyes to see into the dusty windows. It looked just like Jack and her dad. But they didn't have a motor home. A sickening feeling crept up from her lower abdomen; suddenly she wished he could hide her face. She gathered her things as fast as she could before running toward the monstrosity. As she got closer she saw Jack was trying to open a small window. Suddenly his young shrill voice rang out.

"Isn't this the coolest thing you have ever seen?"

Chloe didn't say anything. She just wanted to get inside and out of the view of her school. If anyone saw her like this, she would never hear the end of it. Suddenly her dad was there, opening the door for her. He wore a huge idiot level grin, but something in his eyes wasn't matching.

"Are you ready to start our adventure?" He was trying too hard. Something smelled wrong with all this.

"Did they open a freeway to Europe that I don't know about?" Her quip was well paced and thoughtful. She almost smiled a little bit. Her father's face lost his idiots smile instantly. For a second she thought he might start crying. The whole thing was freaking her out. *Where is mom?*

"Mom had some work to get done, she's going to join us en route." His tone had dropped severely, he sounded almost depressed. He also sounded more genuine when he said it. His eyes matched his tone. Something was still wrong, but at least it wasn't as obvious. She looked around the motor home. It was much better from the inside. The couch was leather and the countertops were some kind of stone.

"Buckle up Chloe", he father had started the beast. It had more of a low rumble than any car she had ever been in. Blissful air conditioning began to pour down on her and she was grateful for it. She hadn't even recognized how hot and sweaty she had gotten until the cool air started blowing. She sat down in the couch and worked to figure out where the seat belts were. Finally she found them jammed between the backrest and seat. She smiled and gave the thumbs up. She didn't want to say anything more, she couldn't see her dad's face do that thing again. She wanted to see the happy face again.

"Next stop Texas." Jack jumped up and down in his seat, smiling back at Chloe.

"What about school", she tried to ask without any kind of attack. Her father was back to pretending, huge smiles and exaggerated movements.

"You get an extra week of Summer break this year." Now something was definitely wrong. They wouldn't even let her take a sick day when she had horrible cramps, but now they were taking her out a week early? She chose to watch instead of attacking. She would get to the bottom of this.

The motor home rumbled down the road and toward the freeway. For the first time but not the last time she felt the thrill of an untraveled road. Unaware of her destination she was nearly overcome with fear.

"Wait, where are we going, Texas?" It had just occurred to her that she didn't know. The answer didn't make any sense to her.

"Tierra del Fuego."

"Is that in Texas?"

Now it was Jack's turn to say something. "No silly, Tierra del Fuego is the bottom tip of South America." Chloe didn't even know what to say. Years of staring at the ceiling instead of the geography map hindered her ability to comprehend what they were saying. But her dim recollection was that the journey was a long one, like through Mexico and Central America. Images of drug cartels and dusty Mexican towns brought her little comfort.

"So where is mom meeting us?" No answer came for some time. When it did her father's tone had changed again. It was like speaking to another person.

"Somewhere out there, she wanted us to get started without her." And that was it. No more information, just the steady prattle of the road below them. She needed to think. She loosened her seatbelt and turned sideways so she could lie down. Once her head was down sleep came quickly. She never noticed when her father whispered in Jack's ear. She didn't even stir when he reached into her purse and pulled out her phone. Not even when her father opened the slide window and dropped the phone onto the passing tarmac and it shattered into a million pieces did she move. She never could remember what she dreamt of that afternoon, but it always felt like she went to sleep as one person and woke up as another.

Chapter 6

Just after Provo Clark had taken Highway 6 toward a small Utah town called Price. Chloe had fallen asleep almost instantly after the coach started to roll, but Jack had stayed with him until the point of the mountain. It was getting hot, at least the coach sure felt hot with the brilliant sun shining down. That was the thing about Utah, the high altitude combined with lack of humidity made for an intense sunlight. Where it streamed through windows a house would raise five degrees, he guessed the back bedroom was nearly a hundred degrees at the peak that day.

But now finally the sun was at their backs melting into a blood red sunset that spoke volumes about the air quality. As the light faded and faded more the vibrant colors of the Utah terra firma faded to greys and purples. His sunglasses had to be shed then the lights turned on. When he got diesel in Price he decided to try and attack some of the accumulated filth on the headlights. Mostly all he did was ruin the peoples window squeegee. The water was brown and he wasn't entirely sure he hadn't made it worse. He stepped back and wondered how he would ever get the thing clean.

I should have made him throw in a carwash.

He smiled to think of the negotiation. It seemed he and the motorhome had found each other quite by accident. He had not been looking for a motorhome until a moment of inspiration took him. He saw a motorhome driving up toward a house from the back field and barn area. Apparently they had just plowed during a horrendous windstorm, the thing was covered with filth. But there was something about it, like a hidden quality, that made him turn around just a few hundred yards down the road. He had been in a hurry to get back to the IRS, but for some reason he was drawn to this mammoth block of a vehicle as he passed by that dusty road. Clark wasn't much of a dreamer, but he found himself lost in the moment. Rolling along faraway lands in his enclosed home. A mobile base from which to explore the world. By the time the rig came to a halt he knew he wanted to buy it.

The little old bent man that emerged from it sealed the deal. He was wearing blue and white overalls, with a sears and roebuck shirt underneath. Clark was instantly reminded of his own grandfather who had worked until a week before his death. The old man was as wrinkled as a human could be, before being lost within the folds of his own skin. His eyes were still sharp and watched Clark closely as he got out of his car and walked toward him.

"Can I help you?" he called toward Clark.

"Are you selling the motorhome?" Clark tried to ask as respectfully as he could.

"You're in luck my boy, I just moved it out here to put it up for sale."

"How much?"

"Well, that's a good question. When my wife bought it twelve years ago it was almost two hundred thousand dollars." The old man spoke with such a forceful tone that Clark thought for a moment that he should just go, the man would want more than he could pay.

"Oh, I'm sorry I don't think I can pay you what it's worth. Sorry to have wasted your time." Clark turned to leave, dejected. That was exactly the sort of thing that Karen had yelled at him about. He should have known that the thing was out of his meager means. He had no business looking at it anyway. He was almost to his car when he heard the old man's voice.

"Didn't your mother ever tell you it's rude to leave a question hanging like that?" The sharp eyes were trained on him again, as if appraising him.

"I'm sorry sir. To be honest I'm not entirely sure what I can afford, or what I'm doing exactly. I promised my kids a European adventure, but when I saw it…"

"Well, that's a hell of a predicament to be in, better come inside and have a glass of lemonade to work it all out." With that the man turned and headed toward the house, shuffling his steps. Clark wasn't sure he wanted to go into the house. He had been chastised for not answering the man's questions, what kind of etiquette would he break entering into the man's domicile? Then he remembered that he was an IRS auditor, he had been in thousands of hostile situations, within people's businesses and homes. Certainly he should be able to take one old man.

Knocking lightly on the door he heard the man call him in. The screen porch door whined as they must on an old farmhouse. Inside it smelled of old people, the same as his grandparent's house had. A moment of nostalgia and a desire to ask his grandfather for advice hit him like two poorly timed waves. He was looking at pictures of the man and his wife when he came back in with two glasses of what appeared to be lemonade. He took the glass, eyeing the spoon and a small pile of white powder at the bottom of his glass. He stirred as the old man stirred.

"By the way my name is Clark."

"Clark, I'm Lester, nice to meet ya."

"Is this your wife? In the picture?" Clark immediately regretted asking. It had felt like a polite thing to say, but honestly the last thing he wanted to discuss was a wife. The old man took a long draught of the drink. Clark was still busy stirring his. He had a terrible feeling it was going to be lukewarm country time lemonade. He imagined that it would either be so strong that it would immediately strip the enamel off his teeth or so weak that he would taste the nasty well water it was surely made from. As the drink hit his lips he was shocked to find that it was in fact a little warm, but it was quite tasty. Clark took a long draught and remembered that his grandfather had also considered country time lemonade to be top shelf.

"That there is what you might call my Ex-wife." Clark was so surprised he inadvertently choked on his lemonade. He could hardly believe that a man his age could be divorced; it seemed to violate the laws of nature.

"I'm sorry." Clark tried to say when he had nearly cleared his windpipe.

"Don't be. She was an ornery old bitch anyhow." Now Clark really started to choke, but he was laughing with Lester.

"That's her damn boat anchor out there. Needed a fancy top o the line motor coach to haul her fat ass to Branson to watch all them old timey singers." The man's voice was riddled with bitterness. It was possible that she had just left him today to hear him.

"When did she leave?"

"Ten years ago and good riddance." Then Lester drained the remainder of his lemonade like it was a glass of scotch and slammed it on the table. Now he just looked crazy.

"You never did tell me how much you wanted to pay for the old thing."

"I'm sorry, I think I'm wasting your time. I have been planning a trip overseas for the last three years."

"Well, let me ask you something, did you want a vacation or an adventure? Leave those socialist sons a bitches in Europe to their own devices and drive to Tierra del Fuego. That's the adventure of a lifetime. No crowds, hell, you probably won't see another white."

"An adventure," Clark said to himself. He thought to himself of what he wanted, what he wanted for his kids. But in that moment he saw escape more than anything. This might be his chance to catch his breath.

"And just what can you pay?"

So Clark shared with Lester the events of earlier that day. He shared how he had saved up enough to take his family on a once in a lifetime vacation. He nearly wept three times.

"And now it's over. But I saw you driving it out and I just thought 'that looks like an adventure'"

Lester looked Clark up and down as if sizing him for a suit. Clark never was sure what he saw in him, or whether he was just looking for parts of himself within Clark, but he must have found something he liked.

"Since your dream got ruined, would you consider fulfilling someone else's? Clark didn't say anything. He wasn't sure what Lester meant, so it better to say nothing at all.

"I kept that motorhome because I had a dream to drive it all the way to Tierra del Fuego. Furthest point south in the Americas. I spent hours pouring over maps and reading books. I tried to learn Spanish with some tapes I got at the library, got pretty good. Well, after Emma left, I still planned to go, but it just never felt right to go alone and now I'm just too damn old and too damn scared." Suddenly his eyes looked old, as if it were a trick he could play on unsuspecting guests. Clark was speechless.

"Give me fifteen thousand bucks for it. And promise to take pictures of everything."

Suddenly Clark felt a transference, as if the momentum which had shifted so disastrously this day, was now on his side. Clark was tearing up. His own dreams of seeing European architecture and dining in chic Parisian cafes seemed so distant and miniscule now. This was a quest. This was just what they needed. This was why he had taken the kid's passports.

Now staring at the massive front window of this "Beast" he felt an enormous weight of responsibility. He was taking his children on a real exploration, not the fake kind that included safety harnesses and padded helmets. They would drive through a place different from anything they knew. Clark removed the diesel nozzle from the fill port and blinked at the reading on the pump. He hadn't even known that a person could buy four hundred dollars' worth of fuel at one sitting. It was time to take stock of his assets.

Inside the rig he laid all his treasure out on the table. He had almost twenty thousand dollars in cash, five thousand in emergency traveler's checks and his remaining balance in his new savings account. He had a camera, which he was not exactly sure how it worked. He had an old laptop that wasn't really much more than a word processor. He had the three passports and copies of their birth certificates. His phone was the only remaining means of communication. Other than clothes that was it. No jewelry or watches, almost none of the things he had spent a lifetime accumulating. Part of him was so sad to have his life condensed and distilled down to these few things that he ached inside. But a larger part of his heart spoke quietly that this is how it always should have been. That the things he owned had a tendency to own him. That he was better off without any of those items that brought with them social trappings or great admiration. He was free of those things and the labels they brought.

He walked over and tucked a blanket around Chloe. Jack was so light that Clark was able to pick him up and put him to bed in the back. With the children situated, he sat down and checked his mirrors. The rig fired up easily and with some of the dirt wiped from the headlights they actually illuminated the road before him. They were just coming into Moab, the last city in Utah. After that would come Colorado. He was either kidnapping his children or taking them on the trip of a lifetime; it seemed difficult to guess how every individual would see it. He had texted Karen that he wanted to take the kids on a short road trip and she had given her okay. Technically he had never stated just how far, but since Clark had rarely been out of their home city of Ogden, much less outside Utah, she had probably not guessed that he was taking them on an odyssey through the Americas. As long as he got through the Mexican border before she did anything rash, they should be fine.

The road ahead was so dark that it faded into oblivion beyond the shallow reach of the headlights, just the reflective lines on the road glowing ethereally into the distance. It looked a little like Doctor Who, or when they jumped to Hyper space in Star Wars. The notion that this was an adventure sounded much better than kidnapping. For as badly as his day had started, Clark sure had a large smile now.

Chapter 7

Jack was up before anybody else. Chloe was still asleep, even though he had stayed up way later than her, his mom said it was because teenagers were inherently lazy. His dad said they needed sleep because of all the growing they were doing. Either way, when he woke up that morning his dad was snoring softly in the bed next to him, still fully dressed and on top of the blankets. He hadn't even taken his shoes off, he must have been really tired. Jack got up quietly so he didn't wake him. Who knew how long he drove into the night.

They had to be somewhere close to a highway; he could hear the rising and falling sound of semi trucks as they passed by. He found his pants and shoes right next to the bed. The only item his dad had taken off before going to bed had apparently been his hat. Jack slipped it on and moved into the main part of the coach. There were small doors all over the thing, he had tried to explore them after he got in, but had been forced to sit in the navigators seat so he could belt in properly. He opened a couple of them, but didn't find hardly anything. After three doors he gave up, it was making a lot of noise and he knew if he woke Chloe up, there would be hell to pay.

Speaking of waking up, he noticed that in the few minutes he had been up that the amount of light had increased dramatically. The rig had been parked along some road and the sun was coming up directly outside the front window. Chloe already had her hand across her eyes. If the sun came fully up, everyone would be up shortly. Quietly he crept by Chloe and sat down in the drivers seat. He undid the Velcro strap and pulled the curtain around to block off half the window. He repeated the process from the other side and suddenly the coach was dark again. He looked at the controls for the driver, there must have been a million switches. He read what they said only comprehending a few. He knew where the key went, but everybody knew that. He could see the switch for the lights and the buttons to put it in gear. Closing his eyes for a moment he was driving, racing across the desert with bad guys hot on their heels. He pulled on the steering wheel to avoid a booby trap laid by the assassins. Suddenly there was trouble from the side and he looked for the rocket switch, flipping it quickly the lights under his feet came on to confirm the kill. Now he had bad guys on both sides, each driving black spy cars. He twisted the wheel from side to side to knock them off the road, trying to reach across to the rocket button again his elbow came down hard on the button in the middle of the steering wheel.

"Whaaaaaaaa", the air horn split the quiet air of the motor home like a peal of thunder. Chloe sat up and suddenly Jack's dad was standing in the kitchen looking around like the bad guys really were after him.

"Sorry, sorry." Jack tried to get out. He closed his eyes, but heard his father breathe a sigh of relief.

"I guess you found the air horn. That's one way to get us out of bed, probably not the best way." When Jack dared peer out of one eye his dad was smiling at him, stretching. Chloe looked very upset, but she always looked upset.

Chapter 7a

Clark tried to stretch the knots out of his back. He peeked out the window to see where he had landed them. It appeared that they were on a freeway off ramp. In the middle of the night it had seemed a quiet oasis, tucked away from the noise of the world. By daylight, the sound of rushing cars was so loud it sounded like they might be passing underneath. Clark wanted to look for breakfast, but remembered that by the time he and Lester had worked out the sales slip, gotten the coach inspected and registered and started it up, he was already twenty minutes late picking up Jack. Unless Lester had forgotten a can of beans, there would be no breakfast in bed.

"Well, should we go find some breakfast?" he asked. Chloe immediately nodded enthusiastically although seemingly still asleep. Jack just smiled.

Clark went in and used the bathroom, realizing that now he would have to solve the age old question 'where does it all go', by emptying the black and grey tanks. Lester had given him the twenty minute tour while it was getting inspected, but he was far from sure in that knowledge. Pull the big one first, then the small one, try not to get it on your shoes.

Maybe we should just use the bathrooms at gas stations.

Clark decided that he ought to do a once around the motor home before setting out. He was surprised by the blasting sunlight that accosted him when he opened the door. Shielding his eyes he made his way around, checking the tires, pretending he knew what to look for. Suddenly he noticed that the passenger side bumper was sticking out further than it seemed like it should. On closer inspection there was yellow paint and a definite bend in the metal. Clark started to get mad, wondering who in a yellow vehicle had hit him. Then thinking on it more, he guessed that it was in fact he who had hit an immovable object, probably on one of those tight right turns. They were the worst; he had to almost take up the opposing lane of traffic to swing wide enough to avoid situations like this. He gave the offending metal a solid kick, which repaired nothing, only leaving a small black scuff about where the yellow paint mark ended.

Opening the door the step made it's mechanical moaning and protruded the small metal platform to help him step up into the motorhome. Clark wondered how long it would be until he caught that on something as he drove by. It would be quite the leap of faith to jump two and a half feet into the coach.

He pressed the button to bring the slide in, Chloe finally shaking off the sleep stare and moving off the couch. It looked a little like one of those rooms in the Indiana Jones movies that keep getting smaller and smaller. Jack loved this part, but Chloe had yet to really smile even once. The sound of grinding gears seemed to indicate that the slide was all the way in. Clark strapped himself into the captain's chair and pressed the button to retract the jacks, now the coach rocked and bounced slightly as they came to rest on the tires instead of the hydraulic lifters. With that he turned the key, where buzzers and lights on the dashboard went crazy. He gave it a second as Lester had told him to, then turned the key and was rewarded by the bone shaking rumble of the diesel motor behind them. This was what it was all about, the ability to get back on the road in just a few seconds. He had driven that night until the very moment of exhaustion, only worrying about being out of traffic. As the rig built up air pressure the buzzing and most the lights stopped trying to alert him. He pressed his foot on the brake, released the parking brake and put it in drive. With a sudden lurch they were back on the road. Chloe was still looking around like she had just woken from a six month coma. Now she sat back down on the couch.

"Is there anything to eat?" she asked.

"I was going to find us a McDonald's", Clark replied.

"Mmmmmmm, the McGurgles for breakfast, my favorite", actually that was usually her mother's line, but apparently she felt it needed to be said. Clark pretended he hadn't heard it, Jack seemed excited by the prospect of the Golden Arches.

Clark noticed a small town ahead and hoped they had at least somewhere to eat. From the backseat he could hear rummaging.

"Dad, have you seen my phone?"

Again, Clark just pretended he had not heard anything and kept driving.

Chapter 8

It was at the McDonald's play land that Chloe first started asking questions. Clark knew it was coming, but had hoped to break the halfway point of Texas first. Now they were in Amarillo Texas, with hours to go and Chloe asking questions. Clark was trying not to panic, but once he took them out of the state, he may have become a felon. It would depend on when Karen reported the kids missing, but since she had not filed any paperwork, he thought she might not have the legal right to press charges yet. Of course he was basing his entire legal strategy off his faithful viewing habits of Law and Order. He needed some private time to Google it, but Chloe was watching him like a hawk. Somehow she knew.

Chapter 8a

Chloe was looking at her dad, but after a moment she decided to just watch Jack. She had asked a very simple question, just wanting to know when her mom would join them, but her dad had gone into another thousand yard stare. He seemed to be like an ostrich some times, if he hid his head long enough people would stop asking hard questions. It made her really sad, because her mother had done this to him. He wasn't much of a fighter and when he started getting railed on, he just stared off into space. She hoped he wasn't mad about her losing the phone. She had searched her bag twice, looked where it might have rolled out onto the floor, but nothing. She was sick to think it might have gotten trapped under the sliding part of the room. Her mother would kill her if she lost another phone. It would probably be better not to bring it up again.

She looked over at her dad again, he looked older. Something in his eyes that reduced the glimmer. She knew he was disappointed about the trip to Europe falling apart, and now apparently throwing together some silly little road trip. Chloe couldn't even guess what her mother had said to spur him on this doomed trip. She had a hard time believing

39

her mother had the creativity to come up with something like this. Thinking about the nagging and negativity that she would bring, deep down she hoped her mother stayed at home most of the trip, or missed the whole thing. Chloe resolved in her own mind in that moment to be nicer to her dad, after all, somebody had to.

Chapter 8b

This was awkward. Jack looked over at his dad and sister watching from their seats. How old did they think he was? He had told them that he was fine, that he was too old to play on the kiddie toys at McDonalds, but his father told him he needed to "get it out of your system". Now he was stuck being the creepy older kid at the play land. He was eight years old, this place was for five year olds. He walked from slide to slide, giving each a turn, always allowing two or three of the smaller kids to go in front of him.

He found a spot in the crawl through and looked at his dad. Something was going on. Jack had felt like there was some secret mission when he stole Chloe's phone last night. But now something about it just felt wrong. He couldn't put it together yet, but it wasn't like his dad to take Chloe's phone and then not say anything when she asked about it. It didn't seem very grown up to Jack. And why wasn't mom here? He hadn't wanted to seem like a baby asking for his mother, but it felt like there was a hole without her. She kept everything organized and running efficiently. Just then a boy pushed past him saying "tag, you're it", and they were off. The blissful forgetfulness of youth threw all thoughts of logic and consequence from his mind. By the time he finally tagged the boy back Chloe and his dad were standing up beckoning him with a smile. He walked over to the shoe station and put his shoes on.

Walking to the motorhome they were almost halfway across the parking lot when Jack tripped and fell. He grabbed his knee, just having slightly skinned it.

"Ouch", he said hoping it wouldn't bleed. His shoelaces were dragging behind him like a wedding dress train. All three of them looked at each other, each thinking the same thing but not saying anything.

Mom wouldn't have let him leave McDonalds without tying his shoes.

"Let's get out of the parking lot, but then you need to tie your shoes. We don't have mom here to remind us of every little thing, we need to start being responsible."

Jack nodded as he bent down to tie the shoes. Clark unlocked and stepped up into the motorhome. Jack went up second. Chloe noticed that Jack had only put a single knot in his shoelaces.

Something is going on, and I'm gonna find out what.

Chapter 9

At least when they were going though Utah there had been an occasional pine tree, the majority of Texas might as well have been the face of the moon with a slightly better irrigation plan. Long, flat, hot and dry would have all been words Clark would have used to describe the area they drove through. Clark was getting used to driving such an enormous machine, it had been steadily shrinking in his mind since he got it. The first few turns he had made were so wide that he was completely in the other lane of traffic, but now watching his mirrors he was staying in his own lane for the most part, which was a good thing considering he was on a two lane highway much of the time.

Although he was in a hurry he was trying to enjoy the ride. This seemed to be what might be called 'God's Country', at least it seemed like that to Clark. That term seemed most applicable when the area in question was essentially unlivable, but some stubborn people turned their suffering into devotion. Unfriendly stares with downturned mouths came from nearly every person he passed, as if warning him that a poorly placed stop would mean his end. Regardless of their level of Deification of the land, the farms along the sides of the roads looked like a lot of work to Clark. First of all he wasn't sure exactly where they were getting the water. The sides of the road were dead and brown, only sometimes dotted with desiccated foliage. He had heard the farmers of Texas were having a bad year, but this looked like a dust bowl like the one that came across Oklahoma in the 1930's might do everyone here a favor.

Just as he had written the place off though he noticed how the open sky and lack of protruding structures or vegetation seemed like a blank canvas. Like it held him open before God. Exposed of all his sins and his glorious imperfection. This seemed like a place where you wouldn't dare to lie, couldn't stomach not sharing your water with a thirsty stranger, where life had more meaning because it held on by the slimmest of margins. Would crops taste better here, knowing that even a couple of days lack of care would have meant their death? Maybe Clark was missing out on the real experience, passing by in his air-conditioned behemoth. Maybe the slivered eyes of the locals, many hidden behind large cowboy hats pitied him. Maybe they held some great truth that he would never understand. What he had perceived as hostility might be how the locals beckoned him to their table. He might pull over and never move the rig again; content to live the rest of his days in what he had previously thought was an uninhabitable land.

The dichotomy of the two schools of thought struck Clark. He was not typically this deep a thinker. Usually his thoughts were laid out for him in an appropriate government manual or form. His world was predicated on rules and procedures, but now he found his mind wandering to the far reaches of his own human condition. He wanted to call Marjorie; to tell her about his new thinking. To tell her that maybe all those crazy people he had dismissed as rule breaking tax filers were right, some rules were meant to be broken. He wanted to take pictures and send them to her; he wanted an adult to talk to. He looked back at Chloe and Jack; they were playing a game of Monopoly they had picked up at the Wal-Mart in Lubbock. He wished for the first time that Karen was there. Not the Karen that had left him, or the Karen that had become, but the Karen that had started. She would have loved this. She would have loved Clark in this moment. She had been young and adventurous, she would have smiled and stuck her head out the window to let her hair blow, and she would have understood when he thought two different things about the same place. But that Karen was gone, all Karen's were in fact gone. Clark tried to wipe the betraying tears before anyone noticed. It was time to grow up, become the person he was going to be, become the man that Karen deserved. Wait, what? No, she was gone, found someone else. Clark knew that, worse yet, he had known for some time without knowing.

For the first time, he allowed himself just a sliver of hope that there might be someone out there he could talk to, experience something with. Feelings of guilt came immediately after, like some cruel penance. *Why should I feel guilty? I'm the victim here, aren't I?* But still the feelings came, as if monogamy were a sickness his body couldn't fight yet. But still, it would be nice to talk to someone. Marjorie would be that person, a safe person that he could share his experiences with. Just then his phone vibrated slightly in his pocket. That meant a text message; unfortunately it was rare that good news came from a text, so Clark winced a little to read it.

'Why are you in Texas?' the message read. For a moment his heart leapt into his throat. Karen knew, he didn't know how she knew, but she did. It was over; he was beaten. He lowered his head almost down to the steering wheel. They were no more than an hour from the border; he had been so close. The coach slowed as his hope faded; luckily no one else seemed to be travelling that section of road. Then from the recesses of his memory he pulled a nugget. He steadied the wheel and texted back, 'Visiting my aunt Jennae, need family in a time like this'. It was an obscure family relation, but she did live in Texas.

'Have kids back by Monday'

'OK' Clark lied. But that gave them three more days to make it at least into the heart of Latin America. Of course he had not idea of what to expect once he got there, but he imagined it would be simple enough.

Chapter 10

Clark waited with more anxiety than he had ever experienced. It was all about the lights apparently. Green light good, no check necessary. Red light, well who knows what would happen then? Corrupt border guards might hold them up, kidnapped by Cartel members, who could say what horrors would await them if they happened to get the red light. They didn't have any guns or drugs or anything that he knew they shouldn't have, but in the end who knew? For the first time he looked at his daughter and allowed his mind to run wild on his fears. If there had been a turn around, he would have taken it. He would have run back to Utah as fast as a motorhome could take him. But at the signal he got the green light. A very courteous man asked for their passports and only then causally glanced at them. He gave Clark the wave, and his heart pounded with joy. They were through. This was it, all that worry for nothing. There hadn't been any hands extended for bribes, no threats or anything. Maybe all the stuff he had heard about Mexico was rubbish.

Chapter 10a

Chloe didn't know what to do. Mexico?? When was the last time she heard something good about Mexico? Never, that's when. And there was something wrong for her mother not to be here right now. She would not have let her father take them across the border without her. Chloe allowed her imagination to run wild for a moment; maybe her father had killed her mother? Maybe he was really some drug kingpin and was finally taking them to his lair. No, that sounded stupid to even her. But this was definitely not normal; they were not the kind of people to just pack up from school and drive into Mexico. When Jack had told her where they were going she had honestly thought he was joking, now all those years of geography classes were coming back to haunt her. This was a nightmare. Her father didn't even speak Spanish. Chloe tried to remember if she spoke it, but her mind was moving far too quickly for that. They were across the border now, she should have signaled for help earlier. Now it was too late, she was stuck with a lunatic behind the wheel. Well, he wasn't going to get away with this. She would figure a way to signal for help. She looked out the window and suddenly the world became just that much clearer, they really weren't in America anymore. Brown faces lined the streets and they looked very unfriendly. Well, if her phone was lost she would just have to steal her fathers. Someone had to get them out of this suicide mission.

Chapter 10b

Jack's eyes were wider than they had ever been. As soon as they crossed the border it was like the world he knew exploded. People were walking everywhere. There were stands selling all kinds of things like fruits, toys and piñatas. He wanted to ask his dad to pull over, but he looked preoccupied with driving at the moment. Jack opened the window to allow the smells of the new place to come in. It really smelled, not all good either. But sometimes it smelled like barbeque or fruits, other times it smelled like poop. His father gave him a look so Jack closed the window. They came to a stop at a light and a small boy about Jack's age came out. He had some kind of fruits in a bag. He was holding it up, hoping they would buy it. Jack looked at the boy; he had very dirty clothes on and only flip flops on his feet. His face was dirty and his hair didn't look like it was combed. They were probably the same age, but the boy just seemed different, like even if they spoke the same language they wouldn't understand each other. Jack had sold chocolates for his school one time door to door, but had been too embarrassed to even sell one bar. His mother had taken it to the gym with her and sold about twenty bars, enough for him to get a poster of a cool jet for his room. But other than that Jack had never sold anything, much less out on his own like this boy. This was a man-boy, out all alone trying to sell his bag of fruit. Jack wondered if he should feel bad for the boy, or bad for himself. They were different, but Jack wondered if the boy could play monopoly. Maybe not, what if the boy didn't know how to do math? Jack wanted to give the boy something, but boy's don't' really have much to give. He checked his pockets and looked down at his backpack. He opened the zipper and looked inside. Mostly it was just pencils and stuff. There weren't any toys or anything. Then Jack noticed a small solar calculator his mother had bought him, but he hadn't used it all year, because his teachers wanted them to show their work. He grasped the calculator and opened the window. The light was about to go green as he signaled the boy over. He reached the calculator down to the boy, who looked confused. Jack was trying to signal that it was a gift, the boy only looked more confused. Jack smiled broadly at the boy and the boy smiled back. He reached into the bag and removed two limes, reaching them up to Jack. Jack took them and tried to signal thank you to the boy. Suddenly they were moving away, leaving Jack's new friend in a cloud of dust and diesel exhaust.

When the dust cleared the boy looked at the calculator, smiled and laughed. When the next cars came by the street corner they found a boy with a bag of limes and a calculator for sale.

Chapter 11

At about twenty miles into Mexico they encountered another border station. At first Clark thought it must have been a trap or something. But it looked very official. He wasn't sure if it was just a checkpoint or what. But what he found from the broken English of the border guards and his own observations was that this was the real border station. There was some kind of tourist zone that extended from the border into here. Now they were really going into Mexico. Somehow it wasn't as stressful, even when he drew the dreaded red light. Somehow he knew that once he was in Mexico it would all be alright. Even when five armed border guards went through every inch and cubby spot on the rig, he felt calm. He felt calm right up until they told him that he couldn't cross. Then he didn't feel calm again. He asked Chloe to help translate for him, but she was not talking to him, only shooting daggers with her eyes when he tried to speak to her. It was getting dark and Clark was getting scared, he didn't understand why they couldn't proceed and he was running out of energy to try. The guards were asking for his insurance, but all he had was the Allstate card his agent had printed out. Apparently it was not enough. He tried to get cell reception, which he finally did on a hilltop, but the office was closed and the call dropped before he could get through to the 24 hour people. Clark decided it was a good time to call Marjorie.

The phone rang through to voicemail on the first try. The second time a weary voice picked up on the third ring.

"Hey Marjorie, it's Clark."

"I hoped that was you, sorry I didn't pick up the first time, I was getting ready for bed." There was a silence while Clark tried to figure out what to tell her. He didn't want her to worry.

"So far, so good", he lied. Another great silence followed, longer and more painful than the first.

"How's work?" Now Clark had done it, talking about work, this would help everything to move forward.

"Everything's great", Marjorie stated with an optimism that seemed very thin. Clark assumed that she was worried about him in Mexico. Regardless of the reason, Clark couldn't take this awkwardness anymore.

"Well, we're trying to get across the border, but it turns out there are actually two borders, so we're waiting." Still silence prevailed. "Oh, Marjorie they're calling me, I'll call you later." Clark lied but it just seemed so much easier than having the real conversation.

Chapter 11a

"OK, bye." Marjorie pressed the end call button on her phone. She had printed out the email and was holding it with her other hand. She had tried to put in the paperwork for Clark to have an absence, but it turned out not to be that easy. According to the email, Clark had two days to be back at his desk or face immediate termination. Marjorie set the phone down and read the email again, still no sliver of hope. She wondered for the millionth time if she was doing the right thing, but the time had passed now. She had made her decision and now they would all have to live with the consequences. She folded the letter and put it in an envelope on the kitchen table. She walked over to the kitchen sink to get her husband's night pills and a glass of water. Her hands shook slightly as she filled the glass. Closing her eyes for a moment to still her mind against all the could be's and should'a done's, she walked silently toward the bedroom.

Chapter 11b

Clark walked back down the hill. Jack was fast asleep in the back, Chloe was watching from the drivers seat as Clark sat on the ground beside the motorhome.

Maybe it just wasn't meant to be.

"What are we doing here?" Chloe's voice shocked him; she had hardly spoken in hours.

"We're waiting for something, there's an issue with our insurance or something like that."

"No, I mean why are we driving through Mexico", her look and tone were directly from her mother. This was the 'I want answers' voice. Clark was too tired to lie anymore.

"Mom is divorcing me, she told me to get out yesterday." He felt immediately unburdened when he said it. Like a guilty pleasure, one that he would certainly regret very soon. But for this one moment he was no longer poisoned by the deceit. He closed his eye, feeling the tears slide, his pretense of fatherly notions shattered, open and vulnerable.

"Why?" And there it was, the moment of peace gone; Clark braced himself to possibly destroy his own daughter. Wasn't it usually something like this that people pointed to as the moment their lives spiraled down a dark path? What should he tell her? Karen had made him promise not to tell the kids, so he had already blown one person's trust, what would he do now. Did he want to put all the blame on Karen's shoulders, work to make her own daughter hate her? Did he have that power? Or would he try desperately to shoulder the blame on Karen only to alienate his daughter? At some point she would realize that she was being basically kidnapped, so what to tell her?

"Your mother is going through some stuff, but for now I think it's best if we're apart." That seemed like a line out of the soon to be divorced handbook, maybe it would work.

Chapter 11c

Chloe didn't know what to say. She had been expecting this for months. Did he know about mom's new boyfriend? What had she told him? Chloe was so mad at that moment that tears fell down her face to match her father's. He looked devastated, she should have known. It all made sense now. Mom had finally done it, pulled the trigger. Chloe wanted to have some words of comfort for her dad, tell him that everything would be all right, but what did she know? She had known about the other guy for months and hadn't said a word to him. Was she as bad as her mother? How was she any better? What could she do now, how could she make this better? Suddenly she realized that she could do something to make it a little better anyway. She bent down and kissed her dad on top of his head and walked toward the guard shack.

"Permiso, senor, nececitamos ayuda….."

Chapter 11d

Clark started to get curious about where Chloe had run off to. He didn't think she was storming out in a tirade with how she had kissed his head, but a father never stops worrying about his daughter. He could see that she was speaking with the border guards in the building. He walked over to the building to see if anything had changed. When she noticed him she waved him closer.

"It's not our insurance, we need a special Mexican insurance. But Jorge has a brother in law that can come tonight and get us a policy. Then all we need is our Import Permit and we can go."

She was smiling so much that Clark began to think she had not heard what he said earlier. He had expected her to be devastated, crying in the motorhome, sleeping twenty hours a day. Maybe she was in shock, he heard that sort of thing happened from time to time. But if she was going to get them past this checkpoint, he wasn't about to upset the balance of the universe.

In the end it seemed money really did make the world go round. He paid money at three different places, one a bond to ensure that the vehicle left the country at some point, and they were done. If he hadn't been so tired, he would have jumped with joy. This was exactly how he had hoped it would go. His daughter the translator finding her skills necessary swoops in to save the day. He reached out instinctively to give her a hug, and then she looked at him. She was smiling, but her eyes were so sad. He pulled her tight to keep himself from crying in the Aduana, which was supposedly what the name of the building was.

Outside Clark fired up the motorhome and they backed up until they could make the turn to get through the checkpoint. This was it, he wanted to lay on the horn, but it was late at night and seemingly no one wanted to hear that. As he squeezed the rig through the barricades he noticed that two motorcycle riders were approaching. As they parked it almost appeared that one of them was a woman, but he only shook his head, doubtful that any woman would dare ride a motorcycle through Mexico. Now all he needed was a place to pull over and sleep. When no presentable place presented itself, to took what appeared to be a farm road and pulled a hundred yards down before setting the jacks, extending the slides and plopping into bed.

Chapter 12

The blare of a horn split the peaceful morning like an M-80 might an over ripened cantaloupe. Clark sprang out of the bed, almost with fists up. A half a second later he was angrily looking for his son who had performed the same joke yesterday. But when he looked to his side, Jack was there in bed with him, wide eyed. Clark moved stealthily up the motorhome, Chloe was in bed, somehow still asleep. As he parted the curtains he faced what was certainly the answer. Two Mexican men in an old pickup were trying to get to the road, only their motorhome had the way blocked. He waved to them and they shook their head, but seemed content to leave the chastisement at that. He pulled in the slides and hit the buttons to retract the jacks. It had never taken this long it seemed. He fired the diesel engine and put it in reverse. Slowly he backed along the dirt road until they got to the highway. Unsure of what to do he backed onto the highway. Suddenly there were more car horns than he knew what to do with. He must have picked the gridlock moment of driving, cars seemingly appeared out of nowhere. They were pushing off around the shoulder, keeping him from finishing his backing maneuver to get on the road. Finally he just pressed the accelerator and started to move the machine on to the road. He closed his eyes for a second; it was going to be close. Suddenly he saw the window and put the beast in drive. They jerked forward and suddenly the horns stopped and the road lay out before them.

No need for coffee this morning.

By the hour on his watch, which he was not totally sure was correct; it was just after Six AM. He thought the Aduana had said an hour earlier than his watch, meaning they had moved into Central time, but with all that had happened in the day, the correct hour had been a low priority.

All the signs were in kilometers, so it was taking him some time to do the conversion, but he thought they were about an hour outside of Monclova, whatever that was. In his mind it was the small pueblo style town, with men in ponchos and sombreros on the corners, dust devils and tumbleweeds the only signs of life, just like Desperado with Antonio Banderas. Certainly there wasn't much out here. Clark did notice there was a green bush now mixed in with the sagebrush, but guessed that the offending foliage was mostly populated with thorns and some sticky poison.

As they got closer to Monclova Clark began to laugh at himself. This was a real city; he wasn't sure why he had expected some Hollywood idea of Mexico. The city they had passed through at the border was a modern city, but to the ignorant American it had seemed more likely that any sense of modern sophistication had more to do with leaking sophistication from the U.S. Of course that was absurd, but having spent his whole life living in a place that so worshiped itself, it was hard not to see the world as a shadow of the self-proclaimed and pathetically often restated greatest country in the world.

As if a fast food restaurant sign could provide adequate punctuation to a thought, the golden arches of a McDonalds shone forth at that exact moment. Clark was too late to get off the main highway, but he could figure out a way to get back to it. He hit his blinker and took a subtle right turn into the city. Luckily it was still a larger road he first turned onto. He began to straighten out the motor home when he noticed a bus coming right toward him. He tried to gauge the distance that was left between the bus and the cars parked along the road and got somewhere between nothing and less than his motor home. Unsure of what to do he pushed the coach as far right, until he thought he would hit cars, then watched as the bus adjusted his rear view mirror and kept on driving. Luckily it had not broken anything, but the bus had just kept going, as if that were a normal thing, to pass so close they adjusted passerby's windows. *What the hell, I guess things work a little different down here.*

Ahead was the object of his desire, but now where to park the lumbering beast was the question. Jack was jumping up and down with excitement, probably based upon the fact that the majority of their rations were of the Hostess variety. Clark had told himself that they would eat local, but the familiarity of the red haired clown just felt right. They would get to Mexico later, right now they needed a little bit of home. Only there wasn't a parking spot that could possibly fit their vehicle. Clark had to drive a hundred yards further, until some abandoned buildings had enough open street parking that he could comfortably set up. Finally he was parked and he breathed a sigh of relief. There was something about driving this huge thing that kept him coiled tightly, a wound spring poised for action.

"Let's go get a taste of home."

They locked up the door and headed down the street toward the familiar looking building. Actually the whole city looked familiar, like the industrial side of any small non tourist city. Until someone on a cart being pulled by a donkey passed them, that was unique. They stopped to stare at the man, who seemed to be hauling large bags of something, concrete maybe. Once he had passed they felt they could proceed. The heat was oppressive, with just a hint of a breeze that tasted slightly of dust and diesel exhaust.

Inside the McDonalds they were back in America. Sure the workers spoke Spanish, but it wasn't that unusual in Utah to have minimum wage types speaking broken English. They ordered Big Macs and Cokes; Lester had told Clark that the secret to safe intestinal travel south of the border was to have at least a Coke a day. The same beverage that could dissolve a penny would save you from the dreaded Montezuma's revenge, or so he had heard. It sounded alright to Clark, he didn't drink much soda, but it seemed like a nice treat. They sat down to eat their food and watched the locals.

Whereas in Utah it seemed that this kind of fast food restaurant attracted the bottom tier of society, it seemed this was a middle class level establishment. Many people in pressed shirts and ties were there. They ate their food and watched the locals. To be fair the locals seemed to be watching them as well, Clark and Jack with their brown hair didn't stand out too much, but Chloe had bright blonde highlights that acted like neon signs screaming 'gringos'. Of course they didn't think about how much lighter their skin was, but each person that passed seemed to notice them and then return to their meal without making anyone feel uncomfortable. Finally, Clark felt like they had stayed long enough, that it was time to get back on the road. They threw their garbage into the can and walked back out into the heat, which seemed to have gotten somehow much worse in their absence. Walking up the street to the motorhome was agony, sweat almost instantly beading on Clark's back. When they got to the coach Clark noticed something.

"Son of a bitch." He ran over to the coach to inspect the bottom storage compartment. The metal was bent, the door left slightly ajar. "We've been robbed." Jack looked like he was going to cry, although to his credit the tears never fell from his dewy eyes.

"What did they take?" Chloe asked. Clark opened the door and tried to think. It seemed like there was something under there, but he couldn't remember what.

"The lawn chairs and rug," he stated finally remembering.

"Well, that's not so bad right? I mean they could have stolen the whole thing. They're not inside right?"

For the first time it occurred to Clark that the robbers might not have left. He instinctively pushed Chloe behind him and looked toward the door. It didn't look bent or forced in any way.

Did I lock the deadbolt? Heck did I lock it at all? Maybe I didn't. What if they're hiding inside there until we get in so they can do horrible things to us?

He tried to collect himself, but this was so far out of his comfort zone it felt like an episode of the Twilight Zone. Clark did not have interactions with robbers, unless they were people robbing the IRS from their fair share of the tax burden. Clark didn't have a gun, hell he didn't even have a stick to poke at them. He grabbed the door and shook the handle, which held fast like it was locked.

Does that mean I locked the door, or I didn't lock the door and the robbers did? What do I do now? This was the stupidest idea ever. What have I done to my family?

Slowly, like he was defusing a bomb he reached into his pocket and withdrew his key. He slipped it into the lock silently, gingerly opening the lock, hoping not to disturb any nefarious types that might be lying in wait. Once the deadbolt was retracted he grasped the handle and slowly pulled the door open. He closed his eyes, as if bracing for some unknown attack from all angles, but when nothing came, he opened it further and peered inside. It looked like he had left it, but that's just what a clever thief would want him to think. He signaled for the kids to stay put while he checked out the coach.

Chapter 12a

Chloe was regretting helping her dad get past the border. It had been a moment of weakness; her desire to make amends for not telling him about the other man. But now look what she had done. Obviously her father was overreacting, but they had been robbed. Robbed on their first day in Mexico, a country they planned on passing completely through. Maybe she could talk some sense into him, convince him that while this had been an amazing adventure, it was too much for them. She was lost in her thoughts when her father's sweaty face appeared in the doorway.

"It's okay, let's get back on the road."

Chloe followed Jack up into the coach. Jack was being really quiet, but she guessed that was normal for a kid. Suddenly there seemed something not right, something that made her stop walking, look around.

"Why are there feathers everywhere?"

Suddenly her father looked a little embarrassed, but used the moment to throw a well-worn steak knife into the sink. Chloe looked at him and tried not to, she tried with all her might, but suddenly her eyes were watering and she was doubled over laughing.

Clark shook his head and felt his eyes water at the relief of laughing himself.

"I thought it was somebody hiding under the blanket. We probably need to buy another pillow."

Suddenly Jack sprung up and ran to the back bedroom.

"Holy crap dad, you killed it."

"Okay, let's get back on the road." With that Clark went outside to secure the broken compartment door. Within a few minutes they were fired up and trying to figure out how to get back on the highway. Only one close call later they were back on the highway headed for Monterrey.

Chapter 13

Clark wasn't sure where it had started, but somewhere about Monclova Mountains had sprung from the ground, though seemingly not recently, as they looked very old indeed. Their brown rounded tops seemed to tell an old story of rain and erosion. The whole landscape was barren, but as he had noticed earlier, there were occasional splashes of green, though very little seemed watered here. Clark knew the copper canyon was somewhere in northern Mexico, but he wasn't really sure where that was. The further they trekked the more picturesque the barren landscape became. No more vegetation grew, but the color seemed to spring from the ground itself. Long veins of purple rock opened to offset the taupe dirt and olive sage. It was beautiful in the way that unforgiving terrain can be, always followed by Clark saying 'but I wouldn't want to live there'. Only he could see living here, he didn't know how, but something felt like home here. Maybe it was the lack of civilization that was inspiring him to start a ranch or homestead, but it called to some unknown part of him, enticing him to reach his hands deep into the soil to rediscover that lost part of his humanity, his connection to the earth. Just then they passed a small corral and horses and he could see a clear picture of himself, surveying the landscape from atop his mighty steed. A man could probably go hundreds of miles without being bothered by anyone. This was the kind of place where no one would discover your body, where bleached bones stayed discarded because it was just the way of the world. A sign ahead indicated they would have to make a left to visit Monterrey. For a moment indecision plagued him, instead of taking the left he turned right toward a sign labeled only 'agua'.

The agua turned out to be something different from what he had expected. He turned the ignition off and walked toward a three foot brick cube and a blue barrel. He wondered if the hose for the water was in the barrel, or if you had to bring your own. Only as he got right next to them he realized that there was no hose. The blue barrel was a garbage can, which reminded him that the needed to dump the McDonalds leftovers, they were starting to smell. Looking down into the brick cube it suddenly came clear to him, it was a well. The idea of it seemed at first awesomely novel, some romantic notion of how water should spring from the ground. In application, it was going to be very difficult to get any of that water into the motorhome. In fact, given that the water was some distance down, he wasn't sure exactly how he was getting that water at all. Now that he had pulled over he felt it was a point of pride. Going back to the motorhome he looked through the compartments to see if there was a rope and bucket. After a few moments of futile searching, it was obvious that there was no such tool. He sat dejected on the stair while the kids played out their endless game of monopoly, usually punctuated by cries of cheating and unwillingness to continue playing. But lack of options seemed to bond them to the game.

A truck of many colors of bondo and rust pulled up in front of Clark right next to the cistern. A man got out of his vehicle and went to the camper shell that was somehow attached to the rusted, who knows what make truck. From the back he pulled a long tube and a section of hose. He dropped the section of hose into the water and pulled out what looked like a gas can and put the other end into it. Then he pulled the handle on the tube section, which came out about a foot and a half, then he pushed it in, a few more and it appeared water was flowing into the can. Clark was so mesmerized by the simplicity of the contraption that he walked over instinctively. The man smiled a mostly toothless grin, signaling Clark to pump the actuator while he held the hose in the can. Clark noticed that it worked amazingly well, although the water was not as crystal clear as his dream of it had been. When it was full or near enough the man signaled to stop. He smiled again and gestured toward the motorhome. Clark smiled and dismissed the idea, after all how would they possibly fill the tank, and would he want the tank filled anyway. But then an idea struck him and he held up his finger to indicate that the man should wait one minute. Clark found the empty gas cans that had been in the back compartment. He had bought them in case they needed extra fuel capacity, but water seemed as or more important here in the desert. He tore off the caps and once again the two worked their water pumping magic. Clark was really enjoying this, feeling like he was experiencing some authentic piece of a culture here. Then it was full. The man pulled him pump out and drained the water from it. He placed it carefully back into the camper shell of his vehicle, then put the water in and without a word drove off. Clark didn't know what to say, he had imagined there would be some kind of exchange of information between the two, but he was just gone.

"Well there goes our chance to be friends" Clark yelled after the man with a slight chuckle. He picked up the plastic jug and prepared to haul it back to the coach. Just then the sound of dueling motorcycle engines came over the crest of the hill. They were awfully loud for how small they were, and got even louder as they approached. Clark expected the bikes to go thundering by, but as they got closer they seemed to be slowing down. As the bikes rode around the motorhome it seemed like they were coming toward him. Then a second later they were parking within a few feet of him.

The two riders seemed about as different as two could be. One was on a beautiful black Harley Davidson, full dress and throaty as a lion. It was simple, without any of the cheesy leather streamers or airbrushed eagle feathers. The rider was young looking from his clothes. His jeans were appropriately distressed for a twenty something, with a leather jacket that somehow had been similarly distressed. For just a moment Clark shook his head at the youth of today.

The second rider was on a bike that looked like it was stolen from a museum. Military green, it looked like a bike straight out of an Indiana Jones movie. It had been quiet in comparison to the Harley, but it did have a sound of authenticity. When the rider dismounted it became obvious that it was a woman. The pants were just too tight for a man to bear. The full faced helmet kept her face from view, but the ballistic style jacket was unzipped just enough to make Clark blush. When she unfastened the helmet strap and removed it Clark felt a small agonizingly pleasurable pain in the pit of his stomach. She wasn't just a beautiful woman; she was a radiant creature. She had a quick, devious smile and perfect teeth.

"Did you leave any water for the rest of us?" she asked.

"Well, yes, there's plenty, but. Do you have a bucket and rope?" Anne looked at him with a hidden smile, looked back at her bike, and looked back at Clark.

"Nope, didn't think to bring one. I guess we'll douse ourselves at a future place." Even with her hair matted and sweaty she was still, well, Clark couldn't say exactly what she was. Unique was the first word he would have said, but would have felt that lacked proper description. "Thanks anyway". She turned to put her helmet back on.

"Please take some of mine" Clark blurted out, sounding much less cool than he wanted to.

"You mean you have a bucket and a rope but you aren't going to let us use it?"

"No, I don't have anything; there was a man with a pump, earlier." Anne was giving him a hard look. Clark instinctively looked at the ground.

"Oh quit it", the young man with her said. "We're much obliged, just need to rinse the road dust off our faces and maybe wet our jackets. My name's Jordan and this is my mother Anne." Jordan reached out his hand to shake. Clark noted the comment and tried to mentally digest it, from an outside prospective it seemed like he was trying to do calculus in his head.

"My name's Clark." Clark reached out and shook the young man's hand. There was something in his bearing that made determining his age difficult. Sometimes he seemed younger, sometimes older. Clark tipped the container down to allow water to pour out the spout. Jordan quickly rubbed his hands together in the water, and then pushed it up to his face, scrubbing and wetting his hair as he went. Clark was almost laughing to himself; the boy had damn near taken a bath. He shook his head, sending water down onto his jacket and the dusty ground. Clark could only imagine what it would be like to ride in this climate without air conditioning. He went to pour again, Jordan signaling a question as if to say, 'Okay if I go again' to him. Clark nodded and Jordan repeated the process, this time also pushing a few handfuls onto the shoulders of his jacket. Now he really was a dripping mess. Clark thought he had an extra towel, maybe he should go into the coach and get him one.

"I can get you a towel," Clark offered.

"You kidding, this is twenty minutes of air conditioning." Jordan smiled pleasantly, as if he were using words he had saved for that occasion.

"Anne, are you ready for your bath?" Clark's question shocked even him, maybe mostly him. He wasn't the kind of person who made such comments, even in jest. He knew he would have gone red faced, so he focused on pouring the water efficiently and effectively. It seemed like an eternity that Anne took to walk over to the water spout. He assumed she was furious, as was her right, his comment was inappropriate. It was a foolish thing to have said and he wished there had been some way to take it back.

"Alright Clark, get to pouring so I can get this goat smell off me." It took Clark a second to realize that was the signal to start, he had thought he was being reproached, but it seemed she was a good sport after all. *Beautiful women aren't usually good sports about anything, much less a comment regarding their needing or wanting a bath. I guess there really is something different to this one.* While less vigorous than her son's face bath, she seemed even more grateful for the clear water. He poured slower, watching her splash the water over her face and pull her hair back. Even with short hair she was a hot mess right now. Her makeup was very slight, but still a small black line ran from both eyes. Clark was sure that she smelled 'goatish' as she had claimed. But still, there was something about her. She walked like a gun slinger, confident and sensual. Her face held the first lines of what would probably be a spectacular set of wrinkles, right at the corners of her eyes and just a couple on her cheeks. She smiled a lot and always like a child who had just been found innocent of raiding the cookie jar due to a lack of prosecutorial evidence. She was thin and fit, but more than that, she held herself well. It was so rare that it was hard to define, but a generation of women who believed they should wear their pajamas to the grocery store had caused Clark to forget how a woman was supposed to look. Anne looked like a female adventurer, and the fact that she had ridden here on an old motorcycle seemed to confirm it. Clark wanted to ask her questions, follow her and worship her. She was a goddess, a sweaty, smelly, hideously beautiful goddess.

"I could get you a towel," he offered. Mostly he just wanted an excuse for her to stay, to linger a moment longer in his company.

"I can skip the towel, but if I could use your bathroom it would keep me from having to find a big sagebrush to squat behind." Clark laughed out loud.

"Of course, please, help yourself." Clark tried to be gentlemanly as he pointed her in the direction of his RV toilet. It only occurred to him as he heard voices inside the motor home that he should have made introductions. Instead now he was forced to sit outside, lest he be some creeper trying to listen to a tinkling woman. No, certainly he would not be that person.

Jordan and Clark sat there, next to the well, looking at each other, not really speaking. Certainly they had questions and stories for each other, but it seemed wrong to leave Anne out of their witty banter. Suddenly there were voices inside the coach, it sounded like Anne. He was hoping something wasn't wrong. He wasn't sure what the protocol was for leaving Jordan with the water, but he nearly jumped from where they were into the motor home. As he popped into the coach he found the three of them sitting at the table, discussing proper playing etiquette for Monopoly. He had expected something, but this hadn't been it. Clark thought to make introductions, but it seemed like they had known each other for some time. Anne was explaining to them how she had seen the game run in competition. Her explanation seemed far more entertaining than the game itself, both Chloe and Jack were laughing and asking her questions. Clark tried not to interrupt, instead sitting in the driver's seat to watch. Pretty soon he stopped listening to the words, instead just watching the three of them laugh and joke with one another.

How long since Karen laughed like that with the kids? When did we become such grown-ups?

He got lost in a moment of self-pity. Wishing for a future that left the past unremembered, he wondered what the world actually held for him. Maybe he was going to go to prison, he never Googled the legality of what he was doing. Suddenly he noticed that Jordan had also come inside. He was sitting in the passenger seat, a sad smile on his face. There was more to that boy than met the eye. Some kind of unnatural depth in the way he treated the most basic of human interactions, like he treasured them. Clark realized suddenly that Jordan had lost someone, nothing obvious, but Clark would have bet anything. Now Clark was watching Jordan, who was watching his mother play with Clark's kids, who were probably thinking about their mother. This was getting complicated, over nothing more than a rinsed face and access to a porcelain toilet. He needed to get rid of these two as quickly as possible.

"So where are you guys headed?" Anne was speaking directly to Jack, although the question seemed to hang out there, allowing for anyone to answer it. However, only Jack seemed excited to share their personal details.

"We're driving this thing all the way to Tierra del Fuego." He spoke the words just as one might expect a young boy to proclaim his exploration of the world. He said it like it was easy, done in short order and with much bravado. When he heard the name from his son's mouth Clark was immediately devastated. It hadn't occurred to him how impossible a task he had laid out for himself and his children until Jack had said it. *I don't even know where we're going; I don't have a map, speak Spanish, know the way, have any friends or anything of value for this trip.* Right then he wanted to end the adventure, somehow not the first or second time in two days.

"We're headed down that way too; maybe we can hang out sometimes, share information, and pool our resources." She was saying this for Jack, to make him feel good. But it was Clark that needed to hear it. He dared to allow himself a little hope for their adventure. At least now there would be another adult in the vicinity if something happened. He looked up at Anne and found his tongue swelling. She made his mouth go dry every time he locked eyes with her. Either he was attracted to her, or she was giving him Dengue fever. "Where were you headed first, Clark?"

"Uhm, I thought we would head over to Monterrey. I heard the food was great." Clark was proud of himself for being able to come up with a name, but Anne's smile faded almost instantly. She looked at Jordan, as if having an unspoken conversation.

"Clark, let's get your water loaded back up and head toward some dinner." She was smiling again, tussling Jack's hair as she squeezed her way out of the dinette. Jordan was already outside waiting for them as they came down the steps. Now the three were together Anne got closer to Clark.

"I don't think it's a good idea to go to Monterrey." Anne was speaking close and low enough that Clark assumed the kids couldn't hear anything.

"Why?" Clark asked, not intentionally trying to draw out the conversation or even allowing that he had any valid argument, but Anne smelled so good he couldn't help himself.

"I take it you don't read the newspapers?"

"I guess not." Anne gave him a wry smile which he returned at the appropriate interval.

"Drug cartels, murders, piles of bodies, ring a bell?" Clark got a little nauseous for a second. He had not considered that actually. But Monterrey was such a big city, he had always heard great things about it.

"Well, where to then?"

Anne smiled, which Clark could never tell whether it was from his capitulation or just him, but he knew that with that smile something in him had shifted. Like a switch that went from one position to another, part of his heart had just gone dark while another sprung back to life after years of dormancy. That smile, along with an unknown quantity of her smell and the way he reflected in her eyes, had him in a hell of a lot of trouble. He loaded up the water and prepared to follow Anne Carter to where ever this road ended.

Chapter 14

Saltillo was another major city, continuing the trend of bucking Clark's idea of Mexico. The city was large and with possibly narrower streets than Monclava, if that were possible. However, unlike in Monclava, now Clark had allies in Jordan and Anne, who were able to find him places to squeeze through and even secure him a parking spot near the restaurant. The bikes tucked in front of the motorhome seemed like a natural fit. Jack was so excited to ride on one of the motorcycles. He had hardly let Clark think on the drive there. It was when and where and when again. Looking back at Chloe he noticed that there had been a slight change there as well. He was having a hard time putting his finger on it, but there was something different about Chloe as well. Maybe this was how it was all meant to work out. Walking in, Clark noticed they seemed like one big family.

They were having dinner at La Canasta. Clark was shocked by the level of service. It seemed like every time he turned around, someone was asking him what they could do to help. Finally he stopped doing anything. They all talked about the trip. Anne and Jordan had only planned on going as far as Buenos Aires, but that was practically all the way anyhow. Jack begged them to come all the way, and Anne seemed to be struggling to tell him no. Jack seemed to hold a lot of sway with Anne.

It was with some alarm that Clark finally realized what was different with Chloe. She never wore much makeup, but tonight she had definitely done more than usual. He might not have noticed, but Jordan and she had been speaking together in hushed tones all night. Suddenly he didn't like Jordan as much; his smiling face now seemed to hold evil plots and future ruinations. He would have to keep a closer eye on that boy.

Dinner was phenomenal. He expected to regret his choice of Chile Verde sometime around 2AM. The sweat beaded on his nostrils indicated that this was slightly hotter than he was used to, but he couldn't stop eating it. The pork was tender, and such a dark red color that he thought it might have been smoked first. The sauce was a beautiful green, flecked black where the Chiles had been roasted. There were handmade corn tortillas from that morning; they met only polite nods when Jack had asked for flour. Limes were plentiful and made a great addition to Clark's Sol cerveza. By the time they introduced him to the Michelada, he knew they would not make it far from Saltillo that night.

At the presentation of the check, Clark was faced with a dilemma. He would not have the money to support two other mouths. He needed to pay cash for everything, else Karen would know where they were. So he was glad when Anne asked for a separate check. He felt bad when he glanced over and saw her pulling a credit card out of a wallet that seemed to contain less than a hundred dollars American. They both paid and Clark first started to wonder who this woman was, and how she saw getting to Buenos Aires on no cash.

In the parking lot Anne pulled him close.

"Are you out of your mind?"

"What, I didn't…." Clark was flabbergasted. He was used to being attacked, but usually he had some idea of what his offense had been.

"Don't ever have that much money in your wallet. You'll get us all killed. Find a place to stash the bulk of your money, then a couple of hiding spots for emergency money." Anne was shaking her head at him, as if reprimanding a silly teenager. Clark hung his head, it was obvious now. He shouldn't have had that much money flashing about. He had put them all in danger. He would have to be smarter.

"I'm sorry, I didn't think about it."

"Well, Clark, I'm not mad. I just thought someone should tell you, that's all. But if you want to make it up to me, boil me some water for tea." Now she was trying to be overly nice, like she was propping up a rag doll. This was not at all how he had planned for this to go. He was going to show her how strong and successful he was, so she would fall helplessly into his arms. He was the hero here, that's how it should have gone. But Anne was already putting her gear on. Clark had thought to sleep right there on the road, but Anne was apparently intent on driving. Clark gave himself a couple of slaps, just for good measure. He would be fine.

The diesel roared to life, destroying the silence of this quiet area of the busy town. The bikes nearly drown him out and they left in a haze of exhaust and good intentions.

A few miles outside of town Clark noticed they were headed East. They were supposed to be heading South, always South, that seemed a simple principle. He would have said something, but he knew he was a little overly drunk to discuss directions; he was having a hard enough time keeping the big rig on the road. Slowly the temperature dropped and they actually started to see small trees, junipers maybe. The roads cut deep into the mountains, even through a tunnel, before heading further up into the Mexican mountains.

Finally there was a small dirt road, which Clark had serious questions about taking the motor home on, but when they signaled, he followed. About a hundred yards in the road turned and went behind a small rise. Now he understood, the rise kept them invisible from the road. He put the parking brake on and leveled the coach. Another button popped out the slides and he was ready for bed. His eyes hurt, as if they had a thin coat of acid applied. Anne and Jordan hadn't said anything to them since the restaurant. Jack was already asleep in the bed. Clark looked outside, not sure what to say. For a moment he thought of the dangers outside, but also that he didn't know Anne or Jordan, maybe they were dangerous. He turned the deadbolt, noticed that Chloe had already fallen asleep, gave her a kiss and went to bed himself.

His dreams tortured him, visions of a woman that must have been Anne. She was always maddeningly out of reach. She was teasing him, telling him how she wanted him, only him. He could almost feel her hands on him, making him ready; almost hear the sound of her knocking…. *Was that real?* Clark sat up in bed, straining his ears for any sound that didn't come from his mind. He slipped out of bed and put his pants on. He crept slowly, trying not to wake Jack or Chloe. He went to the door and pushed aside the drape. There was Anne with her sleeping bag around her. Clark unlatched the door.

"Okay, so it might have been a little colder than we were prepared for."
Anne was smiling, but her nose was bright red. Clark opened the door
and she walked up and in. She kept the sleeping bag tight around her.
Clark was without words, he was sure there was something he should
say, but he had no idea what. She looked so cold, shivering beneath the
cocoon of her sleeping bag. His fatherly instinct kicked in first, he
wrapped his arms around her, trying to use his body to warm hers. He
was surprised, she was softer and smaller than she had seemed. Even
with the bag around her, his arms could have almost circled her twice.
He felt her shivering next to him; he should have offered them to stay
much earlier. As was his ritual with cold children, he rocked her softly
from side to side, unconsciously humming something soothing. He felt
something soften within Anne, as if something made her let go, she fell
into him more. Suddenly her mouth was on his, the cold trembling lips
dancing on his. Her mouth was so small, the kisses exacted painful
precision on his mind. He was having sensory overload, trying to
remember the last time he had really been kissed. He tried to remember
what to do, not too much tongue, advance and retreat, soft and hard,
but all he could feel was Anne. Her smell invaded him, possessed him.
It was as if the world stopped spinning to allow that kiss to endure. As
if they had absorbed all the heat in the world, all its energy and fight, as
if there was nothing for those seconds but their mouths on each other.

A light knocking on the door shattered the moment, the stark
realization coming to them both simultaneously. Clark stepped back,
the demon possession having passed. He wanted to say he was sorry,
but he wasn't. He knew he was about to face her son, but all he could
think about was how to make that thing happen again.

Clark went to the door and opened it. "Are you taking frozen
refugees?" Clark nodded stupidly, like a child trying to respond on
Christmas morning after having gotten exactly what they wanted. He
didn't know what to do next. To say it was awkward would have been
to elevate the definition. Eventually Anne saved them all.

"We'll just setup here on the floor, thanks Clark." Clark was too busy
sorting himself to do anything but nod and walk back to the back
bedroom. Looking at his son he felt a slight wave of guilt, which he
strongly countered with a dose of self righteousness. This was going to
be a long night.

Chapter 15

Morning seemed to very slowly, but once it was there, Clark immediately wished he could try to sleep again. He had tossed and turned, but as everyone else seemed bright eyed, he did his best to hide how tired he really was. Apparently he had unwittingly agreed to do some hiking today, which didn't sound right to him, but even his own children were against him on this. Anne talked him into boiling some water so she could make her tea while Clark dug through the bottom of the motor home until he came up with a couple of old army backpacks and three canteens. He rinsed them out twice each, and then sniffed; it smelled just like water inside a metal canteen. Jack didn't seem to mind, drinking it down and needing to refill it before they even left. Somehow their camping spot was close enough to set out from there. Clark was amazed by Anne and Jordan's ability to pick a spot. They locked up the coach and set off. The early morning cold wore off within the first few minutes, the sun doing its best to blind them as they hiked almost directly east.

The ground was ideal for hiking until the ragged pine trees took over. The trails seemed sporadic and poorly maintained. Clark tried to console himself with the knowledge that the return trip would be downhill, but the memories and fear of the night's Chile Verde plagued him. The trees did offer some relief from the sun, and the higher they climbed, the more it looked like an alpine forest. Clark would never have thought this place existed. It had a rugged beauty to it, again like much of wild Mexico, it left you with the sensation that not many people came here.

Jordan was on point, occasionally checking his map and a GPS, with Clark at the rear. Then they came to the top of a ridge, they had made it. Everyone had nearly caught their breath by the time Clark made it. He wanted to reward himself by dousing his head with water, but he knew the return hike would be hotter, so he might wish for that water back.

"Whew, quite a hike. You guys wanna have some lunch before we head back?"

Anne was chuckling softly to herself. Jordan was making a sour face as he informed Clark that they were only about half way. He pointed through the trees at another distant top. Clark sighed heavily; this was entirely too much like work.

By the time the group crested the actual peak Clark was nearly through his water. He had tried to be resourceful, but he hadn't been able to unstick his tongue from the roof of his mouth. But now on the knob that had been hidden from his earlier vantage point, he understood why they were there. He could see for miles in every direction, an entire mountain range laid out before his feet. Suddenly his feet didn't hurt as much, his legs weren't as tired. Jack still had running around energy, endeavoring to find bigger and better things to throw down the mountain. Jordan was exploring with him, leaving just the three to take in the view.

"Thanks for bringing us here Anne". Chloe surprised Clark; he hadn't thought her the kind of girl that thanked people without him or Karen asking her to. Maybe he had misjudged her. He often wondered how she behaved when she was out of pocket. Right at that moment he couldn't have been more proud. He put his sweaty arm around her, which she only slightly winced at. This was a lifetime memory, the kind he had denied his kids all these years. This wasn't him, but maybe he could become the man that did things like this. The spontaneity of it all was his favorite part. Karen wouldn't have done this in a million years. This would be his and Chloe's and Jack's forever. He looked over at Anne, who had been watching them. She looked sad, lost in some thought that wasn't all that pleasant. He wanted to say something to cheer her up, some light hearted way to express his gratitude. But he wasn't funny, wasn't witty and charming. What did he have to offer at this juncture?

"Did I tell you that I'm an IRS auditor?" Suddenly Anne's face snapped its stare. Apparently she had not thought he was. She was just softly chuckling and looking at him.

"No, but I believe it. Is this how you tell me I'm getting audited?" She smiled that little half smile, it seemed so devious, so deliciously devious.

"Well, now that you mention it…" Clark tried to bait her into one peal of laughter. He wanted to make her laugh with him, not just at him. He knew he could be funny if he got enough practice with someone who wanted to laugh with him.

"Did you hear the one about the IRS Auditor?" He asked Anne. Chloe looked at him like he had just sprung horns from the top of his head. Anne shook her head no and turned to listen.

A buddy of mine audited this guy named Ralph. The IRS auditor is not surprised when Ralph shows up with his attorney. The auditor says, "Well, sir, you have an extravagant lifestyle and no full-time employment, which you explain by saying that you win money gambling. I'm not sure the IRS finds that believable." "I'm a great gambler, and I can prove it," says Ralph. "How about a demonstration?" The auditor thinks for a moment and says, "OK. Go ahead." Ralph says, "I'll bet you a thousand dollars that I can bite my own eye." The auditor thinks a moment and says, "No way! It's a bet." Ralph removes his glass eye and bites it. The auditor's jaw drops. Ralph says, "Now, I'll bet you two thousand dollars that I can bite my other eye." The auditor can tell Ralph isn't blind, so he takes the bet. Ralph removes his dentures and bites his good eye. The stunned auditor now realizes he has wagered and lost three grand, with Ralph's attorney as a witness. He starts to get nervous. "Want to go double or nothing?" Ralph asks. "I'll bet you six thousand dollars that I can stand on one side of your desk and pee into that wastebasket on the other side, and never get a drop anywhere in between." The auditor, twice burned, is cautious now, but he looks carefully and decides there's no way this guy can manage that stunt, so he agrees again. Ralph stands beside the desk and unzips his pants, but although he strains mightily, he can't make the stream reach the wastebasket on other side, so he pretty much urinates all over the auditor's desk. The auditor leaps with joy, realizing that he has just turned a major loss into a huge win. But Ralph's attorney moans and puts his head in his hands. "Are you OK?" the auditor asks. "Not really," says the attorney. "This morning, when Ralph told me he'd been summoned for an audit, he bet me $20,000 that he could come in here and piss all over your desk -- and that you'd be happy about it!"

Anne's smile and laugh seemed like music to Clark's ears, like hearing birds chirping or angels singing. He wished at that moment that he knew another joke, but his mind was empty. He saved that one for any especially difficult audits. He found it broke the ice with a certain kind of taxpayer.

He smiled at himself, very pleased that he had made her laugh. When he looked at Chloe, she was doubled over, laughing so hard that her eyes were watering. Suddenly she was wrapping her arms around him, like she used to do as a little girl. Then it didn't seem like laughing as much as crying. "I'm sorry dad, I knew about it. I should have told you." Then the tears started for real. Shaking tears that left her almost totally in his arms. Clark was trying to pretend she wasn't saying what he thought she was saying. *How could Karen do that to her?* He was so angry, so heartbroken; wondering if this would be the thing that ruined relationships for his daughter. He also didn't want to have this moment in front of Anne. He looked up, but she was gone.

"It's okay honey, everything's okay." He just stood there, trying to love Chloe enough, trying to absorb the pain out of her. He would have done anything to have saved her from this. Chloe pulled away, trying to dry her eyes and save what was left of her makeup. She wasn't a total wreck, but she was close. Looking at each other, it was like they were staring at new faces, or faces that kept evolving anyway.

Chapter 15a

Jack was on the trail. He knew there was some buried Aztec gold somewhere here. Jordan had said he wasn't sure, but Jack knew. This was just the kind of place he would have hidden the treasure. If only he had a map. Before long Jordan called to him, "Hey, we better get back, we don't want to get too far from the group." Jack was devastated, how would they find the treasure if he couldn't explore. When he got back to where Jordan was standing, Jordan had his hand out. "I have something for you", he said.

"Really, what is it?"

"Close your eyes." Jack squeezed his eyes closed so that nothing got through. He felt something slip into his hand, it was heavy and metal. Opening his eyes he saw the biggest Swiss Army knife ever. It must have had a hundred different tools.

"Mine, to keep?" Jordan smiled, though his eyes looked sad.

"It's yours, for keeps." Jack sat down immediately and started to open the different tools. There were scissors, all kinds of knives, screwdrivers, files and even something to take the scales off fish. Jack had a lot of questions about the knife. Jordan found a spot close to him to sit on the hard ground. He went through all the different tools, although some of them left him wondering. Finally he jumped up and waved for Jack to follow him. Jack was close on his heels, Swiss Army knife in his pocket. He saw a really great place to throw one last rock, so he knelt down and picked up a nice flat one. He walked over to the edge and tried to get a run at really launching this one. Just as the rock left his fingers he felt his tennis shoes slip on the loose gravel. He let out a little scream as he got closer to the edge.

"Kaden!!" Jordan cried out. He grabbed at Jack's shirt and pulled him back. When the dust cleared they were both sitting on some nice bruises and Jack had slightly twisted his ankle. Jordan's heart was beating like crazy, Jack could feel it. Jack just wanted to get back to his dad, he felt tears welling up in his eyes, but didn't want Jordan to see him cry. They stood up, Jordan brushed him off. Jordan gave him a drink of water and took one for himself. They walked back toward the peak. They were much quieter than when they had left, Jack couldn't help but wonder, *Who is Kaden?*

Anne stood on the edge of the overlook, it was really quite impressive. Only she wasn't thinking about mountains or breathtaking views. She was trying to remind herself that she couldn't take some things back. She was trying to remember that she was worth forgiving. Watching this family suffer as she had made her own family suffer was more than she might bear. She resolved to take Jordan their own way when they got back to the camp.

Back together at the peak, everyone was quiet. Clark ran to check out Jack's injuries, luckily it didn't seem like he had injured his ankle too bad. With an eerie silence they started the return hike. Down the mountain they all hiked, each seemingly lost in their own world. When they got to about the halfway point, Jack was limping on his hurt ankle. Clark loaded him on his shoulders and they continued on. They could almost make out their camp when Clark couldn't take Jack anymore. Without a word Jordan loaded him on his back. Clark could see that Jordan was tired, but he simply couldn't go another step with the boy's weight. When he saw the outline of the Motor home, he almost cried with relief. His water had gone dry some mile back and his mouth was about glued shut. Like a flash of irony, he felt the drops of rain on his lips first. At 100 yards out it was a light mist, 50 yards out raining, and as they hit the door they felt they might just be swept away in Noah's flood.

Chapter 16

The storm raged all night long. Because they weren't sure where they might get fuel next, Clark didn't dare run the generator. So as the dark afternoon passed into a black storming night, they sat huddled around two flashlights and a game of Monopoly. Clark thought back to the Wal-Mart in Lubbock Texas, wishing he had bought more than just one. He loved Monopoly, but there was only so much wheeling an dealing on Real Estate speculation that he could take. After the end of the third round he took his leave and sat in the driver's seat. Outside he could just make out the motorcycles, sitting like obedient animals, huddled together in the cold wet misery. He had never been a motorcycle guy, but he had to admit that it sure looked like fun. Maybe not this very moment, but other times anyway. Occasional lightning flashes backlit the old mountains in the distance, it was hard to gauge whether the storm was coming or going. He tried counting the seconds between lightning flash and the resulting thunder, but his results were inconclusive at best. Suddenly someone was there beside him. Anne had joined him, sitting in the passenger seat. For awhile she didn't say anything, content to stare out the window alongside him. It felt nice to have her there, reassuring. He looked over and smiled, not a huge smile, a hidden teeth smile. The kind you gave people at funerals, sort of a 'well this sucks, but it's nice seeing you'.

"Jordan and I are going to break off and go in a different direction tomorrow." She said it with such cold clarity that it hurt Clark, like a pin drawn in and out of his chest. Clark didn't want her to go, he hadn't realized the enormity of what he had signed them up for until he met her, now he couldn't imagine how he would do it without Anne.

"If you think that's best." Clark's training had kicked in, men weren't to beg. They were to appear powerful and all knowing. He would have to tell the kids that everything would be fine, that it was really for the best after all. But it wasn't best for Clark; he didn't want to be alone.

Anne shook her head, as if agreeing with him, but her eyes didn't seem to match the sentiment. Clark knew he had to say something, some combination of words that would magically change the situation. What he was really good at was coming up with the words in the days and weeks to follow. He was the master of the far too late comeback. Sometimes it would wake him up at night, some explosive thought or realization that he 'should have said'. Just like every other time, he was blowing it now. Anne was getting out of her seat, to head back to the game. Suddenly he didn't care about using the right words, didn't care if it sounded witty or pathetic. He grasped her arm, too hard he was sure, but it was done now. Quietly, almost under his breath he spoke.

"Please don't go." He wasn't even sure if Anne had heard what he said. It was said quiet enough to keep everyone else from hearing. He couldn't look at her while he begged, keeping his eyes transfixed on the ground.

"I don't think I'm good for your family." Her response was as quiet as his. So quiet that he thought he had misheard her, some trick of his subconscious. Surely she knew how good she was for them. She was wonderful with all of them, she made them better. He wanted to tell her how great she was, how much her guidance and personality reinforced their faith in their own journey. But there was something in her response that scared him, something that went unspoken. Regardless, he needed her.

"I don't know if we can make it without you." There it was, Clark had said it. He hated himself for letting the words fall out, but he knew that he would turn around sooner versus later without someone like her to spur him on.

Without another word she broke free of him grasp and rejoined the game. The storm raged outside while Clark stared on into the dark. He wondered and questioned and doubted and hoped. Finally the storm outlasted their abilities to fight their yawns and they all found a place to sleep.

The storm had passed when Clark woke up. It was still pitch dark, just the smallest amount of moonlight shining through the window. He had heard something, he was sure of it. He tried to keep his panicked mind under control, but visions of coyotes and banditos immediately popped into his head. He slipped on his pants as quietly as he could. He pushed his feet into the still laced shoes and threw a sweatshirt on.

As he crept forward he tried to open his eyes wider somehow, hoping to avoid stepping on Anne or Jordan. But when he came to the first sleeping bag it was empty. His eyes immediately sprung to the bed his teenage daughter was asleep on, but she was alone. Jordan would live to see another day. He crept forward and saw the boy sleeping in the next bag. Clark's heart pounded at the thought of Anne wandering about. Their encounter the other night had taken him back to a place he hadn't even known still existed within the confines of Clark. He wanted desperately to go back. He opened the door handle, cringing at the sound it made. People rolled, mumbled in their sleep, but no one woke up, not even when he walked down the steps and shut the door.

The outside felt frozen in comparison to the warm motor home. He pushed a vapor trail before him with his breath. Anne was just ahead. He hesitated; she had not invited him here. This was her moment, was he intruding? Unsure, but unwilling to go back he cleared his throat to let her know he was there. Only she didn't turn, or acknowledge him. He wondered if he should do it again, but knew that there was no way she had not heard him. Instead he walked forward to see what she was looking at. The moon was just about to dive below the horizon, sort of a lunar sunset. It cast eerie shadows on the barren Mexican landscape. Clark wondered what she was thinking about, but didn't dare ask. He felt outmatched, unworthy to intrude upon her personal space. He wondered if he was blowing it by not kissing her, he heard that fortune favored the bold, but thought that was probably made up by rapists. Instead he stood there, waiting for her to say something, for her to make a move. It took a very long time.

"I was married once," Anne started, "to my high school sweet heart. I had my boys, years passed by and pretty soon I was nothing more than a shadow. All the things I wanted to do got tossed out with the leftover pizza and dirty diapers. It was like I was asleep. When I woke up one day the woman that looked me in the eye was old, lost, past it. In my heart, I still felt like the young girl who had followed the neighborhood boys when they rode their motorcycles in the gravel pits behind our house. So I followed my heart to tragic consequences, it hurt people and did things that can't be taken back. I heard you and Chloe talking, I know you've been hurt. I'm not your cheating wife and you're not my dead husband. I don't want us to get confused by all the bad stuff that has been done to us and that we've done to others. I can't hate myself anymore, there just isn't enough left for that. But I would like to share this journey south with you, if you still want me to."

Clark wanted to say yes, but somehow he just couldn't get himself to speak. He hurt, inside, hurt for her and himself and her dead husband and all the hurts in the world. It wasn't fair, none of it was. Sometimes it felt like all there was left was the hurting. He felt for Anne's hand and clasped it. Slowly the moon went down and the first purple glow of daylight came up in the opposite direction. Clark wasn't crying, maybe he had run out. His father had always said that men had a finite supply of tears. He just wanted to get back on the road, to make progress. For the first time that trip the sun rose upon a new Clark, one that refused to be dogged by doubt and fear, today he would be a lion. He reached his hand over and pulled Anne close, he kissed her mouth and felt the initial stiffness of her mouth melt into his. He felt her lips tremble and he hoped it was from more than just the cold. Today Clark would be the lion.

Chapter 17

The light of day brought blue skies and a sense of renewal to their little group. They had shown remarkable teamwork getting Jack back to the camp and everyone sensed that they had settled into a foreign, yet pleasant rhythm. They had some breakfast and stowed everything for the day's journey.

They were on the road before 8AM, which seemed like a minor miracle to Clark. Through the large picture window of the motor home he watched the mountains dissolve into the desert. The vegetation became more and more scattered until all that was green were the bushes and occasional trees. Small farms started to spring up along the road; with inhabitants that seemed t have skin more like an old leather glove than anything human. When they grinned it was often showing only a few teeth, but he was surprised how often they smiled at him. None of them seemed to be in a hurt, some just standing in place as if waiting for a bus that never arrived. Again Clark tried to imagine a life here, trying to irrigate the barren landscape enough to feed a family, it sounded awful to him. He could see living here if you had money, but to try to force anything to grow in the ground here, that would be an uphill battle.

Around noon they stopped at a small restaurant that sprung up from the desert like a mirage. Anne had signaled for them to slow down then pulled into the parking lot. Clark loved following her; it was so much easier and less stress than having to figure everything out on his own. He might have made the same decision on places to eat, but now if the food was terrible it wouldn't be his fault. Anne and Jordan both took several minutes of stretching before they were ready to go inside. Clark felt tired, but they looked ragged and depleted. Four hours behind the wheel of a motor home with air conditioning was apparently quite different from four straight hours on a motorcycle. He had assumed they would have stopped if they needed to. He would have to make sure they knew it wasn't his idea to drive straight through each day. They set their helmets inside the motor home and walked as one group into the restaurant.

"Buenas dias" the gentleman that greeted them was wearing jeans and a soccer club shirt. He had a round brown face and an easy smile that revealed two gaps where teeth should have been. Clark didn't have to look at Chloe for a translation to get to the table, he was becoming quite adept at greetings. They sat at a plastic table with plastic chairs, but at least everything looked clean.

"Para tomar?" The man asked. Clark even knew how to answer this question; his Spanish was tripling every day.

"Coca's por todo", he answered. Chloe looked over at him and smiled. Clark was rather pleased with himself. Only when the menus came out, Clark's display of proficient Spanish was over. Without pictures he could only grasp at a few words, and knowing how little of an animal went to waste here, that wouldn't do at all. The Cokes gave him something to do with his hands while everyone else scanned their menus. Even Jack seemed to be reading his menu. *Does Jack speak Spanish?*

"Okay, what are you guys getting?" Clark asked, hoping to cheat off of someone else's work. He was happy to see other confused faces looking up from menus. Suddenly a chorus of shoulder shrugs indicated they were all as lost as him. Even Chloe seemed to be having very little luck.

"Does anybody actually speak Spanish, other than Chloe?" Clark asked the group in the lowest whisper he could manage, trying not to publically shame anyone. Jack raised his hand a little.

"I know how to count and most my colors." A mountain of silence seemed to be coming out of Anne and Jordan; Clark had assumed they both spoke at least marginal Spanish. But the hurried shakes of their heads indicated they spoke almost none, which was on par with his, which was not good. How was this group driving through Latin America? They couldn't even read the signs.

When the waiter reappeared with his little pad of paper it was like the greatest reinforcement of stupidity Clark had ever felt. They had no idea what they wanted.

"Do you speak English?" Anne had asked the obvious question, which was brilliant. Only when he shook his head no, many faces went back into their menus. Clark looked again; he knew a few words after all.

Tacos, Chile, Colorado, he knew some of the words, but the descriptions ran so long he figured there would be an eye ball or intestine slipped in there somewhere. But someone was going to have to step up; someone was going to have to be the Lion today.

"Tacos, por us. Chicken, bok bok, beef, mooooooo." Clark even made the wing flapping motion and the horns on the head for the beef. He felt pretty happy with himself. The man was blinking hard, looking now around the table for help from someone other than Clark.

"Puedemos sacar tacos por nosotros, cinco? Res y pollo." Chloe had stepped in to fix her father's ordering attempt. Now Clark felt foolish, he should have just asked her to order in the first place. He wanted to be proud, but he felt laughing eyes on him. The waiter had written down something on his pad and headed off toward the kitchen. Clark was staring at his plate, unsure of when he would be able to pick his head up again.

"My mom thinks just adding an 'O' to everything makes it Spanish", Jordan quipped. "I would like'o a large'o Coke'o." The table began to shake slightly as their laughter finally broke the awkward silence. Clark looked up to see Anne laughing, she didn't look ashamed and she didn't seem to be defending herself either. She winked at him, which made his chest hurt a little. She wasn't trying to make him feel stupid, she was trying to let him in on a little secret, she spoke Spanish as poorly as he did. Suddenly the whole table was talking at once. Anne was asking Clark which route he thought was best, Jack was trying to listen and tell them his thoughts. Jordan and Chloe were talking about something, Clark couldn't hear clearly and besides, he was trying to focus on what Anne was saying. He looked at Jordan and Chloe. Together now they appeared about the same age. Jordan's youth only really showed when he was speaking to Chloe. He could have been talking about going to the mall or the new video game he had gotten for Christmas, or the current Socio Economic climate in Vietnam for all he knew.

When the food came out the table quieted down, but only slightly. It seemed the plates and containers multiplied exponentially. By the time the waiter had finished the entire table was covered with containers of foodstuffs. Clark was surprised, he hadn't thought they had ordered this much food. Once he started to open and explore the dishes he found that it was a Mexican taco bar. Everything was there to make tacos until someone vomited. The chicken was in a red sauce, still on the bones. A stack of tortillas three inches high made him wonder what other families would be joining them. One taco at a time he started working his way through the myriad of sauces, garnishes and obligatory lime squeezes. The beef had a hearty flavor to it, but the chicken was the absolute standout of the meal. It was amazing to him that the meat stayed on the bone. The red sauce was so flavorful he gave serious consideration to drinking the bowl. One small container contained some kind of peppers. They were green and sliced up into small rings. He assumed they were jalapenos, so he popped a couple in his mouth to check how hot they were. He was known for his ability to handle hot stuff at work, but that was the IRS. A slight tingle started in the middle of his tongue. As he continued chewing, the tingling changed into what could only be described as a chemical burn. Without thinking he spat the peppers on the plate in front of him, then scraping his tongue with his fingers to remove any residue. The Coke seemed to intensify the burning with those magic little bubbles. People were offering aid, but all Clark could feel was his tongue burning. Slowly the pain became manageable, he ate a plain tortilla. That was easily the hottest thing Clark had ever come across in his four decades on this planet. He pushed the peppers to the far side of the table, far out of his son's reach. Jack had laughed and said, "I wanna try one", but Clark couldn't be that cruel.

The rest of the meal tasted like pain for Clark, that demon pepper sealing his doom. He hoped he had not swallowed much of it; the idea of facing that pain in 8 to 10 hours was nauseating. When it came time to pay the check, Anne reached her hand for the bill. Clark was not used to such shenanigans and waved to the waiter that he would take it. Only Anne had gotten there first, pulling out a black American Express card. Clark had never actually seen one of those. They were usually reserved for the mega wealthy business traveler. The waiter was shaking his head at Anne, so she pulled out a Visa, which he shook his head again. Anne looked perplexed. There were still a couple of holdout places around Clark's house that didn't take credit cards, he wasn't that shocked. Now the waiter approached Clark.

Clark looked at the bill and to his shock it was over four hundred dollars, this was highway robbery. Clark was going to have to find a

Sam's club or Costco along the route to stock up the motor home. He looked into his wallet, but had to go into his secret stash to get the amount of money.

"Dad, you do know it's four hundred pesos, not dollars." Chloe was saving him again. Clark closed his eyes for a moment to do the math. He had been told that it was about ten pesos per dollar, so it was about forty bucks. Now that seemed reasonable, maybe not unbelievably cheap, but he didn't feel quite as robbed. He put two twenties down on the bill and handed it back to the owner. Again he waved his hands, *oh hell, now what?* Clark reached back into his wallet and pulled out another ten and handed it to the man. Now the waiter looked really confused and acted like he was trying to tell them something, although he never said anything. Finally he just walked away with a slightly disgusted look on his face.

After a few minutes they felt the welcome mat had been removed and it was time to go. Clark got the helmets out of the motor home and gave them to the bikers. He handed Anne hers and their hands touched. For a moment they both stood still, just looking at one another. Neither was at their peak, but there was something reassuring about looking at each other in the full light of day. Something in the night maneuvers that made them feel more like a dream than an actuality. "Be careful out there; let's pull over in an hour or so." Clark felt better having said that, he didn't want them riding to exhaustion. Anne smiled that devious grin and put her helmet on. Even with the helmet on she was drop dead sexy, some mysterious creature from space. When Clark turned to get in the motor home Jack was looking disapprovingly at him. Jack walked closer, thinking he was misinterpreting the signals from him son. But the closer he got the more unhappy Jack seemed to be. Then he folded his arms, which in their house was the ultimate sign of pissedoffedness. Clark thought he might slip by the boy without comment, but just as he passed by he heard him.

"When is mom coming?"

Thunder rolled somewhere in the summer afternoon, but silence prevailed in that spot. It wasn't just silent; it was as if there was a vacuum of sound. The question had been laid down, how long would he have before he had to answer it? He had lied to his son, telling him that his mother would be joining them later. He should have told him the truth, but feared that he wouldn't have been able to process it. The last thing he needed right now was for Jack to have a meltdown and scream he wanted to go home. This could take the whole thing off the rails.

"She's going to meet us in Panama City." Clark knew he shouldn't have said it as soon as the words escaped his mouth. In order to try and sell his lie he continued up into the rig. He sat down in the driver's seat and fired up the coach. Jack was still outside, standing in the dust of the highway, arms folded. Obviously he had seen something or felt something. Clark would have to distance himself from Anne, in front of Jack anyway.

Finally Jack stomped up into the motor home. He walked back into the back room and closed the door. Clark exhaled hard and released the air brake. He rolled off in the direction of Mexico City, although it was unlikely they would make it there today. Chloe was listening to the iPod, bopping her head as she lounged on the couch. For a moment he was so jealous of her, with her whole life ahead, unencumbered by the frailties of others. He turned toward the road and tried desperately to lose himself in the vision of Anne riding before him.

Chapter 17a

Jack knew what he saw. This wasn't the first time either. Mom was going to be so mad when she go there. Dad would tell her how he held Anne's hand and mom would flip out. He was tired of being between the two and all the fighting. Dad knew the rules, he wasn't even allowed to go to the water parks because it always lead to a fight between the parents. Now Jack would have to figure out a way to not let his dad tell his mom. He could do it, but it just seemed unfair. Why did he always have to be the grown up?

There was a lot going on here, some stuff with his family and some with Anne and Jordan. Nobody was talking about it, but they were also not thinking of talking about it, which was worse. Like puppet strings that pulled you in a direction you didn't understand, all these people and their problems were exhausting. Mexico wasn't anything like he had thought it would be. He had expected more churros and donkeys. He had thought they might ride horses or have adventures, but so far all they had done was drive and eat. They had done the one hike, which still made his ankle hurt when he thought about it. But most of all he didn't want them to treat him like a kid anymore. He was too old to be the baby, he was nearly nine years old. Chloe didn't want to play hardly ever, too busy trying to look all pretty for Jordan. But that dad and Anne moment back there, that had taken the cake. He had to get his dad to keep it a secret, even from mom. So he laid there, planning how he would teach his father to keep a secret, until the bouncing of the journey and his full belly conspired to send him into a deep sleep.

Chapter 17b

When the hour was up, Clark flashed the lights and pulled the rig over. Anne and Jordan pulled over a little down the road, circling back. There wasn't much here, just those same houses, seemingly occupied by the same people, brown and wrinkled. They didn't seem as ragged as before, this stopping hourly was the right thing to do.

Jack was asleep in the back, so Clark tried to be very quiet using the bathroom, unzipping and trying to use the side of the bowl as a silencer. A flush was a flush, but coming out Jack was still asleep, success. Jordan and Anne used the bathroom, but when Anne came back she had bad news.

"I think the toilet is like full, full." She made an unpleasant look, which made Clark believe her. He should have known, but now what to do? He had no idea where a dump out might be. Were they so full that when he hit a pothole they would all be covered in human waste?

Clark was trying to think what to do, but growing on his mind was an increasing burning sensation on his, well, manhood. Everyone seemed to be looking at him, waiting for a response about what to do about the pooper being full, but all Clark could think was, *why is my penis burning?*

His mind immediately played cruel games with him, telling him that Karen had given him one last gift, something inherited from her new boyfriend. But no, this was sudden onset. *Maybe it's cancer.* Clark started to run his options for getting checked out in Mexico, maybe the hospitals were nice. The sensation was getting worse, and now everyone was looking at each other, past waiting on his response. Suddenly he looked up, as if a light had turned on, the bulb shining. "The peppers!!" Clark exclaimed and ran to the bathroom.

When he got back he noticed that everyone had a good laugh, Anne's eyes were still watering and seeing his face go red at the realization made her laugh again. Clark was embarrassed, but relieved. "Okay, those peppers were seriously hot", he reiterated. Then everyone laughed.

A mile ahead they found a hardware store where they bought a shovel, and on a flat piece of desert they dug a hole and dumped their waste, stained blue with deodorant. There was a lot of waste there, Clark quickly realized that his hole had not been large enough. The advancing line of blue foul smelling sludge inched closer and closer to Clark's shoes. Although he wasn't a religious man, he prayed that the hill sloped away from him, because if he had to retreat further he wouldn't be able to shut the valve. Luckily the flow broke the other way and the horror show flowed away, staining the ground as it went. Bending down to close the valve, he almost threw up, catching it only at the top of his throat. Anne stood some feet away, sour look on her face, but at least she had witnessed his sacrifice.

Back on the road, Jack seemed in better spirits and didn't bring up any questions about his mother's absence. That was too good, it was too early to start that. It would come, but Clark was hoping to be through Mexico by that point.

Three stops later it was getting dark, so they camped outside San Luis Potosi. It looked amazingly middle class for Mexico. Major powerlines ran along the sides of the road, and trees grew where people irrigated. Clark would have headed into the city, but Anne's plan of keeping them out of the big Mexican cities to avoid trouble seemed wiser. He wondered if there was an RV camp, the idea of hooking the rig up to the utilities instead of running his generator, feeding water in through a five gallon can and dumping his shit into a hole in the ground sounded awfully appealing. But Anne had pointed out that they had not passed another motor home the whole time in Mexico. It hadn't made Clark any more comfortable, now keenly aware how much of a target they seemed to carry with them. They had run into a handful of other Americans at restaurants and passing by on the roads, but not in larger than life RV's.

A taco cart stationed outside what appeared to be a power plant provided their dinner. Clark had never really been one for Mexican food before, but he had to admit he was quickly becoming a fan. Jack had eaten, but was much quieter than he had been. Clark wondered if he was getting sick. When they went to go to bed that night, Jack stayed eyes open, sitting on the bed until Clark joined him. Then Jack had closed and locked the door. Clark started to say something to him, but long before he knew what to say, Jack was curling himself up in the bed. Clark stood there, wanting to tell his son that there was a reason for it all, but he couldn't. He didn't know where to start, couldn't face the look of disappointment on his face when he found out about the lies. So instead Clark lay down next to him and said nothing, hoping that somehow tomorrow would be easier and better.

Chapter 18

When Clark had been planning his European odyssey, he had imagined that the best part would be that he knew everything that was coming. Every expense, attraction and novelty that the trip had to offer was held within his spreadsheets, power point files and that damn map. What Clark found now was that not knowing where exactly they would find themselves was his favorite part. The adventure of blazing their own path as the mood struck them was exhilarating. His whole life, he had been paralyzed with fear at the thought of what might go wrong if things weren't all figured out, but he hadn't thought of all the things that might go right. Clark was amazed at how things just worked out. He was also humbled beyond measure at the charity and kindness the people of Mexico showed them. As the days progressed and the world greened as they passed, friends sprung from the ground to let them take water, plug in and even dump the unmentionables. It seemed that the less people had, the more they were likely to be willing to part with it. Clark doubted they would have gotten a drop of water in Beverly Hills, but somehow, here in the south of Mexico, proprietors of cafes that compromised nothing more than cinderblock walls and plastic chairs were willing to give whatever support they could.

Finally, the journey was going as Clark had envisioned it might. Except Jack, who had started a near constant vigil of his father's affection toward Anne. They could hardly sit next to each other at a taco stand without arousing his ire. Clark knew he would have to speak to his son, but in truth he was afraid. He knew things weren't good now, but it wouldn't take much to make them much much worse.

They had been in Mexico just over a week. They had gone out of the standard path to visit Oaxaca. Chloe said that there were ruins just outside of town that were some of the oldest in Mexico. It sounded like a good excuse to escape the long hours behind the wheel for a change. Even Jack looked excited about it. He had been bitterly disappointed that they hadn't visited the ruins outside of Mexico City, but knowing its reputation, they had given the capitol city a wide berth.

Once again Clark found himself on the narrow streets of Mexico. He marveled at the colonial architecture, trying not to remove any of it with his oversized American motor coach. Luckily, on the outskirts of town they found a small restaurant with a large parking lot. The owner spoke broken English, and Clark was able to negotiate parking his motor home in the lot. In return they would eat at the restaurant twice, which turned out to be excellent food at a great value anyway. It was in this restaurant however that a terrible thing reared its head, Mescal. Clark had heard about a powerful type of tequila with a worm in the bottom of the bottle, turns out it wasn't tequila, it was Mescal. Somehow, it tasted even worse than Tequila, which had always turned Clark's stomach. The owner either made his own, or was invested in a company that made it, but regardless by the time they left dinner, the only two who could drink, Anne and Clark, were well past inebriated.

"Let's go see the Zocalo", Anne suggested in a slurred mouthful of vowels. Everyone agreed so they found a taxi. Clark had to close his eyes; he was given the honor of riding in the passenger seat, which afforded him the best view of the oncoming traffic and near misses. His foot went instinctively for the brake pedal the entire trip; he hoped he hadn't dented the bottom of the car when he stepped out. Clark had traded some money, so now he could pay in pesos. The man smiled and drove off to find his next hapless victims.

The central square of Oaxaca was like stepping back in time. Finally the Mexico they had expected came to life. Street vendors lined the sidewalks with brightly colored fantastical animal statues, stone masks, black pottery and countless pieces of jewelry. Unlike the hardened border towns though, this was clean and friendly, the kind of Mexico that people should have spread rumors about. The brightly lit Cathedral on one side of the square stood over them, drawing their eyes up the time worn walls that rose impossibly high. Food vendors were everywhere; it must have been some kind of festival. There were local dances in traditional outfits and tourists with dreadlocks in nearly every café. Clark gave Chloe and Jack some money and told them to buy souvenirs. Clark watched from afar as the two approached the long tables of goods. Money in Jack's hand was a dangerous thing, but at least it never lasted long. He had been drawn immediately to the knives, Clark should have told him anything but that. He was about to walk over and tell him that exact thing when Anne sauntered up next to him.

Suddenly it didn't seem so serious. Jordan seemed to be watching after the kids anyway. Clark liked Jordan, there really wasn't much not to like, except the way he looked at Chloe. Anne's head on his shoulder gave him a warm feeling throughout his chest. It caused a pleasurable numbness that spread out toward his fingers and toes. He let his body relax, felt his shoulders drop and turned to smell Anne's hair. Even with always wearing a helmet she always smelled clean and somehow tropical.

A Mariachi band had gathered close to them. When they began to play it was a slow song. Anne pulled Clark toward the group. Clark was about to protest when she placed his hand on her waist and lined him up. Before he could protest they were dancing. Clark had no idea what he was doing, just trying to shuffle his feet so that he didn't step on her feet mainly. The feel of her body sliding against his was almost too much. Clark had thought this part of his life was over, he had expected a rocking chair on the front porch, grandkids running around the house. He had not expected to be falling for some woman on a trip through Mexico.

"What do you do for a living?" Anne asked.

"I'm an IRS Auditor." Clark was pretty sure he had told her this before.

"Seriously, what do you do?"

"I'm an Auditor with the Internal Revenue Service."

"Seriously, I thought you were shitting me. No kidding, hmmm? My taxes are not completely in order, so let's just play it cool here. Well, for what it's worth, you don't look like an Auditor."

"Thanks I guess", Clark hesitated a moment, "You've never told me what you do." Now Anne looked at him again with the furrowed brow.

"You don't know?" Clark shook his head no.

"I'm a writer. I wrote the Pandora's Lust series." It sounded familiar to Clark, something he should have known. Suddenly a term came to his mind.

"The Slut Poet?" For a moment Anne looked like she might storm off. Clark immediately regretted saying it, it had just slipped out. They went back to dancing, but the electricity seemed to have been disconnected. Clark waited for the inevitable storm off; he began to think of how he could apologize.

"I hate that stupid fucking name. I hope Rush Limbaugh burns in hell." Suddenly she was smiling again. Clark had only been in the beginning phases of his apology dissertation, needing many future reviews, but now it was over. He could get used to this. He smiled broadly at Anne and she took the opportunity to scratch her nose on his shirt. The incandescent lit darkness, the music, Anne as his dance partner; this was as close as he dared to wish for a perfect moment. He tried to cement it in his mind. This was what he wanted to think about when he couldn't sleep, instead of sitting on the couch so many days ago and watching his life drain away. Every sense was engaged in this moment, her smell, the feel of her breasts against his chest, the deep blue of her eyes as she smiled that crooked grin. He wanted to kiss her, to feel the soft sensation of her lips and tongue, to feel that falling sensation again. He wanted her, wanted to tear her clothes off, be with her, love her and make her love him.

"Dad, what are you doing?" Abruptly Clark's fantasy slammed the door and he was back outside in the cold. As if he were a misbehaving child, Clark put his arms at his sides and his head down. When he looked up at his son there were tears in Jack's eyes. Without warning and without advance provocation tears sprang up in Clark's eyes as well.

"Let's go home." Clark couldn't bear to look at Anne; he knew she would be angry or confused. He deserved that, but he could stand not to look at her, he couldn't do that to his son. He knew he should say something, explain the whole thing. He glanced back at Anne once as they walked forward, but he didn't see anger or resentment or confusion, he saw pity. That was worse than any amount of condemnation, the idea of being pitied was akin to being spit on. Clark took Jack's hand and walked toward finding a cab.

"I miss mom."

"I know buddy, I miss her too." At least Clark was being partially honest now. Chloe had caught up to them, started to ask something, but just locked step with them. Slowly the group walked up the narrow streets, it was some distance to the motor home, and Clark knew they should take a cab, but they just kept walking. When Jack tired out, Clark put him on his back. It was almost an hour walk by the time the towering beast poked its head above the parking lot wall. There were no motorcycles parked near the coach. Clark had blown it, made worse by the fact that he didn't even understand why he had blown it. He could have been honest all along, but there was something in him, some stubborn desire to maintain the status quo that was letting everything spoil around him. Clark put Jack into bed, pulling off his shoes and pants and tucking him in. He went to check on Chloe, who was sitting on the couch in the dark. Clark went and sat next to her, saying nothing. Minutes went by without anyone saying anything. Suddenly Clark's shoulders began to shake and he let his head fall into his hands. He had broken like a dam and there was no stopping it now. Like a baby he bawled, finally falling over to be comforted by his daughter. Of all that he had lost, his interrupted dance tonight and what might have been with Anne was more than he could bear.

Chapter 18a

"Oh daddy." Chloe rubbed his back until he stopped shaking. She pulled him down the couch until he was filling the whole thing. She found a blanket and wrapped it around him. Chloe was trying not to feel sorry for herself, but she was struggling with it. Jordan was the first boy that had treated her like a real person. He was handsome, kind and he was here. Well, he had been here. Why was it all falling apart all the time? When would she get to start her life instead of worrying about her parents? She lay in the dark thinking about things until finally sleep took her.

Chapter 19

Jack woke before everyone else. He had dreamed about mom again. He needed to talk to her. He slipped his clothes and shoes on. There on the nightstand was dad's phone. He knew he wasn't allowed to use it without permission, but this was a special case. No one could yell at him for calling mom. He was surprised to find the phone off, but he knew how to turn it on. He held it to his chest when it came on and made the sound. He opened the phone book, selected favorites and pushed the one titled 'my wife'. The phone clicked several times trying to dial. A recording came on, telling him something in Spanish. He hit the end button. He retried her number; this time the phone rang funny, and then rang with a distant sound. A crackly voice picked up on the other end.

"Are you on your way home yet?"

"Mom?"

"Oh, hi sweetie. How's Texas?"

"We're in Oaxaca now, Texas was over a week ago?"

"What? Did you say you're almost home?" What was she saying? Jack felt very confused.

"When are you coming? Dad says you're not coming til Panama, but you could come here, Oaxaca."

"Panama, honey I don't know what you're saying. You're supposed to be home tomorrow, let's talk about it then." Now Jack was really confused. She acted like she wasn't even planning on coming to Panama. How could they be home tomorrow?

"Mom, we're in Mexico. WHEN ARE YOU COMING?"

"You mean you're in NEW MEXICO?"

"MEXICO, MEXICO. We'll be in Guatamala like tomorrow."
Suddenly everything was moving very fast. Chloe was sitting up looking
at Jack, a look of horror on her face. She was making the hand across
the neck motion. Jack suddenly wished he had asked permission to use
the phone. He heard his father moving toward the room, suddenly he
appeared at the door, clothes wrinkled and wiping the sleep from his
eyes. He looked more scared than he had ever seen him.

"Give the phone to your father." His mother did not sound good, she
was almost screaming crying. Something was seriously wrong. Jack's
eyes had started to water as he handed the phone to his father. He was
going to get in a lot of trouble for this. He sat very still on the bed.
Chloe had her hands to either side of her mouth.

"Why did you do that?" she whispered pointedly. Jack shook his head
to signify that he didn't know. Of course he had just wanted to ask his
mother to come sooner, but he hadn't meant to make them fight. It
didn't seem right to make this kind of thing without mom there.

From the other room it sounded like his father was doing a lot of
apologizing. He heard something about the police and suddenly
everything was bad. Jack was really getting scared, why didn't mom
know they were in Mexico? Suddenly his dad was screaming, Jack just
wanted to get away from it. He was saying terrible things, all about
mom. He was using words that Jack would have had his mouth washed
out for using. What had happened? Jack started to cry, hoping this was
just some horrible dream he might wake up from. He wasn't very good
at it, but he tried to prey, asking God that if he would make everything
alright, Jack would never tell a lie again. But still it raged on, time
seemed to have stopped on this most horrible of moments.

Then it changed again, now dad was crying. He was saying that he
needed to do this for his children. He was asking her how she could do
this to them? Jack thought this might be worse than the last, he put his
hands over his ears to stop hearing. He didn't want to know or hear
anything more. Then he felt the weight shift on the bed. Chloe had
gotten up and was walking toward dad. He peeked, dad was on the
floor with his head almost between his knees. Chloe walked up and
took the phone from him. His shoulders were shaking, something had
to be wrong, dad never cried. Chloe took the phone and went outside.

Once the latch closed on the door, there was only the muffled sound of someone speaking. Chloe was talking to mom? That never helped anything. Jack let his hands slip off his ears and opened his eyes. Dad didn't look like he was still crying, but he was lying on the ground with his knees up against his chest. Jack walked over and stood in front of him, looking at his own feel because it just felt like what he was supposed to do.

"I'm sorry dad." Jack could feel wet tears falling down his nose; he didn't mean to, it just seemed to be happening. He lay down next to dad, putting one arm around him and patting his back with the other. They sat like this for what seemed like an eternity. Then the handle turned and Chloe walked up into the coach.

"Three weeks, then mom is flying us back."

Jack wasn't exactly sure what that meant, but it sounded optimistic. He rubbed his dad's shoulders, hoping that the news would break him out of the silent stare he was in on the floor. But as the minutes passed Jack began to worry that something was wrong. Maybe he had a heart attack? He tried pressing his shoulders, as if pushing him to stand up. Still the pile of human tissue on the floor that was his father didn't move. Time passed, Chloe only stared at the floor. Then as suddenly as it had started, his dad sat up. He smiled at Jack, who was still trying to rub his back.

"I need to tell you some things. I didn't want to tell you because I thought it might ruin the trip. But the more we go, the more I can see that I should have told you in the first place." Jack tried his best to ready himself for whatever this was. Jack knew it was something big, his dad's eyes were filled with water and he was having a hard time speaking, like there was something in his mouth.

"Mom has fallen in love with another man and she's divorcing me." Jack shook his head to acknowledge that he had received the message. Only the message seemed flawed. Jack had plenty of friends whose parents were divorced, but his parents had been together forever. What did this mean? Would Jack never be going home? If he did go home would his dad be there? If his dad wasn't there, who would mow the grass? Would he be getting another dad? Lindsey in his math class had recently gotten a new father, and she didn't have anything nice to say about that. But in the near term, he was confused about why his mom wasn't here.

"So is mom still coming to Panama?" Now his dad looked away, not at his feet which was how he looked when someone yelled at him.

"Jack, I was not totally honest when I said mom was joining us in Panama. Mom isn't coming on this vacation at all. I should have told you the truth all along, but I was afraid you wouldn't want to come. I didn't tell mom because I didn't think she would let me take you two." Jack's head was swimming. He needed a nap, this was just too much information at once. Since when didn't mom come on vacations? Since when was mom seeing another man, someone who wasn't his dad? The more he thought the more questions he had that he didn't really want answered. He didn't want to hear anymore. Suddenly Jack realized that he had been unfair to Anne. All the lock tumblers rolled into place and he saw that had been his dad dating. Jack thought he might faint, it was just too much.

Chloe surpised Jack by wrapping her arms around him. He couldn't remember the last time she had hugged him without a direct order from mom or dad. In that embrace though, came the peace that at least he wasn't in this alone. Chloe would watch out for him. Jack knew there was something he should say.

"I'm sorry I yelled at you and Anne last night, I didn't know." A sad smile spread on his dad's face. It would be alright, if they could smile at all this, they would have to be alright.

When they were all standing, it was time to go, no one had said anything, they just all instinctively knew at this point. Like an orchestrated dance team they moved in separate directions to prepare the motor home for the road. Jack moved the items in so that the slide outs wouldn't get caught, Chloe pressed the buttons that brought the groaning sections inward like in the Indiana Jones movies, Dad fired up the engine and brought the jacks up.

Within minutes they were on the road, only they had lost their guide. He looked over to see if anyone else knew where they were going. On the dash a small dome indicated they were heading south, Jack supposed that was good enough. According to Chloe, all roads heading South eventually went to Tierra del Fuego. Jack wondered if they would see Anne and Jordan again. There still seemed to be something wrong with seeing his dad hold her hand, but deep inside he had liked how happy dad had looked. Maybe he was supposed to apologize to Anne, he thought he would know if he saw her again. Straining his eyes on the road laid out before them he tried to spot two tail lights in the distance.

Chapter 20

Out of Oaxaca they descended fast into a different landscape than they had travelled yet. This was the beginning of the jungle portion of their journey. Tall trees with vines and undergrowth so thick Clark wondered if he should buy a machete. He wondered if this would limit or destroy their ability to camp. Some areas were so thick with jungle vegetation, it seemed if he had been able to park the coach in the thicket, it might overgrow and swallow them before they could escape.

On the dashboard Clark had discovered a map for the entirety of their journey. Anne must have worked it out and left it for them before she and Jordan split. Clark had thought it would be the end of the world if Karen found out about the trip, if Jack found out about Karen, but really his deceits had been the worst choice he had made. Clark wondered what Chloe had said to Karen to get three weeks out of her. Karen had almost been hyperventilating when he had spoken to her, she had threatened to call the police and start an international incident. But what she had said last somehow was what had broken him. Thinking of it now made him sick to his stomach.

"Clark, the IRS fired you for leaving your job. I'm holding your official termination."

Clark was trying to reconcile the two, Karen telling him about the letter and Marjorie telling him that everything was fine. He wanted to believe Marjorie so badly, but deep down inside he knew that Karen had been honest with him. Clark had not been sure he was able to take an emergency leave of absence, now he knew. He still had three days to file an official appeal, if they all flew home now he might beg for his job back. He might claim temporary insanity, but most likely he was done. Now Clark was spending money he didn't have, when this trip was over he would be starting from scratch.

What was so great about your life that you're going to miss it?

Clark started to think about all the things in his life. He would miss seeing Marjorie at work, but she was retiring anyway. No one would miss auditing people, it wasn't work that humans were supposed to enjoy, Clark never trusted anyone who enjoyed being an auditor. He would miss his house, but he hadn't seemed to have a choice in that anyway. At least he didn't have to mow the lawn anymore; he hated that more than anything. He was allergic to grass, as the mower made its passes his eyes would water, his nose would flow until he 'farmer blew' his snot into the verve. That was a net gain; Clark needed to start thinking about more of those. More than just more of those, Clark made a silent promise to himself to start looking for the silver linings. He had always been a positive person, but years of trying to anticipate Karen's hot buttons had made him into a nay sayer, but no more. There was yet another.

If I get another shot with Anne, I'm not going to blow it. Clark smiled at just the thought of her name. He hoped he had not seen her for the last time. There was something about her, something in the fearless way she took her life that he wanted desperately in himself. She seemed to live life without encumbrances or apologies. That would be a live to imitate, but how much better to entwine their lives? It seemed a little early to be thinking long term, but Anne was the kind of woman that inspired passion. The soft line of her jaw flowed into a nearly perfect neck. Her face was painfully beautiful, perfection without an ounce of makeup. She was like fresh air and her lack of presence now made Clark's breathing painful and unpleasant.

Suddenly Clark realized he was fantasizing about her, and not only in some metaphorical and platonic way. He could hardly remember the last time his fingers had caressed a woman's naked body, but it had been far too long. Her image was still so fresh and bright in his mind that he could nearly feel her flesh under his fingers as they traced the exquisite outline of her breast. Breathing deeper he imagined he could smell the clean and faintly metallic smell of her hair. He tried not to close his eyes as he daydreamed of pulling her close, tearing her buttons as he removed the unneeded garments. She was even more perfect standing naked before him, and he was naked before her, not embarrassed or shy, but proud and pleased to see that she was looking at him appreciatively.

Looking around the coach, Clark hoped that no one noticed his inappropriate protrusion. He shook his head, trying to remove the erotic images from his dirty mind. He tried to think of baseball, but then remembered that he didn't care for baseball, he wondered how many guys that actually worked for?

It was almost lunch time, so when he spotted a small building advertising tamales he applied the exhaust brake and in a cloud of dust parked the huge rig just down the road.

Inside was a short Mexican, although he looked Mayan, man in his fifties. He wore a white ribbed shirt and spoke excellent English. The three of them ordered and sat with their Cokes, the bottles so cold they smoked in the humidity. Jack drank almost all of his before the tamales made it out. Karen would have yelled at both of them, Jack for doing it, Clark for allowing it. But that was yesterday Clark, today Clark was letting his boy do more of what he wanted.

When the parade of plates started flowing from the kitchen they were presented with several dark green packages and various bowls of varying sauces and chopped vegetables. He had expected tamales as he had always been served, wrapped in corn husks the color of midday sun. The small gift looking packages in front of him were dark green and the size of a large mans fist. Clark tentatively started to unwrap one, Chloe and Jack waiting for him to give them the sign to proceed. A few days earlier there had been an issue with some tripe tacos that had left the kids slightly hesitant in their culinary appetite for adventure. Clark unwrapped and unwrapped, whatever this was the leaf was almost two feet square, nestled inside was the familiar off white semi gelatinous tamale innards. It didn't have the crumby appearance that old tamales had, when Clark put his fork through this one, it held its shape admirably. Clark could see sections of what looked like potato and peas, with flakes of some light colored meat. He looked across the table at the various sauces, rolled the dice and spooned a small quantity, no larger than a dime, onto his bite. Chloe gave him a shoulder shrug, apparently for confidence, Jack just smiled, he was probably secretly hoping it was insanely hot so he might see the 'show' again. Clark smelled the bite, just to ensure he didn't put any Peruvian insanity peppers into his mouth. As the bite passed his teeth a strong smell of roasted peppers filled his sinuses. Chewing the tamale brought the rest of the flavors to light, the hearty flavors of vegetables and what he guessed would be chicken. It was the texture that really made it stand out, not a hint of graininess, the tamale almost melted in his mouth.

Clark had chosen wisely on the sauce, its sharp smokey pepper flavor contrasting nicely with the delicate earthiness of the tamale. He signaled for the kids to dig in, although it had to be nonverbal as his mouth was full and it was going to be some time until it was empty. This was very likely the best thing they had eaten in Mexico. Clark noticed the further they moved south, the gentler the food became. The Tex-Mex of Northern Mexico had been delicious, but his stomach was unaccustomed to the level of spice. In truth, Clark was a meat and potatoes kind of guy, this seemed to be the perfect balance of his diet and Mexican food, finally he wouldn't have to face two hours of stomach pain as they drove.

"Se gusta?" The proprietor had come to check on their progress, which was ravenous. Clark took a moment to chew and swallow before he could give a proper response.

"Claro", he smiled at the owner and he seemed to be immensely pleased. Clark was happy that he had not only understood the man but had been able to respond correctly and been understood. This was how it was supposed to be, so much better than trying to explain why the pile of pig or cow intestines (yet to be determined) were left untouched. It was one thing to send back a meal at a Chile's or Applebee's, the servers and kitchen staff there didn't invent the dish, at the places in Mexico your waiter was often the chef, owner and torchbearer of their mother's secret family recipe. Other than that first day, they hadn't been to an American restaurant, they had seen Golden arches in the distance, along with any number of American chains, but they never seemed to be the best choice.

After finishing four tamales himself, Clark waved the white flag of surrender. The check was a pitifully small amount, less than twenty dollars. Clark looked around at the concrete building, it was sleek modern taken to a minimalist extreme, just plain concrete walls and plastic tables and chairs. Clark thought about leaving a huge tip, but he didn't have the money. Instead after settling his bill he extended his hand.

"Gracias por los mas Buenos tamales." Clark knew his Spanish was horrible at best, but he hoped the man would understand enough to appreciate the sentiment. The man smiled at Clark and shook his hand in an almost formal motion. They stepped back out into the intense sunlight, the humidity pressing down on them like a physical weight.

If it had been hot and humid outside, it was doubly unbearable inside the motor home. The diesel rumbled to life, raising a cloud of dust behind them. Clark started down the road, noting that they needed fuel at the next Pemex. The idea of only having state run gas stations was at first troubling to Clark. But when he saw their frequency and how evenly they were spread out, even in remote areas, he was glad for it. Instead of having clusters of stations and then huge distances in between, they were able to put the stations where they made sense. Clark didn't notice any difference in price, in fact if his calculations were right it was slightly cheaper. At pesos per liter, it was hard to do an effective calculation in his head; somehow his calculator had gone missing.

He pulled into the Pemex, allowing the attendant to direct him in, as if he were landing a 747. It was much the same at every stop. The attendant prattled on for a minute, of which Clark understood nothing. Instead of asking the man to stop, he just did the dumb tourist look. Finallly the man understood and used his hands to intimate amounts of pesos. Clark handed the man a thousand pesos, which would have been a huge amount of gasoline for a car, but in diesel for a motor home it wasn't even a third a tank, but that was all he needed to be full.

Clark looked at the windshield, the further south, more vegetation and exponentially more bugs. He thought there were at least thousands, many beautiful butterflies that had committed windshield suicide today. The attendant had a bucket with a windshield brush. Clark wasn't sure it would last more than twenty minutes at the rate he was accumulating dead bugs, but he guess it was better to try and get on top of it. As he tried to work a small space for him to see out of, he heard running water behind him. For a moment Clark feared the fuel was spilling out of the tank. He jumped back only to have his shoe filled with water from the hose the attendant had drug over for him. Clark nodded appreciatively, spraying to windshield to at least loosen the dried bug matter. After the big bugs were hosed off, Clark motioned to use the hose to fill the coach water tank, or at least he hoped that was what the attendant understood. The man shook his head yes and Clark lifted the door to the water tank area. Clark connected the hose and the big beast began to drink. The diesel had long since been filled, and yet the tank continued to drink water. The attendant and two apparent friends came over to watch with amazement. They pointed and spoke words Clark didn't understand. They laughed and clapped Clark on the back before heading back to their shady corners. Clark tipped the attendant a couple of dollars and they were off. When Clark realized they were only a short distance from the border, he was surprised to find himself apprehensive, now that he was used to Mexico now, what would he find in Guatemala?

That little ball of apprehension took seed and fully blossomed as darkness fell and the signs seemed to indicate the border was coming in 100 Kilometers. Clark could never be sure about what the signs were saying, but piecing the data from what had followed similar sounding signs seemed the best way to predict future events. Clark wondered if it would be easier to get across the border at night or during the day. Clark spied a large parking lot next to what he hoped was an abandoned building. He knew he could just part the coach there for the night, but wondered if he might miss something. He knew Anne and Jordan would be coming through this border, he had been thinking all day that if he could make it to the border before they got through eh might have the chance to explain things to her. He might have a chance to save it all.

Oh what a miserable creature longing makes of men. Oh, that's good, I ought to write that down and show Anne. Oh dear Lord, you are hopeless.

Miles rolled on, the monotonous hum of the tires pushing eye lids down until only Clark was awake. The border loomed close, they passed signs indicating that guns were prohibited, it seemed that this border was very similar to crossing into Mexico. They had a chance to speak with the owner of a nightclub that had let them park and fill their water tanks, who had indicated that racism was not the sole property of Americans. He told them with a hushed tone that Mexico had the same illegal immigrant problem the U.S. faced, only this was Mexico being overrun by Guatemalans. Clark had suppressed a laugh as the owner told him almost the exact same things a Texas rancher had told him a country away. The similarities were thus:

1. They come take all our jobs
2. They're all thieves
3. They're all criminals
4. They should just go home
5. We need a bigger fence

Clark had wondered if the Canadians said the same thing about the U.S. people sneaking across the border to buy cheap medications. Maybe it was a southern border problem. Would that mean that Argentina then had the worst possible people on the continent?

Now Clark was about to head into the land of the thieving job stealers, but as this was his second foray into that same scenario, he faced it with a much steelier resolve than he had before. Nighttime crossings had one advantage, with the exception of the occasional commercial vehicle, the entries were mostly empty. Mexican officials spent only a few minutes looking over the packet. After the debacle at the Mexican border crossing, Clark had put their passports, the original title to the motor home, their insurance and their special Mexican insurance. With another smile Clark was out of Mexico, having never paid one bribe or extortion, only having been robbed once, and no physical threats of any kind. It almost seemed disappointing, not having any great story of death defying adventures to share.

At the Guatemalan side no English was spoken. Chloe again proved an invaluable asset as they tried to navigate the waters of getting across. Clark was still in the dark, but when Chloe smiled at him, he knew they must be getting through. Once again there seemed to be a special fee they needed to pay in order to get through, but they seemed to be able to sell it to them right there. The uniforms had a homemade like appearance, or maybe more like a movie prop. Machismo lived heartily in the border guards, who all seemed to be even a shade darker than the Mexican guards had been. As they walked outside one of the men suddenly grabbed a commercial looking spray machine. For the next few minutes he went around and inside the vehicle spraying some kind of substance over the vehicle. It looked like they were being deloused, Clark wondered if he had just missed the creepy crawlies or whether this was just a good excuse to charge for something.

Once their passports were stamped the man gestured they could go. As Clark drove forward he thought of all the terrible things he had heard about Guatemala over the years. Civil wars and ruthless dictators seemed likely to be hiding behind every brush and branch. Surely every peasant that walked along was carrying at least a kilogram of cocaine. But like Mexico, all he noticed in the evening hours were smiling faces that looked like they were on their way home. Clark spotted a road that looked abandoned and backed the RV into it. It was visible to the road, but then again, it was visible to the road. He and Anne had debated this exact thing multiple times, whether it was better to be in the open, or hidden away. Clark thought that open was better, after all, who would come to their aid if some bad guy found them in some isolated backwater? Speaking of which, he had not found Anne at the border crossing. He wasn't sure why he had thought she would be there, maybe they wouldn't even come this far, Jordan had said he doubted he could make it all the way to Tierra del Fuego, he had his Sophomore year of college to prepare for. Clark tried to put it out of his mind, it was quite possible that ship had sailed, there wasn't much he could do about it now.

A large faded beer sign towered above them, it seemed peeling paint wasn't just a Mexican thing. He ensured all the compartments were locked and that the jacks weren't over any holes. He closed the door hard and latched the deadbolt. He brought the jacks down one by one until the coach reached as close to level as they were going to get. Chloe stood up obediently as Clark pressed the button to extend the slide. About half way out there was a loud popping sound. Clark removed his finger from the button; that sound didn't bode well for the pop out. It was getting late, so he gestured for Chloe to lie down. He couldn't see anything if he went out to look at it anyway. Clark added it to the list of things that needed repair, which grew daily and rarely seemed to shrink.

Jack was always in bed before him, but it was his uncanny ability to fall asleep instantly that Clark resented most. His whole body was tired, aching from being stuck in that single driving position, but still he knew his mind would torture him tonight. He felt like there was a good cry in him, but his sense of what it meant to be a man wouldn't allow it. He had been sure that Anne would be at the border, some kind of cosmic fate that had to draw them together. But she hadn't been there; and now he had no idea if they were ahead or behind. They could have gone toward Quintana Roo and the Mayan Riviera, or turned around and headed home. Something about Anne told him that she wasn't much of go home girl, but still who knew?

After an hour of trying to fall asleep Clark got up and opened two windows and the roof vents, the smell of the fumigation was getting to him. He opened the door and walked outside. Only a few feral dogs seemed to be roaming the neighborhood, Clark watched them warily as they trotted by. Looking up at the sky the stars twinkled then faded from view as the clouds drifted by. Clark wondered if Anne was somewhere close by, maybe he could just yell out and she would hear him. But what would he yell? Would he yell that he was sorry, or that he wanted her? Each declaration seemed a little sadder than the last. What could he bring to someone who had their life together? He was homeless, jobless, wifeless, basically he was a few thousand dollars away from being a hobo. Maybe it was best if he didn't find Anne. As if on cue the clouds gathered and began to weep. First just big fat drops that hit the ground like artillery, then increasing to a full downpour. Unlike home this rain didn't seem to make Clark cold, so he continued to stand there, hoping that the water would wash away some of him, maybe it would just wash away what was wrong with him. Eventually it seemed the rain would not wash any of him away, only cause his teeth to chatter. He walked up into the motor home, taking off his wet shoes on the stairs. He stripped out of his wet clothes in the bathroom, luckily finding one last pair of clean underwear on a nearby shelf. Tomorrow would have to be a laundry day, or buy new clothes. He flopped down on the bed next to Jack, who continued his tormenting unfettered sleep. Clark started at one, losing track at around 405.

Chapter 21

Morning brought an unfortunate treat for each of them, for although they had left Mexico without gold or treasure, Monteczuma's curse had followed them. Clark's stomach felt hollow like he had never eaten, but his backside was as raw as a baboon's ass. Clark wondered what had done this horrible thing to him, pointing to the tamales, water, anything that could have cast this horrible curse of the cramping colon. He had found a little Farmacia that had pink bismuth, but though they had each had nearly a bottle for breakfast, the fountains continued. When finally they thought they could make it further than ten feet from a toilet, Clark raised the jacks and they headed to the next big city, Pajapita. They longed for the golden arches in the agony of their intestinal issues, as if their former adventurous eating had been a horribly conceived mistake. They were ready to beg that red headed clown for forgiveness and repent with two all-beef patties, special sauce, lettuce and cheese. Alas, there were no arches to be found there.

Instead they found a small café that served coffee and pastries. Eyeing everything closely, they ordered some delicious looking sweet bread, while Clark had a coffee and something that resembled a Danish. The coffee was excellent, maybe some of the best coffee he had ever tasted, and he wondered how close they were to the source. The pastries were disappointing, lacking the sweetness that Americans had gotten used to in their gluttony. The family sat at an outdoor table sipping coffee and nibbling their bland breakfast.

"Are we close to the ocean?" Jack's voice was a nice break from the silence.

"I think we're only like ten miles from the beach." Clark had looked at the map and was surprised the road didn't pass closer to the Pacific. He had noticed a couple of fish sounding dishes on the menu, but his stomach was having none of that today.

"Can we go?" Jack was looking at him with eager eyes. How could he resist? Clark would have to give up on his ridiculous quest to find Anne, with entire countries to scour, it was becoming an impossible quest. His son deserved to see the Pacific Ocean.

"Of course we can, let's ask around for a good beach. Maybe we can camp there." When Chloe asked the waiter where a good beach was, he indicated just up the road, somewhere called Playa Tilapa. Clark thought that sounded suspiciously like the fish he had ordered just two nights ago. They finished their breakfast and headed in the direction of the great Pacific.

Some distance away blue signs with crashing waves started to appear. As they got closer, Clark realized he wouldn't be parking right on the beach, so they started looking for a parking spot on the entrance road. Clark found a spot where three or four cars would have fit, but even as far over as he could get, the rig sat out at least three feet into the road. It seemed pretty dead, no cars blaring horns on their way by, so Clark decided to risk it. They all changed into their beach clothes, which still had the tags on them from the Wal-Mart in Texas. Clark laughed; it seemed ridiculous that they had driven through Mexico without ever sitting on even one beach. They took their things and locked up the coach.

Walking down the road toward the beach they looked a fairly typical American family minus the mother of course. But to those they passed, they must have been a fairly rare sight. Chloe noticed immediately that she was getting all the wrong kind of attention in her bikini. Before they even got to within sight of the sand she had put a cover up over her suit. That seemed to reduce the leering some, but her alabaster skin still seemed enough of a novelty that people stopped to look.

The beach was just over the crest of a hill. Most of the people in the city seemed busy enough with their shops and businesses that they had left the beach for the three Anglo Americans. As they walked out on the sand they were shocked, the beach was filthy. Discarded bottles, napkins and seemingly any kind of available garbage were strewn across the sand. The sand itself was a dark color, nothing like the clean white sand beaches they had thought to encounter. Agreeably this wasn't a tourist beach, this was a local's beach, but still the pig pen conditions were tough for them to stomach. The windy morning was still whipping the wild Pacific into a frothy fury, the waves crashing with an angry and violent sound. Jack was the only one seeming unphased by the filth, he eagerly ran toward the pounding surf. Clark yelled after him to be careful and stay where he could touch, but he doubted the boy had heard a syllable.

Clark and Chloe worked to clean a section of the beach enough that they could sit down without feeling they were inside a large dumpster. The remnants of a beach site proved to be cleaner than most and after only a few minutes they had the garbage forming a ten foot ring around them. The wind kept them from being miserably hot, but the sun shone bright. Chloe kept looking around, wondering when she would be able to sun bathe.

"I'm gonna go for it." She said as the cover up slipped over her head. Clark had to avert his eyes, it was obvious that his daughter was a rare beauty, but it seemed something that a father would rather bury his head in the sand on. He looked up and down the beach; there weren't more than a hundred people in sight. Several families were on large blankets having some sort of meal. The palapa shade structures were all held tight against the restaurants or bars, each shuttered today, waiting patiently for busier days to open. Clark laughed at Jack; the boy was standing at precisely the location where Clark wouldn't have considered, allowing the waves to crash full force into his torso. Soon Jack was jumping into the oncoming waves, getting pushed back five feet at each large break. After an amazing number of wave poundings, Jack came running up to them.

"Dad, you gotta come out with me. I got the perfect spot." He could hardly speak he was so out of breath.

"Yeah, that's just what I was thinking. Maybe Chloe wants to go." He had to try at least.

"Pass". Chloe hadn't even looked like she had heard them.

"Okay, let's go." Together the two ran out into the ocean, which was colder than Clark had thought it would be. Jack was only content when the waves were smashing them in the body. Clark tried to show him how to body surf, but the swimming was more than he could do. By the time they drug themselves out of the water, Clark was heaving like a winded walrus.

Jack found a spot to build sand castles within their circle of sans-garbage. Clark looked up and down the beach, deciding that he could leave the two for a few minutes. The long waves had created a wonderful flat area for walking, Clark's feet making deep impressions in the wet sand. He looked behind him, ensuring that the kids stayed within his sight. The water ran up the beach every few minutes, obliterating any trace that he had walked there at all. He wondered if life was conspiring to wipe all traces of him from the record. A man with no home, job or wife was one data error away from being erased from the whole thing. Clark had always heard that a man died twice, first when his body died, second when the last person who knew them died. It didn't appear that was likely to be anything more than his kids. Watching the two in the distance, it was hard to acknowledge that they were all he had left. All of the hours, days and years he had worked were spent and wasted on the ever increasing cost of living in America. Clark had bought the whole thing, work thirty or forty years, build a retirement, marry your college sweetheart, only they had all turned out to be hollow promises. Clark had killed himself a little every day to afford a house that was taken from him without a drop of blood or even a really harsh word. He thought back to that morning, wondering why he hadn't fought harder. He wondered if he had been happy, or whether it was just contentment. Maybe it was something more like settling. Karen had said that she had 'woken' up one day, Clark wondered if he would, or maybe he was waking up right now.

Suddenly Anne was before him, her long legs bare in the sun, large sunglasses hiding much of her face. But he knew it was her, it really was her. It struck him; he had imagined her so many times, now it seemed unreal. He looked around for Jordan, who was playing in the ocean just like Jack had. He turned back to Anne, his shadow falling across her legs. He needed to say the right thing, this was a critical moment. He fumbled with the words in his mind.

Anne, I can't believe you're here. I'm sorry about the other night, just give me another chance to make this thing work. No. Anne, hey, what are you guys doing here? Crazy bumping into you like this. No. Anne, I hoped we would run into each other again. No. Hey, I guess fate wants us to be together. No...

"Fuck off creep." Anne's voice had ringed out clear in her declaration. She even waved her hand as if she were swatting away a fly. Clark thought he might cry, he knew he hadn't handled himself very well, but this? He was shocked, but angry was trying to make a move up. He gathered himself.

"I'm sorry to have bothered you." Clark turned to walk away, trying to escape before any crueler sentiments issued forth from her lips.

"Clark? Oh my God, I'm sorry I didn't know that was you. I thought you were some asshole standing over me rubbing his tool." She stood up and lifted her sunglasses onto her head. Clark had never seen her body, but instead of making him weak with desire, it juxtaposed his own soft body. She looked like a cheerleader, every line almost perfect in its shape and flow. He knew he had to say something.

"Not just any asshole, your asshole." Clark had the desire to look at his feet; that had come out all wrong. Anne only smiled and shook her head. It seemed she understood he had meant it in good humor, without the benefit of wit. A moment of silence passed between them as they looked at each other. It wasn't the kind of awkward silence that begged to be filled; instead it was the kind of silence where both parties acknowledged they couldn't have improved upon the silence. Jordan finally broke the moment as he trotted toward them.

"Clark, you made it to Guatemala. Good to see you." The young man who wore only a pair of red swim trunks jabbed Clark softly in the arm. His smile was good natured and genuine, damn Clark was always waiting for some hidden blackness in the boy so he could forbid Chloe from speaking to him. But instead he just smiled like a Labrador, faithful and obedient to the end.

"Much easier than into Mexico or at least for us it was." Jordan seemed to smile and nod his agreement, but he seemed to be scanning the area behind Clark for something. His gaze would lock on Clark's eyes for a second, and then slowly drift off in a search pattern.

"Chloe and Jack are actually behind you, about a quarter mile down the beach." Jordan smiled again, just the beginnings of a smirk at the right side of his mouth.

"Well, I better go say hello." Just like that he was off. Clark sighed heavily, he liked Jordan, but he couldn't shake the feeling that he liked nobody better than the best anybody. His eyes traced after the boy who was nearly at a sprint and fading from view like a rocket ship.

"I'm really glad we bumped into each other again Clark, what would the odds be, astronomical I would think." Anne's voice distracted him completely from his trajectory search of teenage/tween lust.

"I've been looking for you since you left, or at least since the morning after. Jack knows everything, so does my soon to be ex-wife. It wasn't pretty, but at least it's done. The kids have to go back in three weeks no matter where we are."

Anne didn't say anything, instead studying Clark's face as she often did. For all Clark knew she might have been some exotic face wrinkle reader, able to tell his future and the course of his heart. If so she never seemed to fill him in on any of the details.

"So what, we should just pick up where we left off, midnight rendezvous and you leaving me on the dance floor anytime someone says boo?" She sounded a little angry, which Clark expected. This was his area; he excelled in begging for forgiveness almost as much as making it up to people.

"I'm sorry how that thing happened in Oaxaca. It wouldn't be like before, Jack knows now that I'm not some philanderer out here. We could actually have something. Just give me a chance to prove how I've changed." Anne laughed out loud, which stung Clark. He was not used to having his pleas laughed at, even by Karen. She had always weighed them against her anger and made a solid judgment, but to laugh?

"Why do you insist that you're the problem Clark? You seem to have some incorrect assumptions about me. Let me assuage those for you. I am no damsel in distress that needs saving. I had the whole marriage, kids, white picket fence; and to be honest with you, I threw it all away. I would take a lot of it back now, but I can't. And I will never be someone's shadow again, ever." Clark had never heard a woman speak like this outside the movies; all the women he knew wouldn't dare be heard saying these things. Clark tried to temper his shock, lest his jaw be on the floor. He liked that he was hearing what she really thought, even if he didn't necessarily like how she said it. At least he knew where he stood with her.

"Clark, I'm just not sure that I'm what you need. You seem like the kind of guy who's going to want a white wedding dress at some point; I don't believe my hypocrisy goes that far. I think you're looking for someone better than me." Clark didn't know what to say, he hadn't thought that far, but if he looked at the plan as far as he could make it out, it did seem to be heading in that direction. Could she be right? Was he desperate to replace his female counterpart? Was he better than her? Was he so desperate that he didn't care who filled it? He sat for a moment, letting the data sort itself out in his head. Anne had been honest with him; he owed it to her to be honest back.

"I'm not sure what I want. My head feels all cloudy, it has since Karen left me, but I enjoy being around you. If all we had was this trip, I would be honored to do it with you." For the first time, the smirky smile on Anne's face faded, with it Anne looked several years older. The wrinkles had begun to accumulate around her mouth and eyes; somehow the smiling caused them to fade away. Anne stared out into the ocean. Clark followed her gaze, but she seemed to be just blankly staring at the water.

"If you want to build a ship, don't drum up people to collect wood and don't assign them tasks and work, but rather teach them to long for the endless immensity of the sea" Still she stared out into the water.

"Did you just make that up?" Anne looked back at him, the smirk back in place and possibly stronger than ever.

"Yeah, pretty good huh? You think I got the title of Slut Poet without having some major skill?" Clark made some sounds with his mouth, none of which were words, much less sentences.

"Where'd you park the beast?"

"The what?"

"That 37 foot beast you drive."

"Couple blocks up from where the kids are on the beach."

Anne slipped a cotton dress over her bikini, grabbed her bag and slipped her arm in Clark's. The two walked along the beach toward the others. Clark knew that second chances didn't happen very often, so he was doing his best to enjoy the opportunity presented to him in this one. The idea of strolling along the beach with your infatuation locked arm in arm seemed almost too stereotypical for him, but it was nice. Suddenly he felt poetic himself, not that he would have dared to tell her anything he could come up with. He thought of a couple of roses are red poems, but doubted they would pass the muster. Clark thought about making up a limerick about how romantic garbage strewn beaches were, even laughing for a moment to himself. Anne looked at him when the guffaw slipped out, not asking just pulling his arm closer. Again Clark felt he should be recording this. He was reminded of the Roman Triumphs, where conquering Roman Generals were paraded through the streets to celebrate their victories. Legend had it that the Generals would have a slave standing behind them in their chariot whispering "memento mori", or "remember you will die" a reminder to the General that he was not a God. Clark felt like a God in this moment, heresy or not. He was glad no one was there to remind him and he did not share his epiphany with Anne.

Jordan and Jack were in the water while Chloe watched them from the safe ankle deep area. Both of them were trying to body surf and damn if the little shit Jordan wasn't doing it. Now Clark felt he had to get back out there, defend his reputation as the King of body surfing, but he felt the tug of Anne's arm coaxing him down onto the towels. His wounded pride took a seat next to him, sulking in the dry sand.

Clark licked his lips and was surprised to find them covered in a thin film of salt, the wind must have deposited it. He looked at Anne, he wanted to kiss her so badly, but maybe this wasn't the time. Maybe they should wait until people weren't watching, until the kids were asleep. Clark was mapping out a small matrix of events that needed to occur for him to put the official moves on Anne when he felt the soft pressure of her hand on his face. As he turned her lips were there, ready for him. Her lips were almost trembling, Clark's heart felt like it might pound its way out of his chest. He felt faint s his mouth opened and his hand encircled Anne, pulling her closer. She tasted like mint and watermelon, it amazed him how she always smelled and tasted so good. Her body rubbed up against his, he could not see her, but he knew which curves went where and again his head swam. Their mouth's became more and more ferocious with each other, Anne bit his lip so hard at one point he swore he could taste blood.

"Take me to the motor home." It was hardly more than a whisper, but she had said it. Clark's brain was firing about reasons that wouldn't work, but still he stood up and rushed her toward the coach.

They were nearly sprinting themselves, heedless of traffic. Clark fumbled with the keys at the door, Anne's hands on his shoulders, her face pressed into his back. Once inside, Anne pounced on him. Their clothes and shoes seemed to be making a trail that led to the rear of the 'beast'. The touch of Anne's skin on his was electric, the goose bumps almost painful they were so tender. A moment later she was on the bed, pulling him toward her. The teenager inside him wanted to plunge right in, but the adult was screaming that safe sex was the only way.

"I don't have a condom." Clark breathed in exasperation. Anne closed her eyes, her Cheshire cat smile in full force. She lifted a small packet to him.

"A girl's gotta be prepared." Clark smiled; trying to abandon a line of questioning that wouldn't lead anywhere he wanted to go right now. Once it was on, he was inside her and time shifted. They were no longer two individuals, but a single entity composed of two things. Their bodies moved independently, but in common goal and effort. Her eyes were amazingly blue in that moment, as if the act had somehow turned a switch and intensified them. Clark pushed the few errant hairs behind her ear. The intense animalistic need had faded, now he felt an older man's reserve to enjoy this moment. His motion slowed and he adjusted his position on the bed. He kissed her again, sure that this time he could taste the adrenaline along with the watermelon and mint. He slowed until it was the sweetest agony, his body begging for him to speed up, her hands grasping at him, clutching and tugging to increase his tempo. His hands found the side of her ribs, tracing along their lines until they rose to the height of breasts, each with an erect nipple. He ran the tips of his fingers along the slow soft curves of her, teasing here as well. He returned her grin. Suddenly her eyes narrowed.

"Okay, my turn." With that she pulled his shoulder down and almost instantly she was on top of him. She pressed his shoulders down into the bed as her hips worked a back and forth motion. Clark began to panic; he wouldn't last long like this. She bit her lip as her hips moved back and forth with reckless abandon. Clark forced himself to sit up, finding a soft plump breast right before his mouth. As he licked and kissed her breast he felt his own pressure rise, he knew he wouldn't last much longer. He lifted his hips to try and force her back on the bottom, but Anne was having none of that. She pressed him back down hard onto the bed. The world exploded in Clark's mind, he pressed his head back into the pillow, his jaw clenched so hard he thought he might break a tooth; his eyes were clamped shut showing the fireworks on the backs of his eyelids. As the waves passed through him and began to fade he noted that she was not stopping or slowing, instead she seemed to be speeding up. He gritted his teeth, trying not to cry out in agony. He was so sensitive that it was hard to say whether this was the greatest thing ever or the worst. He opened his eyes to watch her move, the intense closed eyes, small beads of sweat on her nose, arm muscles flexed rigid. Suddenly she let out a sigh, almost a grunt; her shoulders collapsing every couple of seconds as she coasted toward the end. She collapsed on him, their sweaty chests sticking together. Clark kissed her neck, salt, he wasn't sure if it was sweat or sea spray, but he didn't mind either way.

They lay in silence for a few minutes, until matters of necessity needed tending to. When Clark returned Anne was lying on her side facing him. She was easily the most beautiful woman who had ever looked at him that way, Karen had been attractive in her day, but Anne was the personification of beauty. He hadn't noticed, but she had some words tattooed on her side, almost on the rib line. He was surprised he had missed that on the beach. Now, with their passions spent, he wanted to ask her so many things, hopes and dreams, where she had been, but it felt wrong, Anne was a creature of the now, why ask about the past?

"Do you think we should go check on everybody?" Clark asked.

"Let's just stay here a few minutes longer, come here." She pulled Clark close to her. She kissed his nose and her breasts were just making contact with his chest. He stared at her, trying to see past what everyone saw, to see the something more that he was sure was there. Her toes were rubbing his leg, suddenly he was aware that she was making a lot of contact with his body, and amazingly it seemed to be responding. Clark could hardly remember the last time he had done a "double play", having been years prior. Clark smiled coyly at Anne, who tried her best to look innocent. Just then she held up another foil packet, somehow appearing from thin air.

"Alright, but this time I'm in charge", he smiled as he pulled her under him.

"Good luck with that." Anne was smiling while she said it, but Clark knew she meant every syllable and letter. He would have said something, but some things just weren't worth arguing about.

Chapter 22

By the time they made it back to the beach the boys had tired themselves of the constant onslaught of waves. The three were sitting on the beach blanket talking.

"Who's hungry?" Clark asked the group.

"Dad, where have you been?" Jack's question filled Clark with intense guilt, but Anne's firm arm gave him a small amount of courage. Jack didn't seem to be angry, sometimes Clark had to remind himself, a question was just a question. Instead of responding to the question he continued with his own.

"Come on, you guys hungry from fighting the waves or what?"

"Yeah, I'm starving," Jordan pitched in. Jack followed right behind Jordan in his sentiment. A moment of chest stabbing pain as Clark realized Jack wasn't following him like that. Chloe stood up and folded the blanket into a small bundle.

"What about your towels?" Clark asked Anne.

She shrugged her shoulders, "they belong to the hotel." With that she was apparently done worrying about it. Clark looked toward Jordan, but he only smiled and shrugged his shoulders. Clark knew the fines could be quite severe for lost towels, it seemed reckless to him, but what the hell.

Only one or two of the small Cafés along the beach were open. Without much rhyme or reason they chose one and entered. Café was a stretch, more of a bar inside, it probably only held fifty people. A polite older gentleman came out of the back to greet them. He looked slightly confused and spoke a strange dialect of Spanish that Anne said was more likely Portuguese. The menus were unreadable and communication was at a standstill with the constantly smiling proprietor. Anne eventually took matters into her own hands, literally, pointing and using her fingers to indicate quantities. When the man left she shrugged and set back comfortably in her chair.

Jack was eyeing the two with suspicion; his sense for the off color of their relationship was uncanny. Clark wondered where that sense had been with his own mother. *Don't do that, that's not fair.* Chloe and Jordan might as well have been at their own table, their conversation done in such hushed tones and late model references that Clark had stopped even trying to follow the two. Anne helped both of them by talking to Jack.

"Well Jack, what do you think of the Pacific Ocean?" She turned fully toward him to ask. Clark appreciated that, many adults seemed to only speak to children out of the corners of their mouths, as if conversations with them were some unpleasant necessity, best gotten out of the way. She either was genuinely interested in what he had to say, or was doing a great job pretending.

"It was colder than I thought it would be, and saltier. I got some in my eyes and it burned like crazy."

Anne now really examined him, looking his face up and down. "Are you alright, do you want to go rinse your face off in the sink?" Jack smiled, which made Clark smile. This is what the boy missed about his mother and what he wasn't going to get from his father. A mother's instinct just couldn't be faked, it either existed or not. Clark wouldn't have thought to ask him and would have assumed if he needed to rinse his face off, he would ask. Of course Jack didn't want to seem like a little kid who needed someone to wash his face so he shook his head no.

"Why don't you help me find the bathroom, I need to wash the sand off my hands." Anne's words were again perfect, now she had made him a part of the solution, instead of just another problem. Jack jumped up and started investigating. A moment later he returned and tapped Anne on the shoulder.

"Come on Anne, I'll show you where they are." Anne got up with a knowing smile at Clark and the two walked off. This left Clark alone with Chloe and Jordan. As soon as the two felt his penetrating gaze their conversation stopped and they both smiled as innocently as possible at him. There were several moments that begged for a comment or sound at least, but each of them seemed to be respecting the age old wisdom of polite dinner conversation. None of the three dared break the uneasy peace that pervaded the table with talk of what was, what could be, or what shouldn't be.

"What did we miss?" Anne's voice broke through the oppressive quiet.

"Almost the food," Clark stated as the parade of dishes finally made their way to the table. Delicious blackened barbequed seafood and a dozen bowls of accoutrement got all their interests piqued. Silence was replaced by the sound of mastication and consumption. Clark tried to take it easy, his stomach was still tender from his earlier episode, but he was also starving. He ate things that he couldn't have even described to a police sketch artist, but he stopped early. His stomach was rumbling mightily.

"I'm going to go back to the RV," he stated as he stood up and pushed in his chair. He did not wait for anyone else's comment, instead speed walking to the bar and exchanging money before nearly sprinting out the door. He just made it to the RV before he had an incident.

That was a terrible choice. After, he sat on the couch of the Beast, enjoying the brief reprieve from teenager and child noise. He went to close his eyes, he didn't remember being this tired, but once he got comfortable his lids had become like lead. Suddenly he nearly sprang out of his seat; he had something he needed to do. He put his shoes on outside and locked the coach door. Walking along the road he made his calculations as to where he was supposed to be. A satisfied grin spread when he found the object of his mission, still lying in plain sight. He wrapped up his coveted prize and walked back to the road, stomping the sand out of his shoe treads. Ahead was a small Hotel, the same Hotel that Anne had mentioned at dinner. Nearly inside the front door were two motorcycles, a new Harley and an old Indian. He winked knowingly at the bikes as one might rub the nuzzle of a well-loved horse. He had followed their tail lights with eager anticipation, it wouldn't have been right to ignore them after the absence. The front door was sticky and required a little force to open. Once inside Clark had to ring the bell to get someone.

"Si senor, como puedo ayudarse?" the man asked. Clark stared blankly at him, trying to decide how to respond. Instead he just hefted his prize onto the counter.

"Anne Carter, no charge." Clark's words seemed as foreign to the man as his had been to Clark. But he shook his head, probably just to be rid of the stranger who showed up with two sand covered towels.

Chapter 23

Guatemala faded into the rearview mirrors the next day. Only two days to cross a country, that was more like it. They were making progress now. The rhythm of following the motorcycles was getting easier and everyone's Spanish seemed to be improving, with the possible exception of Clark.

In El Salvador they were able to use dollars and found an even more outlandish border guard uniform. On the roads they passed beautiful farm country, so green it defied belief to people from the desert. Donkey drawn carts and a three wheeled bicycle seemed to out populate the cars by two to one. Motorcycles passed with up to six passengers on board, sometimes entire family units. Taxis were everywhere, along with small trucks that looked more diesel babies. Small simple houses had become the new normal once they passed out of the US. Smiling brown faces dotted the roadsides, sometimes trying to sell something, others just peeking out the open holes that served as windows. Always smiling, Clark wondered how he would survive back home, where instead everyone was buried in their electronic device, freeing them from the burden of interaction.

Gaps between cities were sporadic, so when they found a good parking spot they took it. It had been several days since they were able to dump the holding tanks into an actual sewer, although they had found exactly how deep and wide the hole had to be to keep sewer effluent from getting on Clark's shoes. Then they were at a café just before leaving El Salvador and after using the bathroom Clark wondered at where it all 'went'. Noticing a back door he followed it out and found that it went to an open sewer that flowed out to a river. It relieved any guilt Clark might have had, when he got back to the table he only mentioned one thing. "Don't drink out of the rivers," allowing everyone's imagination to fill in the rest.

In Nicaragua they were back to local currency. Clark wondered if they traveled through enough countries, and lost on every money transaction, he might just be broke without having to actually spend any money. He looked at the pile of money he had brought, it seemed much smaller than the pile that had entered Mexico. He was paying for everyone's meals and it was taking a toll. He wanted to say something to Anne, but the joy of her smile was too precious to him, so he didn't.

They took a day off from travelling to take sailing classes on Lake Nicaragua. After about an hour of trying to understand what the man was saying, they gave up and broke up into two groups for the hands on portion. Chloe and Jordan volunteered to have the small group. Clark rolled his eyes, he was going to have to say something, but he didn't want to ruin the experience. Soon they were all wearing the orange life vests and loaded into two very small boats. On the water the man tried to explain to them what he was doing, but his English wasn't good enough to combat Clark's insanely poor Spanish. In the end only Jack, Chloe and Jordan really learned much about sailing. Anne and Clark had been content to bathe in the radiant smiles Jack had as he mastered each new skill. Tacking and setting sail seemed to come to him quite naturally; Clark assumed it must have been Karen's blood.

Part of the class was an included lunch, which was adequate without wowing anyone. After the parade of exceptional meals they had been treated to, a simple sandwich just seemed to fall short.

Clark gave up trying to get rid of his stomach ailments, instead focusing on keeping the bouts limited to times he had access to a toilet. He had managed to keep from shitting his pants so far, but it had been close a couple of times. He had told Jack that anything that stayed in his underwear wouldn't be counted against him, as long as he never put said underwear in the garbage can without telling him.

In the nights, Clark and Anne fought for every moment of privacy. They had resorted to outright bribery by the time they got to Costa Rica. It had shocked them to see larger building again, having somehow forgotten that Costa Rica was as close as Central America got to a First World country. There were still the small houses along the roads with the brown smiling faces, but there were also large industrial buildings with modern glass fronts. When they found what resembled a mall, Clark and Anne spotted their opportunity for some happy time. Clark had given Chloe an unreasonable amount of cash to spend, both of them quietly acknowledging the blood money had been paid.

Clark and Anne watched the kids walking away through the blinds, much like they had watched their parents leaving, just waiting until they had passed earshot before breaking the rules. They tore at one another, ravaged each other, within the confines of decency, and the parking lot of a major mall. After they lay next to each other, catching their breath, speaking in hushed tones of things that could be and things that should be. This was more forbidden than the physical act, this was premeditated relationshipping. None of the kids would have suffered this nonsense, even Clark thought it silly to speak of such things. But it felt so good to hope, to dream of a bright future full of promise, that he allowed himself to ignore the glaring tactical errors. They spoke of a house on the beach, not anywhere they had seen yet, but some great undiscovered vista yet to be found. Every third sentence caused one of them to kiss the other. Clark's logical mind screamed that it was too soon, too many problems and too much hard road yet to be chewed, but he did his best to silence those voices, reducing them to a nagging itch in the back of his mind that he refused to scratch. They were so close to making another continent, just Panama to go. It felt so close now that he almost began to feel the sadness that came from having all one's dreams come true. What happened when the dream was over? Did real life set back in then? Would he wake up and be back in the life where he was too blind to sense his own misery? Would he be having dinner with his ex-wife and her new husband? Would his kids start calling him Clark and some strange man Dad? Sadly, Clark realized that those nagging doubts had made their way forward, unscratched but not unsensed. His life was a mess; nothing would fix all those things. He looked at Anne, desperately trying to cling to the hope that somehow her presence would solve the innumerable problems in his stable. He kissed her desperately, hoping his rising panic and fear didn't sour the exchange. She kissed him back, redoubling his lust and causing hands to roam, bodies to entwine, passions to engorge. After Clark caught his breath, they just lay there, this time not needing to speak, content to let the tracing fingertips and rubbing legs fill the space of idle conversations.

"I love you." Clark's declaration made even him blush, seeming as surprised as her to hear it. The words hung in the air, the silent air. They hung above them like skywriting, Clark wishing he could take them away once they were out. It was too soon. This should be a casual thing, he had been told that it was nothing more than that and that Anne wasn't capable of giving him more than this. But Clark was frozen, unable to retract the syllables, head swimming in embarrassment and regret. Seconds ticked by, the stupid clock that had come with the motor home clicking off seconds, sounding like the marching feet of destiny.

"Can we not do that?" Anne asked quietly. Clark felt sharp pain in his chest, not only had she not responded in kind, she was telling him not to do it. Clark was no raging romantic, but what was a life without love? He tried to quiet his mind, to accept the nature of their relationship, or lack thereof. Clark's logical mind told him that she had just done him a huge favor, but still the pain persisted.

"Yeah, sorry, that was foolish" Clark hung his head. Anne sat up and started looking for clothing items. She put her bra on before looking back at Clark.

"The kids could be back at any moment." Anne stated. Clark sucked hard on his tongue to keep from tearing up. He sat up and worked to assemble his clothes. His mind was such a jumbled mess he put his underwear on inside out the first time. By the time he was dressed Anne was sitting at the dinette table.

"This motor home smells like sex. Open a window will ya? I hate to give Chloe and Jordan any ideas." Anne's words cut Clark, but still he did as instructed; trying to let the order of tasks needed take over his weary brain. He was getting a headache from overusing his brain. He wanted to take a nap. He wanted to try and forget that he had just been dismissed and then had his daughter's honor taken lightly. Clark wanted to pull his hair out, punch Anne in the face, set the world on fire. His heart was pounding; he just needed to be away from Anne.

"I'm gonna go see if I can find them, we should get going" He said. Without asking if she wanted to accompany him he opened the door, walked down the stair and closed the door solidly behind him. Just that small metal and wood barrier between them made him feel better about the whole thing. Walking between the cars of the parking lot he tried not to look back, not to let his hurt feelings rule his head. About half way to the building he gave in and looked back, but the reflection and glare on the windows kept him from seeing if Anne was watching him go. Clark walked in the glass doors of a store he had never heard of and immediately turned left. Before he found the kids he needed to have some time to himself. He walked along an unused corridor with vacant shop spaces, finding a bench where he could sit in relative peace. He sat on the bench, not thinking, just trying to digest and sort the information as his mind wanted. His hands still smelled of Anne's perfume, his mouth could still feel her lips, how could he not think of her?

"Dad?" Chloe's voice roused him. He sat up, not even remembering lying down. His back was stiff, bench sleeping having that effect on old men.

"Hey," he said back to her, still trying to recover his senses.

"We've been looking for you for an hour, Anne's worried sick." Clark tried to stand up, although his leg almost fully asleep.

"I must have fallen asleep; I was looking for you guys." Clark was fuzzy, but he remembered what had driven him into here. It did his heart some good to know that Anne had worried for him, part of him expected her to be gone when he got back. He was relieved to be wrong for once.

The two of them walked as briskly as they could toward the glass doors. Anne was waiting there, but ran to them when she saw him. She threw her arms around Clark, showing an unnatural amount of public affection. Then as quickly as she had grasped him she let him go and hit him in the shoulder as hard as she seemingly could.

"Asshole, don't ever make me worry about you again." Anne said worriedly. With that she turned on her heel and walked toward the motor home. "Come on, we've got miles to go." Clark shuffled along behind, trying to shake the sleep from his brain and the pain out of his chest.

Back behind the wheel of the beast he was once again Master and Commander of the Universe. The engine roared to life, he pressed the drive button and hit the accelerator. The coach lurched forward, Jack gave a surprised smile. Clark winked at him; he was firmly in control of this rig. The motorcycle were waiting for them on the highway, so instead of pressing forward as he normally would have, slowly and in a creeping fashion, Clark put the hammer down. The entrance to the parking lot was more uneven than he had thought, the coach shook violently as the tires dipped into the gutter. Loud sounds happened all over at once as the slide out's banged in their openings and everything on the tables shifted to the floors.

"Are you trying to kill us?" Chloe yelled.

"Sorry, everybody okay?" Clark looked back, but there wasn't much time as now they were in the flow of traffic. Clark took a mental note to check the slides, the whole coach had racked pretty hard. A few seconds later they were behind the motorcycles and ready to continue.

Clark set a mental note to give the coach a good inspection that night before going to bed.

Chapter 24

"Someday I'd like to be able to make my own mistakes, instead of fixing someone else's." Jordan's words struck Clark. He wasn't sure how he had become the young man's sounding board, but as the two sat in the post-midnight darkness talking, Clark started to see how much Jordan needed someone to talk to. It seemed Jordan and Chloe had suffered a minor speed bump in their romantic endeavors, which didn't really concern Clark much, but as it coincided with the rift between him and Anne, it seemed gender lines were thicker than blood. The girls had somehow decisively commandeered the motor home, a brilliant strategical move. Jordan and Clark were left outside swatting the mosquitos between their complaints. Jordan was filling in a lot of blanks, Anne had alluded to many of the things, but the details seemed to bring into sharp relief why Anne had believed she was the damaged one in their twosome.

What made Clark the saddest however, was how much deep-seated pain seemed to fill the boy. He seemed so strong and even boring, always the even keel, but when really pressed, he was still a frightened little boy.

"Any thoughts what you want that life to look like?" Clark asked the questions he wished someone had asked him. Now on the downhill slide of his career and family life, he was reevaluating everything.

"I don't know. My dad was an Engineer, so I thought maybe that would be good." Jordan didn't sound very confident about it.

"Since I am now unemployed, I'm not sure I'm the best source for career guidance, but I wish I would have spent more time thinking about what I wanted to do. My father was an accountant, so that's what I did. Of course, no one is to blame but me for becoming an IRS Auditor."

Jordan laughed, which was good to hear, Clark thought for a moment they were headed for tears, which he would not have been comfortable with.

"Yeah, no offense, but I don't think I could do either of those."

"Well, maybe you're smarter than you look." Now they both had a good laugh. According to the seven minute rule, there was a long pause. Jordan looked at Clark and then down at the ground.

"I miss being able to ask my dad for advice." Clark worked very hard not to wince, or to look up too fast. This could be Jordan trying to bond, but it could also be an emotional trap. Clark wasn't sure there was any 'Clark and Anne', which meant he needed to be somewhat reserved with Jordan. He was certainly not on tap to be Jordan's new father figure.

"You know, my father gave the worst advice on the planet. Just be glad you didn't have him to look up to." Clark tried to use a bit of humor to escape the genuine moment. Clark wondered if he could get back in the coach yet, but decided against it. He was shocked and disappointed in himself for how shamefully he was trying to run away. He was as scared as a little girl in a spook alley. How could he let this young man shame him with honesty and vulnerability and respond by abandoning him? "I would hate to use my life as an example to anyone, but you can always talk to me." Clark tried to keep his eyes dry.

"Thanks Clark, I like talking to you. I think we're a lot alike." Clark raised an eyebrow, curious how the boy would draw those parallel lines. "We both have powerful women who have been a huge part of our lives, we both suffered losses, and we're both waiting for our lives to really start." Clark almost needed to manually push his mouth closed. The boy had cut him to the quick, he was right, but still he couldn't believe it until it was out there.

"You're right," he said, "we've both lived in someone else's shadow." Clark hung his head, unhappy to have drawn the same conclusion, yet unable to spin it into something the boy could use. He was sure now that Jordan needed a better mentor than he, anyone would be better. He started to recall that morning, the morning it all changed. He remembered how he had wanted to just lie down and die. In those first moments his life had no purpose, was nothing more than a succubus on the essence of life. But he had drawn himself up, he had found the sturdy something that had lain dormant beneath all the years of compromise and defeat. He had found bedrock when he dug far enough and he thought the boy would as well.

But how to communicate that to him?

"I believe there is something in you, something that maybe even you don't know about. Unfortunately it usually takes something terrible to bring it out. Hopefully you can just live a quiet, happy life. As long as you are honest with yourself about what's important to you, greatness seems overrated to me." Clark wondered about his pep speech, it seemed lackluster. But from his current vantage point it seemed true and he couldn't find any better words to convey it. Jordan just smiled.

"I appreciate you talking to me Clark; with my mom around I don't always get a chance." Clark put his arm around the boy, again surprised to feel how thin he was, Clark would have to order him a double helping at the next restaurant.

"Clark, I really like Chloe." With the subject change it was time to break the embrace.

"She seems to like you."

"Do you think there's any chance for us?" Jordan pressed. Clark smiled and wrapped his arms around Jordan again. He lingered the embrace for several long seconds, slightly rocking him, almost like a full body arm wrestling match. He leaned over into his ear and whispered loudly.

"No chance at all." Then he winked at the boy and headed back into the coach.

Inside the belly of the Beast the mood was somber and Clark's intrusion was marked with hostile eyes. They were either done talking or had abruptly stopped when they heard the door, but either way there was an amazing amount of silence in the room. Clark walked toward the fridge to get a bottle of water, eyes following each step and the sound of opening the fridge was deafening in comparison to the vacuum that surrounded him. When he turned around the eyes were still fixed on him, it is obvious whom the women had decided to blame. As it always was, the fault would rest squarely on his shoulders. Clark resigned himself to it, allowing the small light of hope he had kept alight to extinguish, it would be no different with Anne. Clark was nothing more than a bump in the carpet, meant to be crushed low under some woman's boot heel. Apparently it didn't even matter which woman, he would allow any of them to do it. Clark felt anger rising like bile, maybe with actual bile; he tried to drink enough water to wash it away. The water was cold against his teeth, raising a small spike of sharp pain. It tasted clean, ultimate refreshment, washing down the foul tastes that had accumulated in his mouth. The bottle was almost gone by the time he put it down, with only a small gasp for air. Anne was standing right in front of him and the look in her eyes had changed, softened almost to tears it seemed.

"I'm sorry," she said putting her arms around him. He kept his arms at his sides, afraid of spilling the rest of his water if he tried to move. She pulled him tight, almost too tight to be comfortable, but it was nice. Clark allowed himself to melt into the moment, unsure of how long it would last, but relishing the idea that women could apologize, could find fault within themselves.

"It's late we should get to bed," Chloe's voice broke the moment, but Clark knew she was right. It had been a trying day and they had a hard road to drive tomorrow. Clark heard something in the back of the coach. Suddenly Jack was there with a pillow and his sleeping bag. He didn't look happy, but he smiled at his father and made his way toward the side of the couch. Apparently there had been many discussions while he was talking to Jordan. On cue, Jordan came in from checking on the bikes.

"Jordan, can I sleep next to you?" Jack asked. Now it was Jordan's turn to do the math on all the changes that had occurred in his absence. He looked at his mother, at first like a small child hurt in some way, but only a second later the same resigned smile came over his face that was now on Jack's.

"You bet, but remember, no farting." Jack laughed, not a huge laugh, but enough to release the tension that all these changes and shifts seemed to be inducing. Chloe was wrapping up on the couch and the boys were getting situated. Anne walked toward the back, pulling

Clark's hand. He wanted to hug his son, to tell him that he didn't have to sleep here if he didn't want to. But he knew that was self-defeat, it would have worked against his own self-interest, but still that was what seemed right. How could it be that Clark was the last one to be all right with this? Clark closed the door behind him. No light besides what came in from a distant street lamp lit the room. It took his eyes a moment to adjust. Anne was there looking at him. He couldn't make out the expression on her face, but there was a calm sense that filled the room. This was so different from the almost panic sensation that had dominated their relationship to this moment. This felt relaxing, comforting. Suddenly he was aware of motion before him, a slow agonizing unbuttoning of her shirt, followed quickly by her pants. He was mesmerized, the simple act of getting herself ready for bed seeming like the most erotic thing he had ever seen. She walked over to him after removing her bra, his hands reached out reflexively to touch the soft mounds presented to him. She pulled in close and pulled his t-shirt over his head, Clark pushing his arms up like a good boy. But suddenly she pulled the shirt over her own head, the offending garment covering the soft luxury of her body, now covered in what might as well have been a potato sack. She kissed his cheek and slipped into bed. Clark looked up into the sky, as if acknowledging the success of some great cosmic prank. He slipped his pants off and got in bed next to her. She slid over, though turned away from him. Clark pushed his knees behind hers and draped his arm around her and let himself drift off toward the best sleep he would have the whole trip.

Chapter 25

"Okay, you guys need to buckle in for this, okay?" Chloe and Jack both nodded agreement. Costa Rica was giving them some great occasional views of a modern country, but this road was a poor example. He wished they had stayed on the original path and not visited San Jose, though it had been an incredible city. But from San Jose it was shortest to go to Cartaga and then on to San Isidro de General. It passed over what seemed like a huge mountain. The road was wide enough and they had passed enough full size semis to know it was possible, but the further they went up; Clark knew they had to come down. They had pulled off several times when the road had allowed them.

Anne was having her own problems; the altitude change was wreaking havoc on her carburetor. She had to adjust it almost constantly; overall it was giving Clark a bad feeling. The jungle of Costa Rica was amazing though; it felt like driving through a zoo sometimes. Jack would point out some beautiful exotic bird or a monkey leaping from tree to tree. Clark steadied his nerve, this was what they had come to experience, he needed to steel his courage to face the bad that always accompanied. They pressed on, Clark watching the temperature gauge on the motor home as it crept up toward hot. He opened the window and to his surprise it was getting almost cold. The landscape was changing as well, almost to more of an alpine, although the green in Costa Rica never seemed to fade. Fewer birds also seemed to be at the higher altitudes. Suddenly they were at the top and the ordeal was halfway over. They all bundled up and walked around to see what the top of the world looked like this far south. There was a man who passed them walking in front of his llama, now this was an authentic Central American experience. They wanted to ask him what the llama was carrying, but his face was so grim they decided against it. They had bought some meat pies in the last village before the pass and ate them as a thick blanket of fog rolled over them. It brought with it an unnatural silence and eerie feel. Jack asked if anyone wanted to hear a ghost story and they allowed him two before coaxing him into the Beast to carry on. Clark ensured everyone was buckled up before starting off again. The diesel belched a cloud of black smoke as it came to life and Clark let off the parking brake.

Slowly they began to roll down the mountain pass toward destinations unknown. Another pothole that Clark couldn't avoid jarred them and sent the last remaining items on the countertop pouring out onto the floor.

"I'll get em." Jack's voice filled Clark's head. He turned around to see his son on his hands and knees picking up the items. He was about to yell when he heard a loud sound and turned back forward, he had drifted into the other lane and an fully loaded semi was on a direct collision course with him. Clark jerked the wheel to correct them back on to their side of the road.

"Jack, get your ass back in your seat belt."

"Dad, the slide out!!" Jack's voice rang out. Clark dared to look back for just a moment. With a rising horror he watched the wall of the motorhome moving away from him. He looked helplessly at the button that actuated that motion, but nothing was pressing it. He checked his mirrors and to his ever increasing alarm he saw the rectangular section of the coach coming out. Time began to slow down as his brain calculated the final resting place they would make if the coach went over the edge of the road.

Chapter 25a

Jack knew he shouldn't have been out of his seat belt, but as he watched the slide work itself out he was frozen in place. He wasn't sure if he should try and pull it back in or what. He looked at Chloe who was yelling something, but it was hard to hear her over the loud sound of tires screeching. Suddenly Jack was off his feet and the world was rotating. He heard the sound of the wind being knocked from him as he slammed into the kitchen cabinets, then he was thrown back onto the ceiling, then across the dining room table where in some distant land a sickening crunch sound happened. In some detached way he sensed that his arm was hurt and that he couldn't breathe. The tire screeching sound had been replaced with dust that filled the air and a grinding sound that took several seconds to stop.

Jack wanted to breathe, even in the dust filled air, but he couldn't. Panic seized him as he tried to will his chest to breathe, but it wouldn't listen. He tried to reach for his chest, but piercing pain shot through his shoulder. He lay there until finally small breaths would come, then larger and larger until finally he could breathe again. He heard something; it almost sounded like his dad. Jack tried to yell for him, but no sound would come out. Suddenly Chloe was there saying something, but Jack didn't understand any of it. It sounded like she was speaking some language that he didn't understand. Something sticky was running into his eye, Chloe tore her shirt to wipe it away. He wished his mom was there. Jack tried to stand up, but Chloe wouldn't let him. He looked over at the strange sensation that had become his right arm and noticed that his shoulder was different. He became very dizzy and the beginnings of tears started to roll down his eyes. His father's face was close; he was saying something like 'you're going to be okay', but all Jack could do was cry. He hoped Jordan didn't see him like this, boobing like a baby.

Suddenly there were strange brown faces around him in colorful jackets. They hurt his arm as they lifted him onto some kind of board. They pressed something on his forehead, it stung like a fire. He heard the sound of breaking glass over and over. Then he was being moved and he was outside, he saw a monkey in a tree looking at him, Jack wished he could stay and look at it, but the men were loading him into a truck. Jack began to panic, his heart fluttering, where was everybody? Where was he? Who were these people. He wanted his mom. He began to sob, huge tears rolling down his face. He tried to twist out of the hard back but he was tied to it. Then his dad's face was there, held close to his. He felt the truck start moving and he wondered where they were going. Someone should tell Jordan where they were going so he could come see him.

Jack suddenly realized he was in an ambulance, there were all kinds of things on the walls, clear tubes and all sorts of things in white wrappers. He wanted to ask the man about it, but he was so tired. He closed his eyes to just rest for a moment, but loud voices kept him from falling asleep. Tears tried to well in his eyes, but his mouth was so dry he guessed he didn't have any more tears to cry. He tried to ask for a drink, but they didn't seem to be listening to him. The men were talking to each other in Spanish and his dad seemed to be looking at them in hopes that he would suddenly learn the language. Jack didn't know exactly what they were saying, something about a hospital and a half hour. Jack used his good arm to tap his dad's hand.

"Drink", was all Jack could get out. His dad looked around. Then he tried to speak with the men.

"Agua, por nino?" The men shook their heads no, but his pleading looks continued until they opened a small clear bottle. They used their fingers to show that Jack could only have a little. Jack was angry, why would they need all the water for themselves? But the joy he felt when the water touched his lips made him forget it. He hungrily tried to gulp it, only to have it pulled away. The man looked genuinely concerned. The same man said something to the others then came over and started unwrapping items. He tried to communicate something to dad before grabbing Jack's good arm and jabbing it with a needle. There was a sharp pain which made Jack cry out, but a moment later it was over and only a clear tube some tape and a bag of water above him remained. His arm went cold and Jack started to watch the drops as they poured through the clear tube. Jack tried to relax, but it was hard on the stiff board. As he relaxed some, he got tired again, but as his eyes closed they yelled his name. But he was so tired, he was sure that if he could just sleep for a minute he would wake up to find this had all been a bad dream. His eyes went fuzzy and it became difficult to make out anyone's face but his dads. He reached out to pat his dad's hand to let him know everything would be all right.

Chapter 25b

Clark sat alone in the hospital waiting room for what seemed an eternity. Clark had feared they would bring him to some third world toilet house, but his was as nice a hospital as he would have expected in the United States. The brown faces that took his son said things with reassuring tones, although he didn't understand what they were saying. They had escorted him to the waiting room and he sat to wait. His head felt like ants were crawling around his brain. He was worried for Jack, he was worried that Chloe might have been hurt too and he had abandoned her, he wondered why Anne and Jordan weren't here yet. But watching his son's eyes close no matter how much he yelled for him to stay awake had nearly broken him. He needed some information, something to make decisions on, some way he could help. He could donate blood, or bone marrow or a kidney or something.

Finally a man entered the room. He was young with a closely trimmed beard and glasses. His lab coat made him look like a doctor, although at this point Clark would have settled for answers from the Janitor.

"Your son is going to be fine."

Clark sat down again immediately, relief washing over him in pulsing waves.

"Can I see him?"

"Of course, he is almost out of recovery and then it would be good for you to be there."

"Recovery?"

"His shoulder was badly dislocated, we put him under to reset the joint and to close the laceration in his scalp. We ran a CT scan to ensure no intracranial bleeding or injury had occurred, but he seems to be quiet a tough young man." The doctor smiled at Clark. Clark tried to smile back, but there was so much information for his brain to process, he might have flipped him off.

"Thank you, thank you so much. Is his shoulder going to be alright then?"

"Well, I don't know about that. We need to immobilize it then schedule an MRI to determine any damage. Sometimes in children they can sustain this type of injury without any lasting consequences, but there can be ligament or tendon damage. We won't know on that until we get the images."

"Where did you learn English?" Clark blurted. The doctor smiled at him.

"I went to Columbia for Medical school."

"Don't they speak Spanish there too?" Now the doctor laughed out loud.

"Columbia University in New York." The doctor extended his hand, coaxing Clark toward the door.

Down the hallway Clark though they could have been in any American hospital, it had that same bleach smell, a highly disinfected aroma. The doctor pointed toward an open door. Clark peeked inside, Jack was trying to speak with a smiling nurse. He hesitated at the door, not entirely sure what he would say to his son. Clark felt so much remorse right now, he wished he hadn't dragged them here, had just stayed in Utah and begged Karen to change her mind. But that was a child's thinking, Clark realized, he couldn't go back, so why torture himself with thinking it was possible. His marriage was over, there wasn't any use wishing it wasn't, and they were on this trip. The doctor tapped on the doorframe and Jack looked over.

"Dad, they said I can have anything I want to eat." Clark laughed despite himself. He smiled for the invincibility of childhood vigor. He walked in with the doctor who explained to Jack everything he had just told Clark. Jack looked amazed, not nearly as crushed as Clark would have thought. The notion of ongoing shoulder issues would have put an adult on their ass, but somehow Jack's resilience put them all to shame.

Just as the doctor was leaving the room Anne, Jordan and Chloe were running in. Suddenly everyone was talking at once. Jack was informing Jordan of the procedures, Anne was hugging Clark trying to describe how it all had looked from the rearview mirror of her motorcycle, Chloe was the only silent one, content it seemed to just stand next to Jack, smoothing his hair back.

For the next couple of hours they talked about the accident, how they had each saw it, what had gone through their minds and what was to be done now. Anne had stayed long enough to get their passports and cell phones, though Clark's was damaged beyond repair. She noted that the last she saw the Beast, he was being drug onto a flatbed wrecker, after they had pulled it back onto its tires. Clark raised his eyebrows as if to question whether it could be repaired, but Anne shook her head, it was gone.

So someone had lost their life after all, the Beast was no more. The roof over their heads, the wheels beneath their feet, Clark sat down on the uncomfortable couch and began to wonder if this was the end of the road.

Chapter 26

"What the hell do you mean it will take three weeks to process my claim? I paid significantly extra to be covered on this trip, now you're telling me we'll be stranded here for three weeks waiting for my insurance company to help us out?" Clark was growing increasingly hostile, but the lack of answers and delays were leaving them stuck. They had kept Jack three days to observe him, but already his shoulder had some motion back, which Dr. Santiago thought was an excellent sign. The MRI had been inconclusive, which the good doctor also indicated was a good sign, but Jack would need a follow up in the weeks ahead. For now they were the stranded three amigos, one with an immobilized wing.

They had found a hotel close to the hospital, the owner having been contacted by Dr. Santiago. It was nothing to write home about, but when Dr. Santiago showed up at their door one evening they understood the appeal. The idea of a house call was so far removed from the American acumen that Clark had almost stroked out when he saw the Doctor. He was sure the doctor must have some deadly news, but instead he had just wanted to check on Jack's mobility.

They had been there for four days when it occurred to Clark that they were not going to make it to South America, much less Tierra del Fuego. They had only about a week and a half left and they were stuck. Clark was down to nearly his last dollar and the hospital hadn't asked to be paid yet. Clark thought he might have to contact the consulate or even Karen to fund their flights home. It was also time for him to call Marjorie; he didn't want her to have to hold her terrible secret anymore.

"Hello?"

"Hey Marge, it's Clark."

"Clark, thank God you're alright. Are the kids okay?"

"You know about the accident?"

"Of course, it's been on the news and in the local paper. They said Jack was critically wounded, how is he doing?"

"Well, he's fine. He just dislocated his shoulder and a cut on his head. I can't believe they heard about it in the U.S."

"Well, I don't think they would have, but when they found out you were travelling with Anne Carter, that seemed to get them drooling. Now really Clark, what are you doing with that woman?" Clark was shocked, first that she had known so much about him and second that she seemed to be judging Anne from almost a continent away.

"I love her Marge." There was a great wash of silence on the phone. This wasn't like her at all, she had always been totally supportive of Clark. He couldn't let the lie go on any more, it was poisoning his friendship. "I know about the leave of absence being denied."

"I'm sorry Clark, I tried to get them to reconsider. I did speak to Tom Johnson over the Western Auditors and he said he would consider a review when you were back to speak to him face to face." Clark lightened, that was better than Karen had lead him to believe, but he supposed what was in writing was always the worst case scenario.

"Well, maybe I'll be back shortly to make that plea. The motor home's totaled, insurance can't process it for weeks and I promised Karen the kids would be back in a week and a half."

"Clark you can't stop, you just can't. You won't get another shot to do this thing."

"I understand that, but I'm broke, without the motorhome I don't have enough money to get there, much less back." A long silence followed.

"Clark, I have to go, I'm sorry about the work thing. Where are you, what hotel are you staying at?"

Clark gave her the information and hung up the phone. Things were so different from how he had planned them. He thought to be in Europe gallivanting across the great cities, instead he had flung caution to the wind and plowed his way south, pushing himself and the people he cared about until something broke, a stupid hydraulic actuator. The mechanic said he had likely broken it sometime earlier and it took until then to leak out the remaining fluid. Clark knew just the moment it had happened. Coming out of that mall parking lot, he had heard it, knew he should have checked it, but instead he chose to work on mending relationships. He let the details slide and it had almost cost him his son. Now here at a pay phone in Costa Rica he would have to pay possibly the steepest price yet.

"Hello?"

"Karen, it's Clark…"

Clark stumbled away from the payphone checking himself for actual wounds. So many barbed comments and screams had come out from the phone that he was sure that he must be from somewhere. Karen had heard about the accident, had heard about Anne, heard about Jack and worst of all had been left for two days without knowing if her son was alive or dead. Clark had understood how upset she was and did his best to placate her. He had thrown himself on the sword until he couldn't do it any more. Yelling back into the phone had been the only thing that quieted her. Karen was not used to Clark standing up for himself and it seemed to throw her off momentarily, allowing him a quick escape. In the end all her threats to send out the National Guard or the Peace Corps were retracted and they agreed that it was time for the trip to be over. Clark would contact the airlines about getting them tickets to come home. For better or worse their journey was over.

As Clark walked back toward the Hotel the skies opened up and fat rain drops fell down on him. Instead of hurrying his pace, his steps slowed and then stopped all together. He stared at the ground. He let the rain fall down on him without wiping his eyes or turning his collar. The rain intensified and wind gusts blew the drops like stinging missiles at his face, but still he stood motionless. People passing by looked curiously at the man, but they were accustomed to 'crazy Americans', so they thought little about it. The warm rainstorm pounded on and soon everyone on the street had run for shelter, except Clark. Still he stood in the deluge until his body racked with shivers. His gaze was fixed on a cracked section of sidewalk, something probably no one would even notice. The more he looked at it the more he related to it. He wondered at the pressures that were applied to break such a seemingly indestructible thing. Time multiplied the maligned forces and one day the concrete which had looked so immovable, so permanent, had allowed the smallest of fissures to run straight through it. Time and weather worked that small crack, until finally the once solid surface was broken and obsolete. Eventually someone would notice the now fatal flaw and slate it for demolition. Crews would come in and beat the thing into manageable chunks, allowing them to be thrown away, no thought or memorial given for its sacrifice. Soon after another would be laid in its place and no more thought would be given to the sidewalk. Clark guessed that was the nature of things that were walked upon. He looked up and started walking again toward the Hotel.

Chapter 27

The group had become eerily silent. The initial joy of having escaped such a close brush with death was quickly extinguished by the realization that the accident had ruined the trip. Clark had scarcely made eye contact with anyone since he returned from his phone calls and everyone else seemed to be following his mood. They got dinner that night at a local café where most people who saw them thought they might have recently attended a funeral.

Enjoying a chicken dish that featured mango chutney, they ate in silence. No one wanted to talk about what lay ahead, because what was coming was probably the end of their merry little band. Clark tried to drink enough of the local beer to numb himself to the realization that he would probably never see Anne again. He tried and tried to see a way through, a way he could still make it work, but in the end he knew he was out of rope. Clark gave Jack his pain pills at the restaurant so they wouldn't hurt his stomach and they walked back to the hotel. Jack's shoulder seemed to be recovering well, but the general sadness was dampening even his ever cheerful mood.

"This sucks!!" Jack's declaration, made like it was in the middle of the street, surprised everyone. Clark immediately felt terrible.

"I'm sorry buddy, climb on my back if you're tired."

"I'm not tired dad; I don't want to go home yet." This was exactly what Clark didn't want to do, debate the pointless. He had fought one too many uphill battles to engage in one that was unwinnable.

"There's nothing for it, your mom wants you home and we're out of money. Come on; let me give you a ride."

"I don't want a stupid ride." With that Jack started fast walking. Chloe smiled sadly at her father and ran to catch up with the boy. Clark maintained his pace, keeping his children in sight. Anne and Jordan were quietly talking between themselves, but Clark didn't care. He expected them to bail anytime now. Anne's words and Jordan's confessions about his mother led Clark to believe that she was a 'when the going gets hard, the hard run away', kind of girl. The most Clark could hope for now was summoning up enough willpower to kiss the Western United States Manager's ass well enough to keep his shitty job. What a goal he had now. He almost wanted to laugh at how dark his mood had gotten, at the amazing amount of self-pity he was doling himself.

The door was shut when the lagging three made it to the hotel. Jordan knocked and was admitted. Clark opened the other room and noted that the adjoining door was bolted from the other side. Once he and Anne were inside he just sat on the bed and stared at the door.

"Clark, I could buy you another motor home." Anne's words tried to pierce the black cloud that had formed around him. He was having a hard time hearing her, as if a distance already separated them.

"I don't want you pity." Anne started to say something, but bit her tongue before it got out. It had sounded sharp and Clark was glad to have missed it. He didn't really want to hear anything she had to say right now. She would say stuff, he would say stuff and in the end they would both just go their separate ways. No romantic ideas of star crossed lovers, this was simply a case of shit happening. Clark gave up on his visual standoff with the closed door and lay down in the bed. He didn't pull any of the blankets back or off, instead just lying on top of them. There was a spot of peeling paint near the floor board that he could stare at when he lay on his side. That was what he was focusing on now. Anne tried to rub his arm twice, but each time he only shrugged her off. Eventually she gave up and turned off the light. He could still just make out the peeling paint piece, a triangle of latex paint that started in the corner and came up almost two inches. Clark could fix it with some adhesive, maybe just a little drywall patch. The longer he stared at the space the more he wished he had something to fix it with. Maybe he could use toothpaste. He could fix this problem, this was within his skill set. Because if he didn't fix it soon, the hole would get bigger and bigger, maybe letting in cockroaches or poisonous spiders. You just couldn't let things like this go or they became huge problems. He would have to speak to the Hotel front desk in the morning. Clark didn't know when sleep finally took him, only that when he slept he dreamt of ever expanding holes and swarms of insects crawling through.

Chapter 28

Clark was woken by the shrill ring of the telephone. He tried to remember if he had set a wakeup reminder, but nothing came to mind. Anne was still there, tucked safely within the sheets.

"Hello?"

"Senor Clark?"

"Speaking."

"Front desk, car, person."

"I'm sorry?"

"Please, front desk."

"Okay. I'll be down in a second." Clark hung up the phone. He looked around for his pants, before noticing that he was still wearing his from last night. It was still early, Anne had not even moved when the phone rang. He felt better this morning and thought he should apologize, but he didn't want to wake her. He sat on the edge of the bed lacing up his shoes, looking back twice to see if Anne would wake so he could make amends. But her breathing remained steady and her eyes were closed fast. Clark glanced toward the closed door, but he knew everyone else would still be asleep.

He tried to slip out of the room as quietly as possible. Once he was in the hallway he hoped the front desk was not reporting an issue with the motorcycles, in that case he should have woken Anne. He thought it back and forth then deciding against it again walked toward the entrance.

The front desk was a simple wooden counter with a smiling young boy behind it that Clark recognized as the owner's son. What was his name, Manuel, or Emanuel, something like that? Clark was preparing himself for musical names and a foray into the fun world of speaking with partial sign language with the young man gestured to the bench across from him.

"Are you Clark?"

"Yes, can I help you?"

"You know, I half expected you to be a figment of Marge's imagination."

"I'm sorry, I don't follow."

"Marjorie Smith, the two of you work together at the IRS. I'm her brother Thomas, nice to meet you." Clark wondered if he looked as stupid as he felt. He guessed that he looked even more stupid.

"It's a pleasure, I'm sorry Marge didn't even mention she had a brother in Costa Rica." Clark reached out his hand. He shook the man's hand, noting that he must have been Marge's brother; he looked like a short haired and unbreasted version of her.

"Well, since I became an expat down here, seems like pretty much everybody forgot about me. Except when they need me, I guess. Speaking of which, here you go." With that the man deposited a set of keys and a manila folder of documents into Clark's hand.

"I'm sorry, I don't understand. What?" Clark asked. Now the man really looked at him, squinting his eyes.

"My sister called and said you were in a life or death need of a vehicle. I had this old jeep that I'd been talking about sellin, so she bought it for ya. This is all the title and insurance and stuff like that. Good luck, it ain't much to look at, but it ain't never left me in a pickle." Clark looked at the paperwork, which looked similar to the packet he had for motor home. He was feeling light headed, this was beyond a miracle. Clark didn't know what to say, instead grabbing the man into a hug, finally allowing a sense of relief to wash over him. The man pointedly did not return the hug, apparently they were not a hug family; Clark had never physically touched Marge in fifteen years of working with her.

The two walked outside to look at the jeep. It was a hardtop jeep and just as Thomas had billed it, the thing looked like it was duct taped together. He showed Clark the latches to remove the top, although Clark wasn't sure exactly where he would put a hardtop. When Thomas jumped in and fired the engine up Clark almost cried, just the sound of an engine, a way out of the dilemma was more than he could bear. He wanted to hug the man again, but the first embrace had left Clark with the distinct impression that he didn't appreciate being touched by another man. Watching the man describe the starting procedure Clark felt like he was back in Texas, the man's vowels skipped with an almost southern drawl. Now Clark wanted to get away to tell everyone the news. He hoped his dour mood hadn't spoiled everything. He wondered how Anne might react to the fact that he could accept this charity but not hers, but this was still good news. Clark thanked Thomas again before wondering how exactly the man would get home. But just then Thomas waved goodbye and got in the passenger seat of a Ford pickup truck. There was another man in the driver's seat. There was a terse conversation for a moment, then Thomas leaned over and kissed the man straight on the lips. Clark tried not to stare, but for all the eye opening and shocking experiences he had in Latin America, that one might have taken first place. Walking back toward the room he was still shaking his head at the number of stereotypes that had been put to shame on this trip.

Outside the rooms Clark wasn't sure how to tell everyone. It felt stupid to play coy, but it felt wrong to pounce on them too. He was thinking about it when the door opened. Anne was in all her riding clothes, bag and helmet in hand.

"Anne, hey, you're not going to believe this." He held up the folder and the keys. Anne looked at them dispassionately.

"And?"

"I have a vehicle, we can continue on our way. We can keep going." Clark said optimistically. Anne looked even less interested in this.

"Why would I do that Clark? So you can have another meltdown in a hundred miles when everything doesn't go your way?" Anne asked. Clark stepped back, wounded.

"The motor home flipped over and Jack dislocated his shoulder, I don't think that qualifies as things not going my way." Now it was Clark's turn to be angry. Anne's eyes focused hard on him, she was thinking of something nasty to say, but seemed to be keeping it to herself.

"You told your wife that you were bringing the kids home tomorrow." Clark started to sputter about the wife comment, but wasn't sure what to correct it to.

"We'll figure it out. I'll have Jack call and talk to her. Don't go, I'm sorry. I was being stupid, but this puts us back on track." He didn't want to beg, but he seemed to be getting close to it.

"Clark, I do love you. I just don't know that you're the kind of guy who can finish this. I need to believe that you'll finish this thing." She was searching his eyes, as if using the human lie detector on him. He could lie to her, Clark had once lied that he loved a girl to have sex, why not lie that he could finish this journey? If he had to bail out somewhere he would have to. But this felt somehow deeper than that, less a promise or commitment to some girl and more a commitment to himself. He stared at his shoes for a moment, which meant he was really thinking before answering.

"Alright, but no matter what we're going to finish this thing." Anne looked hard at him and took in a deep breath, she was just about to say something when the other door opened and Jordan appeared. He was also in is riding gear.

"Oh, sorry. Are we leaving?" he asked his mother. Anne swallowed whatever she was going to say to Clark and turned to Jordan.

"Good news, Clark has secured himself a vehicle. Tell those two miscreants to get their stuff together. We're hitting the road." Clark breathed a sigh of relief. He wanted to hug her, but she still didn't look like she was in a hugging mood. He pushed the door open and started putting his things together. They had bought some duffel bags for their things; Clark had saved what he could two days after the accident.

The door burst open; Jack's smiling face shining above his immobilizer brace. "For reals, we're not going home?"

Clark smiled. "For reals, but I need you to help me talk your mom into it. You're going to have to tell her how much better you are."

"No problem." The boy smiled and returned to his room to pack.

Clark looked back at Anne, swallowing his pride. "If that offer for help is still out there, I don't have enough to cover Jack's hospital bill. I can pay you back…"

"I already paid it." Anne smiled with as much innocence as she could muster, which was not actually that much.

Clark sputtered for a moment. "Thank you, I'll…"

"Clark, let's get one thing straight. You paid for the first half of this thing with your wad of cash. But that wad is gone now based on what I saw in the motor home and what you said last night. The rest of this trip is on me. Shush now, I'm not taking debate on it." Clark was trying to speak but couldn't as his lips were occupied with Anne's. He tried to speak for several seconds before giving into his body's commands and kissing her back. He let the curtains part and the sunshine in, today would be a new day, the first day of his own private renaissance.

Chapter 29

Touring in the jeep was quite different from the motor home. The large picture windows in the motor home allowed such a massive view of the countryside as they passed it was like watching a movie, the jeep in comparison was like watching television. The view was much smaller, but they were more a part of the environments they passed. The beast had entire rooms for escaping the world, drapes for shutting out the light and even its own weather system. It was like being in a glass bottom boat, you could see everything while remaining safely at a distance, dry and content to sip your margarita. The Jeep on the other hand, as they soon learned, was not even really water resistant. More it was able to channel water away from them so not every drop made it into the cab. Jack joked that now they understood how Anne and Jordan felt. Clark had smiled at that, this was better. He liked the more visceral experience of being subject to the weather and air as they passed. When the sun shone they would open the windows and allow the smells of Latin America to waft through the Little Beast. Jack had also come up with that nickname for their ride.

Of course he wasn't in the Jeep now, he was standing out on the deck of the ship they were on. The Darien gap had proved as difficult as Anne had said it would. The overland portion of the Pan American highway was never completed, after Panama City the roads went further south, but eventually just ended. Anne had wanted to brave it, thinking that there must be a way through the jungle, but in the end Clark's clearer head had prevailed and now the Little Beast, the General and whatever they were calling Jordan's bike were all strapped down in a shipping container. The small charter plane bounced and jerked so often it seemed it would only be a matter of time until they fell from the sky. Luckily it only lasted an hour or so before putting down in the small city inside of Colombia.

Since they were going to have to wait for the transport ship anyway, they decided to fly across the border and spend a day aboard a small ship. Clark hoped it was a real cruise and not a 'Shanghai' pressed crew scam. The cool breeze off the ocean felt good after so many days in the oppressive heat of the jungle. The fine salt mist left a lingering taste on Clark's lips. Just like Nicaragua, good things happened when he was next to the ocean, he mused. He put his arms around Anne who was leaning over the front balcony. Kissing her head he tasted the briny sea again and thought it made her even sexier.

Clark looked around for the kids, but he knew where they were. Chloe was not faring well with the motion and had spent most of it firmly planted against the railing, expelling her breakfast into the vast ocean. The cruise to Cartagena took several hours, Clark shook his head to think of the misery that his daughter must be enduring. He wondered if he should go and take care of her, but in truth he would only have been in the way. Jordan seemed at his best in this when things were the bleakest. Clark wondered at all the things the boy had told him, wondered if there was any hope for a boy raised under such trying circumstances. Maybe he was ruined forever, constantly seeking problems he could solve. Suddenly he hoped that hadn't been what attracted the boy to Chloe, she didn't seem broken, but maybe no one was broken to their parents.

Clark was really out of his depth here in the land of dysfunction. He had been raised by strict but fair parents, both accountants. Obviously there had not been much excitement in their household, save tax season, then his parents often took side work until the wee hours of night. But still, his well calculated life had worked out just how he had thought it would, right until it had all imploded. Looking back it hadn't been much of a life really, but then Clark had not been born or raised to dream of anything greater than a simple life. His greatest act of rebellion had been to take a job as an IRS auditor, showing his parents that now he would judge the validity of those unauthorized tax breaks. Clark laughed despite himself, how painfully boring that life seemed now, how pedestrian. But in it, he had been happy, or close enough that he couldn't tell the difference. Maybe that was it, he wasn't aware that there was anything better, so by comparison his life was the pinnacle of human existence. Could ignorance be the foundation of true contentment?

"Let's go see if we can get the kids anything," Anne yelled over the sound of the ocean the ship and the wind. Clark nodded unhappily; he had hoped to avoid them. The smell of vomit was not his favorite, or more appropriately it called to his stomach, 'vomit with us'. Down on the lowest passenger level they found the three of them, Jack and

Jordan talking happily, Chloe lying down on a bench, he head resting on Jordan's leg while he smoothed her hair. Clark breathed a sigh of relief that there didn't seem to be any active vomiting going on in this area. Karen had laughed at him and even shaken her head in disgust, but Clark would have rather swam in a poop filled diaper than see or smell someone throw up. Seeing Chloe now lying down he was reminded of a time he had been holding her, she couldn't have been more than three or four, and she had been sick all down his back. Karen had laughed until her sides nearly split, Clark running around as if he could somehow outrun the vomit running down his back. The thought of a laughing Karen always shot Clark with a pang of guilt and pain, especially when he was with Anne.

Anne leaned down to Chloe's level, "Honey, do you think you could eat something, just enough to take some Dramamine?" Chloe's eyelids fluttered and her mouth moved, just enough that Anne could make something out. Anne came up shaking her head from side to side, apparently it had not gone well, there would be no food for his daughter. Anne tried to lighten the mood, "We could get you a suppository?"

"Pass" Chloe's voice was clear on that. Clark looked out across the water. He tried to calculate how long it would be, but he knew they had a long way to go still. It was about a seven hour journey, they had only been going about three, which left more time for vomiting ahead than behind.

Anne and Clark found the food area mostly by using their noses, since the amount of Spanish they spoke between the two of them would hardly find a bathroom. They ordered blind, or ignorant, but as with most meals since the journey had begun, rice and beans were 80 percent of the meal anyway, so even if they skipped the savory component, they never went hungry. About halfway through the plate Clark had to push his away.

"Uh oh, like daughter, like father?" Anne tried not to smile as her witty comment hit Clark's fully fledged stomach turn. He swallowed hard, staring out the window at the distant shore. Some damn fool had told him that would work. He tried to calm his mind as the rising sweat condensed in droplets on his nose. Anne's face went from laughing to concern. "Are you okay?" Clark tried to shake his head yes, but then shook it no as he was sure the whole thing would not end well.

Suddenly there was an old woman trying to hand Clark something. A few leaves pressed into his hand and the woman smiled a mostly broken and toothless smile at him. She motioned for him to chew the leaves. Clark was not in the mood to play with the locals, but courtesy wouldn't allow him to just disregard the woman. He took one of the leaves and placed it in his mouth. She was indicating to chew but not swallow. So chew he did, the bitter taste filling his mouth. But a moment later he did feel better. Suddenly the world wasn't moving quite as much, either the ship had hit a smoother patch or he was doing better.

"Let's go up and get you some fresh air." Anne pulled him up and they made their way up onto the deck. He felt even better being out in the ocean spray once again. He stared into his hand.

"I should go give these to Chloe." Anne smirked. "What?"

"You know those are Coca leaves right?"

"Like Chocolate?"

"Like Cocaine." Anne now smiled and laughed as Clark looked at the leaves in his hand. He made a sad face as he spit out the chewed up green in his mouth and let the two remaining leaves blow out onto the water.

"There goes my next drug test" Clark noted. Anne squeezed herself close to Clark, nestling against the cooler air as the sun went down.

Chapter 30

South America loomed large below them. It was time to start the second portion of their journey and some decisions had to be made. With the time left to them, it seemed impossible and dangerous to try and make Tierra del Fuego. Chloe and Jack had made much noise at this, but the reality of the distances involved was quite clear. They would have to fly out of Lima, Peru.

"It's a miracle we made it to South America, at all." No one could really argue with that. Instinctively Jack rotated his shoulder in the way the Doctor in Costa Rica had shown him. It was getting better, but Clark knew the boy needed to have further work if that shoulder wasn't going to bother him for the rest of his life. Cartagena was a beautiful ocean city and Clark wished they were spending a few days to explore. The turquoise waters of the Caribbean still called to him. He was disappointed to be heading inland again.

The Little Beast wasn't starting very well, so they found a small auto parts house outside of the large city. Jordan handled the buy easily, even getting them to swap the batteries. The man that did the work was named Amado and he was so short it almost looked like he was going to climb inside the engine to do the work. When he finished he flashed a toothless smile, it seemed that dental care had gotten progressively worse since Mexico. The man came out a moment later with two bottles of oil. Jordan tried to translate but the man spoke some kind of strange dialect which was hard for any of them to understand. Instead he grasped Clark's hand to pull him under the jeep. He pointed at a black path making its way down the engine. Clark was no mechanic, but it did seem like a lot of oil. He assumed the man was suggesting keeping the oil full on their trip. Hoping he had gotten the man's message they thanked him and pressed on. The man watched them drive down the road, shaking his head worriedly.

The realization that they were driving in Columbia, the demonized drug capital of the world was not lost on Clark. Recent news had focused the war on drugs to Mexico, but anyone who had lived during the 80's remembered Medellin as the capitol of the drug world. In Clark's mind, every inch closer they got to the infamous city was as step closer to the infamous drug czar. Of course Pablo Escobar had been killed many years prior, but logic had a way of leaking out like the oil from the valve cover.

The landscape was beautiful, much like Central America it was poor, but the people were friendly and the hotel rates were reasonable outside the main towns. There were empanadas everywhere as he had been warned, but no one had told him about the Arepa. A type of bread, although it seemed to be a catch all phrase to mean any kind of fried bread as if it was ordered might contain any combination of ingredients. Clark supposed it would have been similar to someone ordering Pizza in the US, not understanding that it came in at least twenty thousand different combinations.

The quality of beef seemed to be improving, although on this side of the Central America / South America line there were some bovine diseases to watch out for. Anne had been told that as long as you could hear it sizzling and didn't order anything rare, you would probably be alright. This seemed like dubious advice to Clark who stuck to ordering his cooked all through.

Anne stayed true to her word, paying for everything. Even when Clark tried to pay he found the check had somehow already been paid. Anne seemed to have an unfair advantage, some woman in the states that sent her money to pick up at various Western Union and similar offices.

The Little Beast was staying true to its name and true to the nature of Jeeps in general by causing them problems any time it could. The battery was just the beginning of its odyssey it seemed. On a particularly bumpy stretch of highway just before Cali the dash went completely dark. In the back of Clark's mind he thought of the accident and how he had not exercised his best judgment. As he signaled the motorcycles and started to pull over the ignition cut out and he coasted to a complete stop. He was just barely off the road now. He turned the key back and forth, but nothing was happening. No sounds or lights or anything. He scratched his head and decided to pop the hood. After a minute of searching he found there wasn't a release, instead the hood was held by spring clips.

It should have seemed obvious that he wasn't qualified to maintain a skateboard, but in the absence of a real mechanic, he would have to suffice. Clark was actually quite adept at a few mechanical actions such as and not only, changing brakes on domestic vehicles, oil changes, spark plugs on a motorcycle. So when Clark finally got his first glimpse of the engine compartment of the Jeep, he was totally lost. He started an orderly scan of the engine components, just thinking that maybe something was loose and he could retighten it with his hands. Anne poked her head into the fray.

"What's the problem?" She asked him like she actually expected him to fix something.

"Not exactly sure, just went dead" Clark replied. They both sighed and redoubled their staring at the engine.

"Do you know what you're looking at?" Anne asked hopefully.

"Not really, no" Clark replied honestly. Anne shook her head as if that were the expected response. Karen would have been furious, telling him how a real man knew how to work on cars.

Clark thought *I really need to stop comparing the two of them; it's not fair to either.* The two looked up at the same time, smiling at each other. There had been so many disasters that this seemed mundane, an everyday type of adventure.

When an empty truck came by, Clark was able to talk the man into towing them toward Cali. As they approached the city Clark was surprised by how large the city was. In the distance the skyscrapers seemed like any modern US city, he had expected it in Cartagena, but figured Cali to be an impoverished town. It was dark by the time they came to a mechanic shop. The driver had to get on, accepting their money for his trouble before setting off. The gates were locked and no one was around, but the shop looked like it was still in business. The area seemed pretty nice, so the group decided to leave the Jeep there and find a Hotel. It took about ten minutes of waiting for a Taxi to come by. He recommended his brother in law's hotel just down the way. Clark noticed that everyone in Latin America had a brother or relative with some kind of service you needed.

The Hotel turned out to be a beautiful Neo Modern building. Ricardo, the onsite Manager, let Anne and Jordan pull their motorcycles into the courtyard. Once they were settled into their rooms they convened downstairs to discuss their plans for the night.

"We are long since past due for a crazy outfit night" Anne announced to the group. Ricardo recommended a local shopping area and hailed them a cab. Jack wanted a panama hat and Chloe was dying to have something more feminine than jeans.

Clark smiled that they were doing this. It seemed their whole journey had become about moving. In the beginning that had felt natural, as if the sense of motion dulled the ache he felt. But now he wanted to savor these moments, string them out as long as he could.

Shopping was a different experience with Anne. She shopped as she lived, wildly and with great passion. Clark had never been a great fan of shopping with a woman, but Anne was somehow more than a mere woman. She had meant it when she said crazy outfits. Clark was dressed in a typical South American shirt, which made him look like he was going to start rolling cigars at any moment. The tight pants and pointy shoes were appropriate with the outfit, but he felt just silly, like he was a small child dressing up. Jack was dressed in exactly the same outfit, which was cute, but again, too conspicuous for Clark's simple taste. Clark took the shirt off, he didn't want to spoil Jack's outfit by wearing the same thing.

Jordan noted the sad tone in Jack's words when his dad took off the clothes. Moments later Jordan came out of the dressing room looking like a slightly larger version of Jack and there were many smiles.

Clark felt bad that he was leaving with his original clothes, but nothing seemed quite right to him.

Then the girls rejoined them from the women's side of the store. He had never seen Anne in a dress, but obviously he should have requested it. The thigh length skirt showed off Anne's legs in a way that even her leather pants failed to do. The top was left open almost to a decadent level, but Clark had to agree that it was very attractive. He was almost reduced to a blubbering idiot. He tried to recover his sense until he saw his daughter, who was every inch as beautiful and seductive. Clark had the instinctive desire to hit Jordan, as the boy must have been thinking impure thoughts. Heads turned as the two walked by, even garnering a couple of whistles.

In other cities they wouldn't have been able to dress like that, machismo was very much alive in many places they had been. But here in Colombia, most the women seemed to dress this way. On the streets and stepping out of office buildings, women were constantly in a state of hyper beauty. No women roamed the streets in pajama bottoms or black tights, the official wardrobe of girls who gave up.

Now Clark looked out of place in his American clothes. The salesman was standing behind; Anne pulled him aside to a rack of suits. They spoke hushed tones and the man smiled broadly. He picked out a few hangers and Anne motioned to Clark.

Inside the changing room Clark almost refused to be seen by anyone. The mirrored version of himself looked ridiculous. The tight suit and silk shirt looked like he was headed to a swinger party or something. He had never looked good in red, yet here he was in a dark red shirt and black suit so tight he had to pick which pant side to put his testicles in. Stepping out, he was greeted with whistles and cat calls from his own family. Anne was already headed to the register, no protesting allowed he guessed. Clark approached her to beg for permission to wear his other clothes, but Anne only put a panama style hat on his head and kissed him.

They found an Argentine steak house called La Parilla del Nato, which served ridiculously large cuts of steak. Each was brought out with live charcoal beneath them, so that each bite was hot and delicious. Even after eating twice what he knew he should, Clark hadn't even eaten half of it. Three glasses of red wine helped with the digestion and to erase all the road worries. He didn't even think of the stranded Jeep, or what they would do tomorrow.

Walking out of the restaurant there were some children asking for money. Clark handed them the wrapped leftovers he had insisted they take with them. Anne kissed his cheek; assuredly leaving lip marks the color of her lipstick. But Clark didn't mind, this was a great night.

Walking the road they felt safe, this was a wealthy part of the city. Classes seemed to separate more completely here, the have not's understanding they needed to keep their distance. It was still taking Clark some acclimation to get used to machine guns outside banks and Hotels. Ahead there was a Baskin Robins, so although none of them needed ice cream after gorging themselves, they each got a scoop. The warm night felt like it was meant for walking. Couples walked by, whispering sweet lover's incantations in each other's ears. Benches held more couples and groups of friends; it felt like the whole city was out tonight. Jack looked tired, it was almost eleven.

"You about ready for bed?" Clark asked.

"No, I'm okay," Jack returned with a yawn. Clark tussled his hair. He knew the boy would stay out with them until the grisly end.

"Well, I think you guys should head back, because I'm making your dad take me Salsa dancing."

"I'm gonna what?" Clark began to panic. "I don't really dance."

"That's okay, they'll teach us."

"Ok fine, cause you're not taking me dancing," Jack announced. Jordan and Chloe had been in their own conversation all night; they only nodded their acceptance to this part of the plan. Clark eyed the boy suspiciously, although he acknowledged that he might do the same to his daughter. She seemed to be awfully handsey with the boy; he should talk to her about that.

Clark put the three into a cab, kissing each of his progeny before giving a hard look and smile to Jordan.

"Be good, you three." Then they were off. He was alone with Anne. He took the opportunity to kiss her. He let his hands roam up and down the soft and thin fabric of her dress. She wasn't wearing a bra, the woman was always on the border of indecent. Her blouse clung to her in the moist air of the tropics. He wanted her right there, but he knew there would have to be dancing. Why did there always have to be dancing, first his wedding, now this?

I just made a joke in my own mind; I think this woman is making me crazy.

Clark found a cab, where he tried to ask the man about a dancing club. He ended up having to do a little dance to the man's laughter. He paid the driver and urged Anne over. The man shook his head no, so Clark paid him a little more of Anne's money. The driver shrugged his shoulders.

He took them out of the nice part of the city to a more industrial area. He pointed up a flight of stairs toward a space they could hear music pouring out of. Clark thanked the man. They held their hands tight as they walked up the stairs. Inside was dark and filled with cigar smoke. Obviously the smoking ban had not made it this far south. The music didn't stop, but it did feel like every eye watched them as they walked in. It was dark, even for a dance club. A man greeted them, although he was not very friendly. He led them to a table. They sat down and tried to let their eyes adjust to the dark and smoke filled room. Several couples were dancing on the floor, the salsa music telling their bodies things it was unlikely to tell Clark. Clark wondered how he would ask for the lesson plan. Just then the music stopped and the couples separated. Strangely enough they didn't seem to go back to the same tables. The women were standing mostly up against the bar.

When one of the girls brushed past them she smacked into Anne's chair. Anne apologized, but looked at Clark with a slightly worried look. The woman continued on toward the edge of the room, where she stepped up onto a stage. When the music started again she began to remove her clothes. At this moment Clark realized that this was very possibly exactly what he had asked for, but not what he had meant. The girl was out of her clothes rather quickly. Clark looked at Anne with horror; he had not meant to bring her to a strip club. Anne smiled and patted his arm reassuringly. She pointed toward the girl, as if to tell him it was okay to watch. As Clark looked back the girl was now completely naked. Two beer bottles were thrown up on the stage, when the girl proceeded to do unmentionable things with one of them. Clark squeezed Anne's hand, he couldn't look her in the eye, it was too humiliating. He wanted to run out, but he needed to pay for the two beers that had materialized on their table after the show had started.

"I didn't know, let's get out of here." He tried to read Anne's face, to see how much trouble he was in.

"You didn't know that it was a strip club, or that it was a brothel?" Anne replied. Clark started to say something, just then noticing a girl taking a man to a room in the back, his hand already under her skirt. Clark took out what he was sure was more than enough to cover the drinks, put it under the bottles and pulled Anne out the door.

"Oh, it was just getting good. Nobody even asked me for a dance yet." Her laughter rang as they hurried down the metal stairs. Clark needed to find a cab as soon as possible. Surely someone in the place had marked them as an easy target. He scanned up and down the street, nothing. He knew they couldn't wait, picking a direction he began to walk with Anne safely on the non street side. They passed grocery supply shops, some already there sorting fruits and vegetables. When they passed an office building with a large antique vestibule Anne pulled him up toward it.

"What are you doing, we have to get out of here."

"Come here for a second, I want to show you something." Clark followed shaking his head. The vestibule was large and open, but they could still see the street, it did not appear anyone was following them. Suddenly Anne was kissing him. He tried to pull away, to get her moving again toward safety. Her hand followed the line of his pants, finding his belt and unbuckling it. *She's lost her mind.* He tried to push her hand away, but the damage was done. Her small hand was on him now, he was without recourse. She used her free hand to unbutton her blouse, exposing even more of her exquisite body than he had. Suddenly she worked her way down to her knees, pushing him further into the shadows. Then her mouth was on him, warm and soft and incredible. He tried to think of the danger, but somehow it only made the experience and the realization of what was happening that much more exciting. He knew this was wrong, that it was foolish, but his body was firmly in control now. He pulled Anne up, kissing her hard and pulling at the skirt that had filled his mind since he first saw it. He tried to remove her panties, just then realizing she wasn't wearing any. Then he was inside her, heard her gasp in his ear, felt how ready she was for him. Her legs wrapped around his body and he almost felt they became something different. He thought he might be having a stroke, his head pounding, the taste of her sweat on his lips, the mint of her breath hot in his mouth. His body needed no instructions, he pressed again and again into her, the halting motion bringing him ever closer toward Utopia. He wished this moment could last forever, wished someone was watching. He embraced to wrongness of it all, the forbidden nature of their sexual union. She didn't even know his last name. Then in a sharp flash that bordered on painful the world went silent but for their breathing and the pounding of their hearts. He was dimly aware that she was kissing him, that she was slipping down off of him, as if all in slow motion.

The world came back into focus; Anne's face the first thing he saw. He was a different man now, the man of passion's moment relieved by this more pedestrian fellow. The world came back into clear focus, the dangerous world they had left for those moments. Clark pulled up his pants, buckling them while Anne smiled at him.

"I need to find a bathroom," Anne's words brought him back into another reality.

"Uhmmmm, okay, let's find a cab." Clark looked up and down the road. No lights seemed to be coming or going.

"Wait here." Anne removed the handkerchief from his pocket and dashed down the stairs toward the vacant lot between the buildings. Clark said nothing nor reacted in any physical way. He had some idea of what she was going to do, but it seemed so contrary to the beautiful woman appearance that Anne personified, that he still shuddered to think of it. Then she was done and she met him at the bottom of the stairs.

"Ready?" she asked.

"When I'm with you, I feel like I'm ready for anything."

A half dozen or so blocks further the road crossed a major highway and the two were finally able to get a cab back to the hotel. It was well past

1AM at that point and they didn't want to wake everyone, but Clark needed to check. Opening the adjoining door he let just a sliver of light shine into their room. He could see Jack's head, but Chloe was not in the bed next to him, and the other bed was totally empty, still made in fact. Clark's blood pressure started to peak as his mind ran over all the possible things that boy could be doing to his little girl. He might have to kill him; it remained unclear at this moment. Clark turned to Anne, "Jordan and Chloe aren't here."

"Really?" she replied as if Clark had told her it might rain.

"What do we do?"

"Wait up and worry, I guess." Clark frowned at her to indicate that this was not a solid plan.

"Well, I guess we could start combing the city, there are only like 2.5 million residents, third largest city in Colombia, where we don't speak the language. No, I think we should wait." Clark sat on the edge of the bed; this wasn't how he wanted the night to end. He just wanted everyone to be doing what they were supposed to do.

Only twenty or so minutes later they heard laughter and the door to the other room opened. Chloe and Jordan looked very surprised to see Clark standing solemnly in the doorway between the rooms.

"Sorry dad, we just wanted to check out the pool," Chloe spoke as if she knew how upset he would be. They were wrapped in towels, their hair wet as testimony of their actions. Clark tried to read the amount of guilt in each of their faces, but it seemed innocent. Clark was about to say something about them leaving Jack alone when he heard a rustling sound behind him.

"Okay, well go to bed. We have another long day tomorrow." Clark was surprised at his own answer, which left the two perpetrators speechless. Clark closed the door softly. Anne had asked him not to overreact and that was his very best effort. He smiled at Anne and pulled the covers back. Anne smiled at him and he noticed that she was naked. Clark smiled and thought that maybe he could get used to being bribed.

Chapter 31

Clark looked anxiously ahead of him, hoping to see some movement at the repair shop. His heart sank a little when the hood was not up on the Jeep, but that was probably a little optimistic on his part. He was relieved however to see the bars on the doors were ajar. It was a functioning shop.

Inside the building Clark was almost blind, the main door wasn't open and there didn't seem to be any other windows. As his eyes adjusted he noted a short, even by South American standards, man behind the cash register.

"Can you, ayuda me?" The man smiled and spoke words that came so quickly Clark couldn't even tell if they were in Spanish, much less guess their actual meaning. Clark shook his head and the man repeated his indecipherable string again, but louder.

Hmmm, I thought that was an American trait.

Eventually the man followed Clark out to the Jeep, where he was going to demonstrate the problem. Only when he turned the key the Jeep fired right up. No hesitation or problems with the gauges. The man unfastened the latches and looked inside. He grabbed a wrench out of his pocket and put another half turn on the bolts that held the battery cables. He gave Clark a nod, which was seemingly to indicate that they were good to go. Clark did not feel good to go. But there wasn't anything wrong with the Jeep at this moment. They didn't have time to be sitting around anyway. So Clark closed the hood and latched it tight. He pulled out his wallet to pay the man for his trouble, but he just waved his hands back and forth. Clark looked at the shop, obviously the man could use the money, but although Clark pushed it toward him, the man continued to wave him off. Clark put away his wallet and shook the man's hand. He hopped up into the Jeep and drove off, watching the proud little man fade in the rearview mirror.

Getting everyone out of the Hotel ended up being a larger chore than getting the Jeep. They had expected Clark to be gone for at least a couple of hours and had conducted themselves accordingly. Bags were unpacked, Chloe was still asleep, and no one had eaten. Now Clark was the nagger, which had always been Karen's job. Anne certainly wasn't going to take the position; she was the last one to be ready.

On the road finally they pressed on down through Colombia. They began to move up and out of the jungle into the sparse but green highlands. The roads were surprisingly modern, with guard rails and well painted lines. After almost a hundred miles they stopped when a sign proclaiming Pizza lured them. It turned out to be an American Ex-pat owned shop that made a delicious wood fired pizza, reminiscent of something they might have ordered in a high end pizza joint. Clark limited himself to a single beer, although the pizza was far inferior to the imported beer the man offered. It was a Belgian beer that was as complex as any glass of wine. Anne didn't let Clark's conservatism stop her, although he did wave her order for a fourth bottle down. The owner had been in the construction business in Dallas, but after nearly losing everything in the recession of 2008, he moved his wife and dog south and had hardly looked back since. He had a few harrowing stories, but considering they were in Colombia, it seemed quite mundane. Clark had expected drug deals, battles with Contra rebels, or something worth note. Instead, it was more petty crime and bad driving. He was amazed at how fast they had made the journey, shaking his head when they told him about the accident. He was intrigued by the ferry; he had come during a time of "roll on, roll off" ships. He shook his head. "Pretty soon I'm gonna have to go escape to Venezuela, this place is getting too Americanized".

He gave them a detour and some intel about the border crossing into Ecuador. Once again they would be able to use American dollars. He had heard stories from a customer who had been on a business trip to Ecuador during Dolarization, the process where Ecuador eliminated their currency, the Sucre, for dollars. Of course the people of Ecuador had watched their currency devalue to the point that it took a stack of bills to buy a loaf of bread. He told them of plumes of smoke, fires set in laid down tires filled with gasoline. Even in 2010 there had been a Coup of sorts, but he urged them to stop in Quito. Apparently he either didn't care about their security, or felt it was safe.

He waved them off and Clark felt bad not having learned his name. He had been slightly crazy, but then again what would one expect of a man making pizzas on the Colombian plateau? On and on they drove; the humidity excruciating even at speed. As the sun went down they hoped the temperature would as well, but the heat seemed a constant. Clark hardly noticed the people anymore, he had become accustomed to road crews in flip flops, donkeys carrying bananas, bicycle taxi's and the ever present smiles on even the seemingly poorest passerby's. Somehow even border crossings ceased to cause him much anxiety, of course he wasn't smuggling anything, nor had anything to hide. They always found some fruit or something they didn't like, but he was used to that now too. So at the border into Ecuador Clark thought of nothing besides getting through to find a hotel. They had driven nearly two hundred miles today and although he was hardened to travel, he felt these miles. As if all the weariness of travel was finally building up inside him, he felt a kind of tired that sleep didn't seem to cure. He noticed hammocks as he drove by and wanted to sit in one of them for a month. He had started dreaming of nothing, not an absence of dream, but of being bored, as if that were something to be devoutly wished. He looked at the kids sitting in the Jeep; Jordan looked even more tired than Clark. All in all, the boy had hung in there, credit should be paid. Just then the border guard brought back their passports and handed them to Clark with a smile. Either this was getting much easier, or Clark's expectations were getting lower. Clark smiled back at the man, noting that at this pace they would need additional pages to their passports.

Anne was putting her helmet on, urging Jordan to get ready. She looked tired, which was bad because they still had a long ways to go to get to Quito. Who had set that as their goal? Oh yeah, it had been Clark and Anne looking on an impossibly small map. They had heard great things about the colonial city and wanted to spend a day there. But the only way they would have time to spend there was if they pressed two days into one. It was early afternoon and the heat was oppressive. Nothing for it, Clark had learned that dousing himself with water didn't work like it had in Utah or Mexico, with 100% humidity the water just never went away.

Ecuador met them with slightly worse roads, but much the same
scenery. They were still making a gradual ascent, but based on the heat
it was gradual indeed. Clark knew that if he could see far enough on his
right he would see the ocean, on his left would be the Amazon jungle.
But in the long hours of driving there was only the road ahead of him,
the red lights of the motorcycles ahead his autopilot. Again he was
drifting off into daydreams of stopping. They saw small churches, some
abandoned and without roofs, but still beautiful stone arches. Clark
thought he should stop for a photo of them, but he knew if he stopped
he would have a hard time getting started again. He pressed the small
camera into Chloe's hand pointing to the building as he slowed. She
snapped a picture and he sped up to catch the bikes. Hours pressed on,
the kids slept sitting upright. Clark wondered how the motorcyclists did
it. For a moment he was jealous of them, thinking it must have been so
much fun that they didn't notice the weariness. Maybe the thrill of
foreign winds blowing through their hair was enough to stave off even
the worst yawns. Not for the first time he wished he was on a bike,
thundering down the road on two wheels, people's heads turning to
watch them go by. But then he looked over at the two sleeping children,
his kids. He wouldn't have traded showing them this part of the world
for anything. He had wanted to take them on the trip of a lifetime and
somehow this had been just that. Not a trip with white gloved
concierges and tours of historic sites, but a trip where they knew what
the country smelled like, with visions of thousands of smiling faces.
This was real travel, Clark's only regret that they were moving at such a
hurried pace.

Anne started to slow down, so Clark applied the brake. Jordan pulled
over and Anne pulled just behind him off to the side of the road. Clark
got out trying not to wake up Jack.

"Everything alright?" he asked.

"I need to adjust the carburetor, it's starting to run a little rich. And I
don't know if I can stand one more God Damned minute of riding."
Anne looked on the verge of tears. Clark could sympathize, he was tired
from driving the Jeep; she must have been exhausted.

"Well, can we adjust the carburetor, get one problem fixed anyway?"
Anne was lying on the side of the road, and ignored Clark's question.

He looked at Jordan, who only shrugged his shoulders. Clark knelt down to look at the old bike, the General. He had actually spent more time looking at Jordan's Harley on the trip, it just sounded so loud and impressive. By comparison it was hard to tell the old Indian motorcycle was even running. Looking over the carb and engine he was instantly reminded of an old Suzuki 125 he had as a teenager. There was nothing fancy about how this bike was configured, air cooled single cylinder. He made some guesses about what was an oil pump and where it looked like some parts had been added only to be removed. The frame had also been repaired in several places, the weld marks still visible. The suicide clutch was almost the most remarkable thing about the bike. Instead of using a foot shifter, the rider would press their foot down on the clutch and shift a lever by their leg. It was a terrible idea, removing your hands from the handlebars, which is why it never caught on.

Clark rummaged into the saddle bag to where he had noticed Anne kept the screwdriver, and then swung his leg over the old bike. He oriented his mind to the flow of fuel through the carburetor, and then made a small adjustment before shifting the bike into neutral and kicking hard on the kick starter. A small puff of smoke and a rough idle for a moment, then Clark turned the throttle and it seemed to clear out. He listened as he slowly pulled back on the throttle, like a piano tuner would work their way up the notes. He made one last small adjustment with the screwdriver, then goosed it one last time to ensure his settings were right.

As he shut the bike down, he felt a presence behind him. Anne's hand was on his shoulder. Suddenly Clark felt very uncomfortable; he had treaded on something that wasn't his. Clark knew about the history about this bike, how her dead husband had spent years working on it, he should have just stayed in the Jeep. He should have smacked his head in frustration, what the hell was he thinking.

"I'm sorry; I was just trying to help" Clark pleaded.

"Since when do you know anything about motorcycles?" This was the question before the storm. He had been baited with this kind of question his whole marriage; here was where his words would be noted and used against him for the rest of the night.

"I'm sorry, it wasn't my..."

"I said, since when do you know about motorcycles?" Anne said sternly. Clark inhaled deeply, there was no avoiding this. It would be best to just play his part and take his beating.

"I grew up with motorcycles. My grandparents had a farm with a shed full of old bikes, if I could get one to run I could ride it. I always had a motorcycle til Karen made me sell mine." Anne didn't say anything for a moment and Clark braced himself for impact.

"You son of a bitch, how is it that you haven't been taking your turn riding?" Clark looked up, with one eye first just to see if he was still standing there.

"Wait, what?"

"You heard me; you're sitting back there all comfy in the Jeep while my ass is getting pounded mile after mile." Jordan snuffed a laugh, to which Anne shot him a nasty look that became a full laugh. "Well, that may not be the best way of phrasing it, but you can take your turn riding the General."

"Well, I just didn't, want, to…well you know?" Anne looked at him, her smile softening. For a moment it looked like she might cry again, but instead she just threw her helmet at him, almost forcing Clark to dump the bike to catch it. Then she was in the Jeep.

"You're lucky mom likes her helmet loose." Jordan smiled at Clark as he strapped on his own helmet and mounted his bike. The Harley fired to life, loud and parting the air like Moses and the Red Sea. Clark put the helmet on, which was tight but not uncomfortable. Now he was filled with Anne's smell, her hair product that smelled like an exotic fruit mix and the unique earthy smell of her. His heart pounded as he started the General. He twisted the throttle, and then wondered how the shifter worked. He had been able to find neutral, but that was a far cry from understanding how it actually functioned. Jordan made a motion, showing him how the progression went up as the shifter moved higher. Clark pressed the clutch and felt the bike engage. He slowly let out the clutch, but not slowly enough and the bike died. Clark was embarrassed and expected Anne to run out screaming, but a quick check of the mirrors showed she was smiling and talking to the kids. Clark again started the bike, this time noting where the clutch began to let the engine take the load. He throttled up and suddenly he was off, his feet tucked on the floor boards.

Suddenly the wind was in his face, the smell of the foliage strong in his nose. The sound of the wind was loud, but still he could hear birds and sounds that had been muffled in the Jeep. He allowed the bike a little more throttle, weaving just slightly to get a feel for the turning capacity. His heart and chest felt overly full, what a privilege, what a rush. Jordan caught up to him, riding to his right and just a half length behind him. This is what camaraderie was, two motorcycles sharing a lane, thundering along some foreign road. Clark wanted to write poetry, sing songs. As if on cue music started playing in his ears. He looked from side to side, trying to understand what was going on. Either he was losing his mind or Journey was playing. Then he remembered that Anne's helmet had integrated sound, but where was it coming from. Checking his mirrors he was Anne waving her phone. Clark's illusion of control was shattered; he would be beholden to Anne's choice of music. All he could do now was pray she did the right thing, that no girly pop music marathon would materialize and torture his ear drums. But as the playlist rolled on Anne was being merciful, playful even. There seemed to be an inappropriate abundance of sexual innuendo in her playlist. If Clark didn't know better, he would say she was flirting from the safe confines of the Jeep. Well, he would make her pay for her dalliance tonight.

The sun set on his right, dipping red, orange and purple in the distance. Quito must be coming up as the signs indicated. They decided to press on to Quito for dinner, though Clark's stomach had nearly eaten through to his spleen before they saw the first colonial buildings. Quito did not disappoint his eyes, the city lit up like his imagination of the centers of Europe. Someone could have told Clark he was in Madrid or Barcelona and he wouldn't have doubted them for a second. He wondered if this looked more like his idea of Madrid than Madrid did. Cities tended to modernize and there was very little modern here. Like Bavarian villages outside ski resorts, this might have become the cliché. Anne flashed her lights and pointed to a Hotel ahead, Clark and Jordan pulled their bikes up to the concierge desk. Just when he thought they were not destined for white glove service, two men in fancy jackets and gloves opened the door for them.

If it had been Clark in charge of where they were going, he would have immediately left and headed toward somewhere he could afford, but he was too tired to argue. Clark helped the men get the bags out of the Jeep, although they seemed personally affronted when he tried to actually carry one. Anne was back almost instantly from the front desk, far too quickly to have sorted all their details.

"Let's go eat; they said there's a great little Italian restaurant next door" Anne said as approached the group.

Clark was trying to shake the cobwebs out of his head. "How did you check us in that fast?"

"I have my ways" Anne said with a small crooked smile. Clark was too tired to argue about a happy turn of fate. The restaurant was right next door and they weren't too busy, things really seemed to be going their way. The food was good, although even Clark's shoelaces would have been appetizing to him after not eaten in six hours. He wanted a beer, but he was so dehydrated that even an overly committed waiter couldn't keep his glass full. He brought bottle after bottle for the thirsty crowd.

Sitting in the afterglow of their culinary orgy, Clark was struggling to keep his eyes open. His blood sugar was probably over a thousand, he couldn't be far from a sugar coma. Suddenly he stood up. "I need to go snap a couple pictures." Like that he was gone. No one said anything.

"What was that all about?" Anne asked Chloe.

"The pictures for the guy." Anne looked at Chloe as if she might pull her hair out.

"Sorry, what guy, what pictures?"

"Dad told the guy he bought the motor home from that he would take pictures along the way. Most the time he gets the pictures before anyone's up. It's kinda dumb." Anne sat back in her chair, looking toward Clark's exit. There was always something more to discover about him. The first time she met him she thought she would know everything that mattered about him in the first fifteen minutes. He was always surprising her in a thoughtful and sweet way. She wished she could kiss him right then.

"I don't think it's dumb at all," Anne's response was too late for Chloe to even acknowledge as part of the same conversation. She had moved on to talking with Jordan and trying to get the marinara sauce off of Jack's face. Anne thought she should tell Chloe how lucky she was to have a dad like Clark, but that really wasn't the sort of thing one could be told, it had to be seen in retrospect. Humans were just kind of shitty like that, Anne supposed.

"Come on, let's get back to the Hotel, tomorrow we see Quito." Anne was trying to play cheerleader, although she wasn't much good at it. Eventually though everyone moved out of their seats, up the street to the Hotel, the concierge running their keys to them as soon as he locked eyes with Anne.

Inside the room, Clark had not returned yet. Anne opened the door between the rooms, Jack was in the shower, Jordan next and Chloe to follow. They knew the routine. Anne wondered if anything had happened between the two, the tension was so thick it could have been spooned on top of ice cream. But looking at her son she didn't think anything had. He just wasn't that kind of boy; he had too much a misplaced sense of honor. Anne probably should have felt guilty about that, but it was hard to look at Jordan and feel anything but pride. He was exactly what every mother wanted, loyal and chaste, smart and good looking. Obviously she didn't deserve a great son like him. She softly closed the door; Jack would tell them if any shenanigans went on.

Anne sniffed her armpits, and not detecting anything too noxious decided a shower could wait for morning. She slipped her pants and shirt off, removing her bra and panties last before peeling back the sheet and slipping between the crisp white linens. She tried to pose seductively, but now she was feeling the Italian food holding her down, forcing her lids down. She would just lay her head down for a moment, just a minute to rest her eyes.

Clark opened the door quietly, the lights were on and to his surprise there was a naked woman in his bed. She was not in the most flattering pose, he mouth partly open and crooked how it laid on the pillow. But she seemed more beautiful than anything he had ever seen in that moment. He didn't just want her, like a Playboy centerfold, he wanted to do things for her, buy tampons at a major grocery store, paint her toe nails, fold her towels. Most of all though, he wanted her to want him. He wanted someone to look at him and need his close presence, want to smell his neck, kiss his mouth. He wanted her to pop the buttons on his shirt, ravage him. He wanted someone to play with his hair like his grandmother had when he was a small boy. He wanted so desperately to trust her, to feel safe next to her. But he just wasn't sure if Anne was ever a safe bet, she seemed fickle to him. Maybe he was nothing more than a fling. The thought was exciting and depressing all together.

Regardless of their future or what it held, he was glad she was with him now. They wouldn't be where they were, he would have given up several countries ago. Clark began to undress, first sniffing his armpits, which didn't seem over the line horrible, he could wait on a shower. He turned the light off and slipped between the sheets. His heart was pounding, which felt so good, to know that it still excited him just to be next to her. He planned all kinds of romantic gestures and overtures for that night, but in the end he settled for a vigorous spooning.

Chapter 32

Quito had been everything they hoped it could be. It had in fact been so good that they had finished the trip there. Walking the streets, they felt transported to a different time, where grand balls were held and sword or musket duels must have been happening just around the corner. Pirates rambling down the cobblestone roads would not have seemed that out of place. But they had found more than just a pretty tourist stop. They had encountered wonderful people and a beautiful culture that they could not part with after just one day. No one spoke about Ecuador to any of them, but the people they had met made it a travel worthy destination. The staff at the hotel alone could have been worth making the trip.

Clark wasn't sure where this left him and Anne, but she had known it was coming. She had been sweet about the whole thing, having her agent make the plane reservations and paying for the tickets. She had been good to her word; she hadn't let Clark pay for a thing since Costa Rica. Per the directions from Maggie's brother, they were planning on just handing the keys to some random at the airport.

A heavy weight hung on the group, Anne and Jordan had only talked in hushed tones to each other about their plans. Clark somehow doubted they were going to finish the journey, which made him sadder than anything. Someone should have finished this thing. He considered staying, but then who would get his kids back safe? No, his path was set, laid out before him in all the ways a parent's life seem to be. It was a burden he was happy to have. He tried to pick his chin up; he had to reestablish a life back in Utah. He would need to beg for his job, find a shitty apartment, try to avoid bankruptcy; maybe he shouldn't think about what was yet to come. Everyone packed their bags without a word, they had done it so often and with such great efficiency it now happened without Clark even having to ask. They had shed everything that wasn't essential, now only carrying three changes of clothes and the most essential toiletries. If nothing else, Clark was looking forward to a new toothbrush. Years of using a Sonic powered toothbrush left this third world off brand toothbrush quite wanting.

Walking down the corridor they encountered a bell hop who seemed affronted that they had not called for his services. He stopped them in their tracks, loading all their bags on his shoulders. He looked like a Sherpa making his way toward Everest, while the lazy tourists followed, carrying only their own weight. As Clark passed a mirror he was shocked, he had lost at least twenty pounds, he looked at least ten years younger. It was odd, he stared at himself in the mirror every morning, but until that moment had not calculated the sum of the changes he saw each day. He smiled, *no wonder Anne thinks I'm hot stuff.* He smiled; he needed to remember to laugh more. They rode down the elevator and Clark looked at Anne. They had not spoken about the future; she seemed to forbid any of that. He wondered if he would ever see her again. She had family in Utah, so it seemed possible. But Anne also seemed like the kind to get distracted easily. Looking at her in the elevator it occurred to him that he might be seeing her for the last time; he tried to make her image burn into his mind. He wanted to remember her smiling.

Check out went simply enough, Anne wasn't disputing any charges and left them a sizeable tip to split between the staff. Clark was jealous of her, she was so free with her money and there seemed to be an endless supply of it. Clark had always had just enough to get by, it had never bothered him, but he had never tipped above fifteen percent in his life. He always fretted about the cost of everything, as if his planning could somehow make things free, if only he put enough research in. He tried not to think of what was coming, allow himself to bask in the present where Anne was so close he could touch her anytime he wanted.

They were almost loaded when it occurred to Clark that they shouldn't just find a random person to give the Jeep to. The bellhop who had caught them that morning had been quick with a smile since they got there. He had carried their bags in and out and there was no way he made enough to have a car. Clark smiled, that had occurred to him, maybe he was starting to think more like Anne. The thought pleased him; usually it seemed influence was only of the negative variety, romantic endeavors should have the ability to lift people up.

"Let's give the car to Rodrigo." Clark knew it was the answer for sure as soon as he spoke the words. Anne smiled pleasantly, walking over to give him a kiss.

"Whatever you want, it's your car after all."

"Jack, go ask Rodrigo if he can help us to the airport" Clark yelled across the hallway. Jack smiled; he liked Rodrigo best of all. When they passed him, he would joke about taking Jack out on the town, making him a real man. Clark had always cringed a little bit at that, having seen the kind of place where boys were made in men in this part of the world. But it seemed good intentioned and Jack had seemed genuinely fond of him, so to do something nice for him now felt appropriate.

"Time to take little Yack out and make him a man?" he joked when he got back to the Jeep.

"Could you help us with our bags at the airport?" He nodded, as if stating 'claro' would have been unnecessary. Driving to the airport Clark was lost between feeling magnanimous and feeling depressed. On one hand he had never given someone a gift like this before, but he had never walked away from someone he loved either. It felt momentous, like he was on the precipice of a life changing event.

The airport came too quickly, not allowing Clark enough time to rehearse what to say to Anne. He would have to say what came to him in the moment, but that was rarely a good thing. Clark was more often bound to say something well intentioned, but off putting. This should be a moment for great poetry, or maybe a sonnet, but not for quoting Star Wars or something equally inappropriate. They unloaded the bags from the Jeep. This part Clark felt prepared for.

"You want me to carry the bags in to the Airport?" Rodrigo seemed as confused as he had when they asked him to accompany them. Clark didn't want to play around with it anymore. He dropped the keys into the man's hand. "Drive it back to the Hotel?"

"It's yours" Clark said with a smile. The man smiled a polite smile back that seemed to assume Clark was joking with him and he thought it was mildly funny. Clark smiled again, the flat smile that indicated that he was serious.

The man's eyes started to water; suddenly Clark's were as well. The man embraced Clark and Clark put his arm around Rodrigo, because he didn't know what else to do. He wasn't really used to this much contact, but it felt nice. When Rodrigo broke the hug he looked for Jack.

"Yack, next time you in Quito, you can stay with my family" Rodrigo said haltingly. Now he went around and hugged each one of their group. Clark felt overwhelmed; he wasn't giving the man a million dollars. The way the thing was always breaking down, he would probably have to scrap it in a month. Eventually Rodrigo drove off and Clark had only the slight scent of exhaust to recall his good deed. He kicked himself for not taking a photo.

Now all that was left was to say goodbye. They had the bikes on the curb. Clark thought about what to say, how he could salvage what they had. He knew it needed to sound romantic but cool, somehow leaving her wanting to be with him, not feeling sorry for him. He needed to stand upright, not look at his feet. He needed to annunciate his words, he checked his breath, and it was tolerable. He walked over to where Anne was looking through her bags.

"I can't believe it's time. It seems like only a few days since…"

"Yeah, I'm gonna miss the kids too." She had cut off his declaration of love and fate. This was not a good beginning. Why hadn't she mentioned him, was this how the end really started?

"We're just two lost souls…" Clark started.

"Pink Floyd? Really, you're going to use Pink Floyd lyrics?" Anne quipped. Clark laughed, as if it had been nothing more than a well-timed joke. Clark changed techniques, instead pulling her close. He held her body close and rocked her from side to side, all the time whispering, "it's okay, it's okay". Anne exhaled audibly, but Clark expected her to bristle at his first moment of vulnerability. She would snap and nip, but he could love her enough for the two of them.

"It's okay, we always knew I had to leave," He told her softly.

"But you're not going anywhere" Anne whispered. Clark held her even tighter; denial was a sign to him that he was really breaking through. How many stages of grief were there? He smiled, knowing that if she cared enough to be grieving, they had a chance.

"Oh Anne, I'll wait for you. I'll wait for you." He was almost crying now, his heart felt full, almost like a bad case of birthday cake over indulgence. He didn't really have a plan, but something told him it would all work out.

"You're literally not going anywhere" Anne whispered back. The tone of her voice was almost irritation. He was sure that if he could get her to anger they would have covered another one of the stages.

"I have to go" Clark stated tenderly. That would put her over the edge; they were getting closer to resolution by the second.

"You don't have a ticket" Anne whispered this so close to his ear that he thought for a moment he had imagined it. Clark stopped rocking her. *Was this just something people said when they were sad?* That seemed awfully mean. Clark's heart had jumped a little when she said that. Was she kidding him or just trying to be mean? He separated their bodies and looked at her.

"What does that mean?"

"Well, it means you're not flying out of Quito today, that's for sure. I wanted it to be a surprise, so surprise" Anne smiled. Clark could feel his blood pressure rise. He knew that Anne was emotional and prone to selfish stupid things, but Karen would be waiting at the airport to pick the kids up. This would be a disaster.

"Why would you cancel our tickets?" His lip was quivering he was so mad. If he had suspected something like this, he would have booked the tickets himself.

"I didn't cancel anyone's tickets; Jack and Jordan are on the flight as promised. I just purchased Jordan one instead of you." Anne stopped smiling; now just looking at him plainly. Then she smiled as innocently as he could have possibly imagined. She looked far too innocent for someone who was dealing in such deceit. "You said you wanted to go to Tierra del Fuego."

Jack walked up behind him, putting his hand on his father's sleeve. When Clark turned to see him, he was smiling sadly. "Don't be mad dad, it was my idea." Chloe walked up behind the boy.

"It was our idea." Chloe added. Now it seemed a conspiracy against him. How much else was going on behind his back. He would get to the bottom of this conspiracy.

"I needed to get back for school anyway Clark," Jordan threw in his sentiments as well. Just like that he was the only one left out of the conspiracy. He had many unanswered questions, but try as he might; people were just saying their goodbyes. Chloe was crying and Jack was trying not to. Jordan and Anne were making a final hug and Jordan worked to put his motorcycle gear in a neat pile.

"Take care of the Captain. He might not be an antique, but he's awfully special to me" Jordan pressed the keys into Clark's hand. He was still trying hard to catch up; everything seemed to be moving in fast forward before him. He felt himself handing the kids' passports, and he heard words come out of his mouth, but it was not until they had faded from sight into the airport that he fully understood that they were gone. Even then he half expected them to run back out, although he knew they would have to be moving toward the ticket counter if they were to make their flight.

He looked at Anne with sad eyes, her own were still a little red from all the goodbyes. She smiled at him and pointed at the gear. The Jacket fit and the helmet was just a little snug. Clark tried to pretend it didn't smell like teenage boy sweat. He attached his bag to the back seat, holding it tightly with the bungee strap. He sat down on the blisteringly hot seat, trying to ease his way down on it like one might a hot bathtub. He pressed the starter and the deep throaty engine caught immediately. Twisting the throttle made a sound like thunder, with buildings behind him echoing the sound. Heads turned as he pulled away from the curb. In the small mirror he could see Anne and the General following close behind. Once they were away from the airport Clark pulled over. He hadn't worried about course after Quito, which had been the end of his road. Now he was torn between the wonderment of being able to continue his odyssey and the sadness that Jack and Chloe would not be here to see it.

Anne pulled ahead of him and gestured forward, apparently she had expected this. He released the hand clutch, much more standard than the General, and settled into the right side follower position. Clark wanted to do some deep soul searching, but he found that the constant barrage of things that came at him kept his mind focused on the bike, the road and Anne. He had no idea how many miles she had planned for today, or if she had really planned for today. He allowed himself the luxury of not thinking, of just allowing himself to take in all the beauty around him. He now was free of the burden of worry, no one could hurt his children anymore; at worst he might lose his own life. By comparison it felt like a great weight had been lifted from his shoulders.

They continued their march up into the mountainous regions; they seemed to skirt the jungle area and Clark wondered if the road builders had just head up to keep from having to chop down all those trees. They drove through cities with obvious Indian names like Tanicuchi and Latacunga. The faces inside the cities had sometimes shown African ancestry, but in the long roads of South America the mostly toothless brown faces that smiled at them were undoubtedly Indians.

They had lunch in Riobamba, although neither of them ate much and there was an unnatural silence that hung over them. It was always hard to be left behind, but Clark seemed to really be struggling with it. Anne looked at him and even grasped his hand a couple of times during lunch. He had not eaten his hardly any of his papusa, which was not usual.

Back on the bikes they continued on, broken asphalt littered with potholes the only continuity. There seemed to be less here, fewer people, more land. The light started to fade, the sun sinking into a hazy evening. Clark looked over toward the ocean and almost wrecked the bike. He honked and Anne pulled over with him. Gazing down toward the ocean the whole expanse was filled with clouds. Only a few small mountains or hills poked above the thick white blanket. Just down the hillside from them the green pastures abruptly faded into the clouds. Clark took out the small camera that Anne had never even noticed. He snapped a picture. Suddenly his grief and sadness started to drain out of him. It hadn't been his choice to send the kids away, it had just been part of the deal. If he had left with them he would have missed this incredible moment. He felt silly for wallowing in his sadness. He walked over to Anne and kissed her, he knew his breath still had traces of a partially eaten papusa on it, but it was time. They would finish this thing. Anne wouldn't let him quit, even when the world conspired against him. Come what horrors might, he would end this thing in Tierra del Fuego.

Chapter 33

Clark tried to adjust himself on the seat, but whether he sat further back and his tailbone stabbed pain, or he leaned forward and crushed his male parts, he couldn't get comfortable. They had been riding for hours and although they had been doing it for days, Clark's behind refused to harden to the saddle. If that had been his only ailment from riding he could have lived with it, but it seemed that each day revealed some new torture. His hands had been the next in line after his butt, somehow the vibrations from the handlebars echoed in his mind so that his hands tingled for an hour after riding. Tapping his fingers felt like bending a spring, sending concerning but not painful sensations up into his wrists. His deafness was growing rapidly. Anne had made a joke that they sounded like an eighty year old couple, yelling at each other in the restaurant, trying to compensate for their mutual ringing. He had thought blessings were at hand when he found a store with foam ear plugs, but three hours in they felt like they were splitting his ears in half from the inside. Certainly riding had given him a greater appreciation of Anne and how she had handled all the previous miles without a complaint.

The exhilaration of riding the Captain wore off quickly, but even with all the discomfort, there was something freeing about riding. When all the worlds' sounds and thoughts were replaced with wind and engine noise, it just seemed like a better place. Clark was freed from thinking about Karen, or how he had been forced to send the kids away. He couldn't torture himself about what the future held, instead there was only him, the bike and the road. It seemed to be the purest form of causality, turn the throttle, move forward; pull the brake, slow to a stop. By the second day he noticed the bike shrunk in his mind. It had seemed so huge when he first swung his leg over it, but now it was neatly tucked between his legs, an appendage. On the lonelier and flatter sections of highway it almost felt like flying. Of course there weren't too many perfect sections of road. The quality of the road seemed to vary given socio economic factors, richer cities had better roads. Most the potholes could be avoided with some clever maneuvering, but some were so evenly and closely spaced that it seemed the road was made of holes, with just a few errant sections of asphalt to snare unsuspecting drivers.

Once they passed into Peru Clark felt more at home on the bike. His heart didn't race every time an obstacle loomed large in his vision, and he and Anne had worked out a predictable pattern of who would lead and who would follow.

At night they both seemed to sense their missing journey members. There wasn't as much laughter and they no longer felt the necessity of sneaking around to be together. Clark began to have pangs of guilt, which took him some time to track the source. He felt like a cheater, he knew better, but still he could not get the thought of his unfaithfulness out of his mind. It occurred to him that he had not been in a one on one relationship for twenty years. He tried to be patient with himself, understanding that some small interior portion of his brain was digesting Karen's leaving him slower than the rest. Although the guilt plagued him, it only made his passion for Anne burn brighter. Some element of danger or uncharted waters surrounded their nights. Sometimes he would wake in the middle of the night, surprised to find he was already making love to her.

If Anne suffered any of the ailments or nagging emotional problems she never mentioned them. She would occasionally arch her back after a long ride, but always smiled and carried her own bags. She seemed to find a world of solace in her morning tea, some rejuvenation that was lost on Clark. They didn't talk about the future, or at least not anything beyond what cities and roads lie ahead. They quickly settled into a pattern, if a pattern could be found in their chaotic journey. Small things like setting the others toothbrush out, or pulling the sheets out of the foot of the bed seemed to indicate they were in a relationship. Clark would have liked clarification, but was hesitant after his previous effort.

Midway through Peru Anne asked, "Wanna go to Machu Pichu?"

"How long would that take?" Anne's face had wrinkled at his response.

"Who cares how long it takes?" Clark shrugged his shoulders stupidly.

"Aren't we in a hurry? To get back I mean?"

Anne smiled and wrapped her arms around him. "We have all the time in the world." Then she kissed him and that was the end of the discussion. They left the bikes with a reputable Hotel and boarded the train for Machu Pichu.

Although they purchased first class tickets for the train, it did not seem to them that they were in anything resembling first anything. As the train continued to load Clark came to a startling revelation, First Class tickets seemed to be the only way to be guaranteed a seat. As the train filled and filled he saw that many of the people would be standing the entire trip. He laughed at his own seemingly quaint American sensibilities, still somehow intact even this far south. Anne smiled and commented on the particularly pungent body odor of the man seated next to her. He squeezed her hand, no matter what kind of ridiculous situation they would find themselves in, if they were together he believed they would be alright.

The train shivered and pulled up the mountain passes, Clark tried hard not to think of those final moments in the beast, remembering what it had felt like to watch the world unravel before his eyes. But soon his eyelids were heavy and since he wasn't driving he allowed himself to drift off.

Anne woke him by shaking his shoulder roughly. No time had passed for him, but he was so disoriented and dizzy he almost fell over the second he stood up. Few others seemed to be getting off, but Anne was hurrying him along. Trusting in her he pulled their bags from the overhead and followed her off the train. A few other rough and ready travel types had stepped off with them. Of everyone in the group he and Anne looked the least capable. Anne smiled and shouldered the pack. He looked dubiously at the light green bag; they hadn't even packed the thing. It had come shipped from New York, a gift from her publishing house. His own bag was orange and blue and held the same mystique and potential for failure that Anne's did. Their lives were now in the hands of total strangers who were thousands of miles away.

They moved out through the high Andean mountains, the air somehow lacking what Clark needed to breathe. He huffed and puffed, but never really felt like he caught his breath. The dark green foliage passed by and their feet rolled along, it was a very nice trail. Clark's legs ached and yet there seemed no end to the path laid out before him.

When he finally stood looking at the carved stone ruins he nearly wept with joy. He wasn't sure whether that joy stemmed from the hike being over or the beauty of the ruins, but he was happy either way. The few tourists who had taken the longer route now merged with the throngs of tourists, half in garish outfits that looked like they were heading on a Safari in 1932.

They tried to find their own spaces, to avoid the crowds which seemed to move like sheep, lining single file to worm their way around any obstacles.

Clark tried to see not only what was before him, but what had been. He tried to imagine this place as a thriving center of the Incan experience. He tried to imagine high mountain runners sending messages of the invading Spanish. But try as he might, all he saw was what was before him, beautiful works with impressive engineering, but no more. He looked at Anne, and he saw reflected in her eyes that this was so much more to her. The imagination pulsing within the confines of her skull painted a vivid portrait of Incan life and culture. She saw colors and people and commerce and all the things that Clark's brain refused. Clark was jealous of her in that moment, jealous that she had gifts this way that he could hardly even comprehend. He was grateful as well; he would not have come here on his own. He would have missed the beauty that was around him, that permeated the stones and left the viewer with a sense of awe and reverence. He would have missed this to get a day closer to his goal, Tierra del Fuego.

He wondered how many great things he missed out showing his children in search of that goal. Did that make him a bad father, or just one that didn't understand why flowers needed smelling? Clark followed Anne as they walked up and down the ruins. They found a secluded spot and he kissed her, he never tired of kissing her. He wondered for a split second if their relationship would grow wearisome, if they would become the couple that didn't kiss anymore? It had happened with Karen, maybe it was just the way of the world. But with her mouth hot on him, he still could not see that day.

They started the walk (the shorter route) to the train stop; Anne was adventuresome, not crazy. Suddenly Clark turned and ran back to the edge, pulled out the small digital camera and snapped a photo. Anne had taken hundreds with her camera.

"What is it with you and that camera anyway?" she asked.

"Just something I promised to do."

"For some old man or something?"

"For Lester, the guy who sold me the motor home. He had always planned to travel himself, but never got the chance, so I said I would photo the trip for him. One or two a day, that's all." Clark said it very matter of fact, as if it were the most normal thing in the world. Anne smiled at him. She knew why he took the pictures, but she wanted to hear his interpretation. As always it was clinical and to the point, forever he would be the auditor. Some things did not change with people and for the first time that she could remember, she was glad for it.

They got their seats on the train, where Clark was able to beat his record for speed to fall asleep. Anne watched him sleep and smiled. The smoothed his hair and hesitated. Feeling his forehead she noticed that he was warm, more than just the hiking. She smiled that her mother instinct was not totally dead. The train slugged and pushed forward until they were on their way back to civilization.

Chapter 34

When the sun lit up their room, Clark felt a little better. They knew that they needed to move on and Clark didn't want to be the reason they got stuck in a city. He felt obligated to the trip now, Tierra del Fuego or bust. After breakfast he lifted his leg over the Captain and sighed to plant himself into the seat. This would be a long day of riding.

Out of Peru and into Chile they left the green fertile lands for the Atacama desert. It was bleak like Clark had never seen before. He had thought that the Western Texas landscape had been bleak, but this was like being on the moon. In fact he remembered something about this being the area where they tested the Mars rover. Clark was glad they didn't have the children with them, this was the most unforgiving country he had ever tread upon. Water tasted better there, and they went through gallons it seemed. The lack of moisture in the atmosphere seemed to vacuum the spit out of their mouths, kindly replacing it with a fine powdered dust.

Clark rode behind, trying to enjoy the ride, but in truth he was miserable. His body ached, the landscape was beautiful but desolate, and the wind was really getting to him. The seemingly constant gale that dirtied their bikes and filled their eyes with sand was bad, but as large trucks passed, he thought several time he would be pushed off the road. But according to the map, they progressed. They found new towns with small hotels, or a sign out that there was a room to rent. They were off the beaten path now, only the few crazy adventurers seemed to pass this way.

As miserable as the days riding was, the nights were enough to make up for it. He was discovering more and more about Anne every day. She was funny and horribly honest, that in compound connection with how beautiful she was would have been enough to drive a smarter man away. For what could a mere mortal have to give back to such a Goddess? But Clark was just a foolish little man and instead of overthinking why she would choose him, he allowed himself to just be grateful. This was who Clark had dreamed he would become, not the man who feared tomorrow while wallowing in his past, but the man who has the courage

to embrace the present. Anne was teaching him and he strove to be her
star pupil.

He only wished he felt better. The fever continued a low boil in his
system, relieving him of his energy. Several times as they lie in bed
talking, Anne would look over to find him asleep. When she confronted
him on it, he didn't remember even starting the conversation. Anne
tried to get him to see a doctor, afraid that there must be something
more wrong, but Clark would only wave his hand, assuring her that he
just needed another good night's sleep.

Ride, eat, ride, rest, ride, eat, ride, sleep, that was the rhythm of their
days and when viewed on a map they looked to be ready to climb the
mountain range between Chile and Argentina. They were nearing the
final border crossing of their epic trip. Clark wondered what came next,
but he was too afraid to dare to ask. The future and relationships
seemed forbidden territory. One night he woke up, pouring sweat. He
felt dizzy and sick and almost woke Anne to take him to see a doctor.
He lay in the bathroom, on the cool tile floor until he fell asleep again.

When Anne found him there she shook him until he woke up. For over
an hour she tried to drag him to see a doctor. Clark's grandfather had
been a proud man, living alone until he was over ninety two years old.
Clark remembered him fondly. He still had a small pocket knife, that as
far as he knew was the only gift from the old man. What he
remembered mostly, what he couldn't forget, was his grandfather
pulling him close at the hospital and telling him that they were killing
him. He claimed that the only reason he was sick now, was that he had
allowed those 'quack' doctors to infect him with some money draining
disease. Clark had tried to reason with his grandfather, but three days
later he was dead. Just a week prior to that he had seemed to be the
same healthy, old son of a bitch he had always been. Clark had never
forgotten that. He had allowed the doctors to see Jack, they could fix
broken things. But he had an inescapable sense that he would never
leave a hospital if he entered it. He had promised to finish this ride and
he would if it were the last thing he ever did.

Clark convinced her that they would be in Santiago the following day,
that he would get checked out then. Only when they got to the city, he
told her that he felt fin and she grudgingly allowed them to pass

through their final border station. They had nearly made it, although the map told of leagues to go, they were close. The mountains that separate Chile and Argentina are the major force behind the uneasy peace that has lasted along the much bordered countries. Up and up they drove, until Clark felt so chilled that he thought he might not be able to let go of the handlebars when they stopped. On the downhill side Clark prayed for a close city. He could not ride much further and so when signs indicating Mendoza came into view, he nearly wept with joy. Anne led them to the hotel. Anne stepped off her bike stiffly and stared at Clark. He lacked the energy to put down his own kickstand.

"Oh you stupid ass, why didn't you tell me to stop?" she asked him angrily.

"What, and miss those mountain views?"

Clark half expected his fingers to break off as he pulled them away from the controls. He was shivering so much that Anne had to help him remove the helmet as well.

"Why are you shivering so much?" she asked with concern.

"It's cold as hell" he responded.

"But it's not that cold." Anne pressed her hand to his forehead. Her look of irritation went to one of concern. "We're checking in, and then you are seeing a doctor."

"Okay", he relented. He was just too tired to fight it anymore. Maybe this was the end. "Just let me get a couple of shots of the city from here."

"You will do no such thing." Now it was time for the stern mother voice, which seemed to get Clark right into line.

Inside the Hotel, the manager kindly phoned a doctor, who prescribed an antibiotic, but couldn't see Clark until the following evening. Anne thanked him and set a reminder with the front desk for the appointment. She sent the concierge to get the medicine and helped Clark to the room.

Roan Poulter

Chapter 35

By the time they got into the room Clark was very sick. He was shaking and his body ached more than he had ever experienced. In bed Anne had him lay his head down on her lap, stroking his hair. Even though he hurt so badly and thought his bowels might not contain themselves, Anne's fingers raking his hair with his head in her lap was the most comfortable he had felt in years. He almost hated to pop his head up and sprint for the bathroom, narrowly channeling the tube of vomit that erupted from his mouth into the toilet. Now he really was the most pathetic human being that had ever lived. Anne only coaxed him to lie down again. Anne had to support Clark he was so weak, his hair wet in the back from the sweat that poured off him.

He cursed whatever had done this to him, although for the life of him he couldn't even think of a culprit. Anne seemed fine and she was a woman. But though he could find no reason or cause, he continued to expel everything he had ever eaten, thought about eating, or dreamed of. He marveled at the capacity of his digestive system, somehow there was always more to come out.

Anne checked on him every few minutes, bringing a constant barrage of feel better items; Sprite, Ginger Snaps, Pepto Bismol, along with the antibiotic the doctor had prescribed. Clark felt miserable, but Anne was showing a totally different side of herself and Clark promised himself he would pay her back. Not for the money spent, but for the kindness in the face of his human frailty. He had thought her the kind of woman who would just run away when things got hard, but she was here with a cold rag on his neck, trying to get him to take a sip of soda. Anne really was everything someone could want, she was exciting and adventurous, beautiful and suave, but she still had a deeply caring side, a mother's instinct that refused to die. Clark would marry this woman if he got the chance, he knew that.

Clark spent that evening on the cool tile floor of the bathroom, over Anne's protest. He didn't like the smell of vomit any more than anyone else; he wouldn't burden her with that. Besides, he could rest his burning forehead on the tile and it felt good. After the night from hell the tide finally seemed to be coming to an end. Either that or Clark was just wrung out like an old dish rag. He brushed his teeth for the fiftieth time in twenty four hours, with a new toothbrush that Anne had bought for him. Finally he lay in bed, the soft warm blankets wrapped around him. It was still early morning, Anne was still sleeping. He tried not to get too close, but when she sensed his presence she slid over and pulled him close. Clark was still wet from the shower, wearing only boxers. The soft luxury of Anne's legs stroked his and if he had not been completely exhausted to the point of death, he would have made love to her right then. As it was he allowed a vigorous arm rubbing to take its place. His arms were too heavy to lift to put around her. Eyelids felt like iron weights. Under his breath he said, "I need to get a couple hours sleep, then go get a couple pictures for Lester." Anne laughed.

Clark let the scent of her hair and the feel of her skin point his dreams, he needed no fantasy women. He dreamt of the places they would see, the things they would experience together. A momentary stomach cramp had him eyeing the bathroom, but it passed and he let himself fall into a deep sleep.

When he woke up, he had the feeling he had been out for years. It was possible he didn't even know what planet he was on. But one thing was for sure, he felt much better. His stomach had preliminary indications that it would accept food without refunding it moments later. He opened a Sprite and although it was warm, drank it down, the effervescence burning his throat and tickling his nose. After eating a couple of the ginger snap cookies, he felt like a new man. He could eat, but where was Anne? What time was it anyway? The clock displayed 7:15 and for a moment Clark wondered which it was. Pulling the curtain aside it was obviously the early evening, so then why wasn't Anne here?

Clark found a clean set of clothes and got dressed. Maybe Anne was down at the restaurant in the lobby, she might have thought to let him sleep. He hit the door before remembering to grab the camera, but when he went to find it, it didn't seem to be where he had left it. He looked through a couple of bags, thinking in his delirium he might have misplaced it. Shaking his head, he decided it wasn't that important, he could always get the photos tomorrow.

He pressed the elevator button and whistled while he waited, really other than being ravenously hungry, he felt great. Anne would have her work cut out for her in the bed tonight. Clark laughed out loud at his own joke, which was tacky, but he would have never thought that sort of thing before meeting her. The elevator music was something he had never heard, some kind of South American pop song ruined by the elevator people.

Coming out into the lobby Clark looked around to see if he could spot her, it was a busy night at a very exclusive hotel, there were probably a hundred people. Nothing stood out, there were a handful of Americans, it was easy to spot them, if you saw a fat white person they were either an American or a German. Again Clark laughed at his irreverence and told himself that he would have to learn manners when he returned to the land of the living. Two military or police officers were speaking with the front desk. Clark took a right turn into the Restaurant. The host recognized him and urged him over. Anne's exorbitant tip seemed to keep the wait staff quite attentive to their needs. His English was pretty good so Clark was spared trying to translate into Spanish.

"Have you seen my, uhm, the woman I came in here with?" The man smiled extra hard, Anne must have really left this guy something.

"No Senor, not tonight."

"Could she be at the bar?" The man smiled again, not as wide, since he was probably not used to being questioned.

"No, Sir. I think not, but if you would like to make check?" Now it was Clark's turn to smile. He passed by the man and walked toward the bar. It wasn't filled with people, but it seemed like the beginnings of fairly good night.

At a table by herself there was one of the most beautiful women Clark had ever seen. She had long brown hair and latin features. Her lips were full to bursting as was her bosom. She was wearing what seemed like the tightest possible black dress, she was absolutely stunning. She noted Clark staring at her and smiled at him. He felt his face flush. No one that beautiful had ever smiled at him, deep inside there was a voice that told him he should go talk to her. The voice said that he had been without so long, it wasn't fair to have to pass up on a chance this good. But his good sense came back in the nick of time, reminding him that the woman he was sharing a room with had nursed him back from health, kept him on the road, she had saved his life, such that it was. Clark smiled back politely at the woman and turned to walk out toward the host again.

They smiled but exchanged no words as Clark passed. In the lobby again Clark didn't know what to do. If she had stepped out to the Pharmacy or something, he might miss her on the street. He knew that he should just go back to the room and wait, but something kept him looking through the lobby. He wondered if there was a chance that Anne had left. He thought he saw her bag when he was looking, yes he had. She could have found another man, no, that was silly. She probably just went out to get something for them both to eat. Maybe something familiar like McDonald's.

"Mr. Carter, please sir, come." The front desk was calling him over. They looked disturbed. Clark walked over and they directed him down toward the two men in uniform he had seen earlier.

"Yes?" Clark spoke, but suddenly his stomach didn't feel so good anymore.

They spoke furiously in Spanish for a moment, he caught none of it. They waved another staff member over and again a flurry of Spanish came out that he had no idea to the meaning. They tried to smile at him as they spoke, but although their mouths smiled, their eyes said they had something bad to tell him. Clark had encountered this a million times as an auditor. People thought if they made friends he wouldn't audit them, they were always wrong. Smiles didn't hide anything really, the truth always came out. Numbers didn't lie.

"There has been an accident. Mrs. Carter has been hurt." Now there was a flurry of Spanish again from the other Hotel staff. "I'm sorry, your wife is gone."

Clark wanted to correct her on the relationship mix up, wanted to get his name stated correctly, but he couldn't do anything. All the sounds from the lobby stopped, a high pitched whine seemed to be bouncing around between his ears. He blinked and tried to get enough moisture in his mouth to speak.

"How do they know it was her?"

"She had her room key and her driver's permit." Clark breathed deeply, so deeply that people probably thought there was something wrong with him. He tried to get himself to do something, say something. They had to be wrong, there was some kind of a mix up.

"Can I see her?" The sound seemed to come from his lips, though he didn't remember saying it. He stopped remembering things, how he followed the police men into their car, where they drove to a dark building. He tried to forget the smell of antiseptic and the hum of the fluorescent lights as they walked down a hallway. But try as hard as he could he could never forget the face of Anne as they opened the black bag. Nights would happen when he wouldn't see her mangled face, but not many. He wanted to kiss her, get her somehow to wake up. He felt the first of many tears rolling unbidden down his face. He crumpled to the floor, broken, like a marionette that had its strings cut. He looked at the men with him, expecting to see laughter in their eyes, at how a man could weep like a woman, but instead their eyes were also glistening. Clark became aware of arms picking him up and quiet distant voices speaking toward him. His legs held and they walked back down the hallway where a man in a suit was standing. He said in perfect English that he was from some official sounding place, but Clark couldn't help him. There wasn't a Clark anymore, whomever he had been before was gone now. He just wanted to sleep. The last thing he remembered was a man pressing a small digital camera splattered with blood into his hand.

Chapter 36

At the southernmost tip of the America's there is a wooden sign, informing travelers that they have arrived at the Tierra del Fuego national park. The area is claimed by both Argentina and Chile. Ushuaia, the closest city, is the capital of the province, sort of a last refuge of man, placed in front of the Beagle channel and surrounded by the Martial Mountains. It holds the distinction as the most southern city in the world. Adventurers and explorers have been visiting the region since its early exploration. Before the Panama canal, ships destined for the Pacific had to brave its deadly waters.

The area of Tierra del Fuego National Park is technically an island, as is much of the area there. In summer months they can have almost no light, while in the winter it can shine for as much as seventeen hours, what the locals call 'white nights'.

Most tourists are smart enough to plan their trips during the winter months, which being the southern hemisphere, means it's actually quite warm. So then on a bitterly cold August night, the few houses which dotted the gravel road toward that sign were surprised to see a lone motorcycle making his way toward the end of the road.

The rider was covered in mud and road debris, to the point where it was difficult to say what color his gear had started. He seemed tall by the angle of his legs against the bike. The motorcycle looked to have seen better days. Under layers of dirt there appeared to be some kind of old bike. What might have been a star was almost visible on the tank. The engine ran roughly, backfiring occasionally and making the people who watched it pass from the safety and warmth of their homes if the man would make his destination. The headlight only cast a faint glow and after he passed the red lights were all but invisible. Some chuckled, some shook their head worriedly, but eventually all went back to whatever they were doing. No one thought to follow him or invite him into their homes. In fact beyond a casual shoulder shrug between an old man and his wife, once he passed no one thought about him again.

If they had followed him and kept in the shadows they would have seen him put the bike on its stand just within sight of the sign. Many motorcyclists had done this feat before, so they would have expected to see a bottle of champagne or maybe something just a little harder spring out. They would have expected to see him dance a little, make some kind of grand gesture while friends or a timer took their photo to immortalize their achievement. Many had some sort of ritual, some spread ashes or threw mementoes into the water.

But they would have known from how this man stood that he was not here to celebrate. His head hung so low it looked like he was studying the ground. He limped on his left leg, to the point where someone would probably ask him if he needed help.

They would have watched him walk forward toward the water. A good watcher would have revealed themselves here, yelling to him that the waters were icy cold. As if to drive the point home, the wind began to pick up from its usual pace into something really terrible. Rain, or what started rain and froze on impact started to pelt the man with such ferocity, it would have seemed God himself were keeping him from reaching those waters. The man removed his helmet, letting it drop in the rocky soil that flowed out into the sea. Waters lapped his feet, but he continued walking. Water filled his boots but still he kept walking. Stinging numbing waters splashed past his waist and he paused. His brown hair was a mess and should have been cut weeks or months prior. An untrimmed beard partially hid the unwashed face behind it. Within the dirt there were clean lines that moved from his eyes, only after close inspection were the tears visible. His mouth held firm, but his eyes looked like he had suffered a long illness. He reached down a gloved hand into the frozen waters and pulled up a cold glove's worth to rinse his face.

The wind stopped blowing for a moment and he looked out over the waters. The final rays of sunlight broke through the bottom of the clouds just before the sun dipped below the horizon. There was no audible click, but suddenly his eyes changed and some of the weariness seemed to drain from him. What conclusions he might have drawn would be lost on our voyeur, for the only words he spoke were muttered under his breath, more to himself.

He turned and walked back up the beach, his riding clothes pouring water out of errant pockets and folds all along the way. On the shore he stripped off his clothes, throwing each item into the water as he went, lastly throwing his helmet with two skips. When at last he stood naked on the shore, shivering and nearly blue from the cold, he reached down and wrote something in the sand. Once it was written he didn't look at it, but instead ran back up the bike and opened the saddle bag. Inside were clothes that he pulled out piece by piece until the rider looked every bit the new man. The package that had been strapped on top was now revealed to be a new helmet. He pulled the helmet on and fastened the straps. He kicked the motorcycle a couple of times and it started, after sputtering and backfiring. He reached into the bag and removed a small tool, adjusting something in the engine area until the bike ran smoothly. He put the bike in gear and pulled out, but after only a couple of feet he stopped again. He reached into the bag and removed a small camera. He pulled the memory card from the camera and deposited it in an envelope he produced from another pocket. The address on the envelope was in Utah, United States of America, someone named Lester. He licked the envelope and sealed it. Putting down the stand once more, he ran two steps and heaved the camera into the yawning mouth of the ocean. On cue the wind picked up again and the man smiled. Now the wind would be at his back. He sat down on the bike and put the stand up. He feathered the throttle, put it in gear and drove straight north without ever looking back.

ABOUT THE AUTHOR

Roan Poulter is an writer, adventurer and accumulator of hobbies. He is currently on a yearlong sabbatical with his family, somewhere between the lines on the map.

He is also the author of The End of the Road.

www.ingramcontent.com/pod-product-compliance
Lightning Source LLC
Chambersburg PA
CBHW020240130626
46549CB00005B/1981